The Binding

The Dream Stealers' Trilogy:

Book Two

Kimberly J. Rosengrant

Illustrations by: Paulette Nelson

For Louisa Kimball
Never Stop Believing!

Acknowledgments

Thank you to Jodielynn Kuhn and Robert McKenzie for their endless patience, editing expertise, and advice. Trinity Vigna and Charlotte Benasutti, whose patience and encouragement helped to bring this project to fruition. Thanks to Elizabeth Heckman, Kaitlynn Fair, and Selene Lassell for reading and advice; Paulette Nelson for her amazing artwork, and Shirley DeSantis for her computer graphics wizardry. Your continued efforts have made this story a better adventure.

You rock!

A special thanks to Elizabeth Heckman for her assistance with this project to the end.

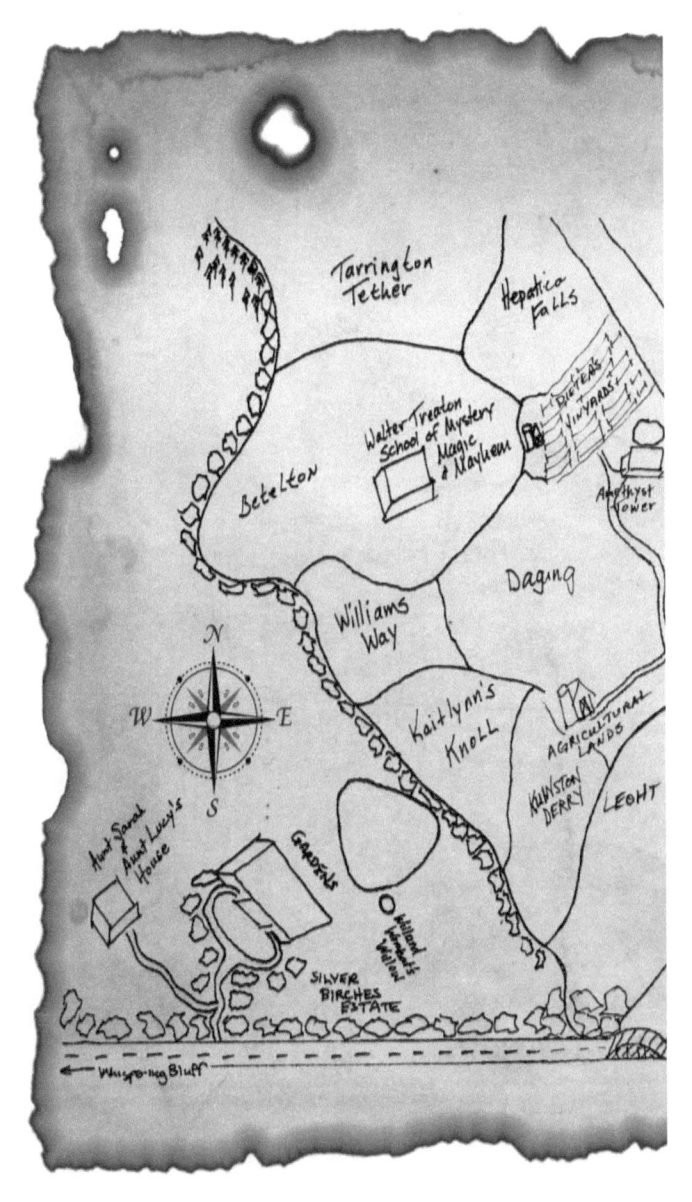

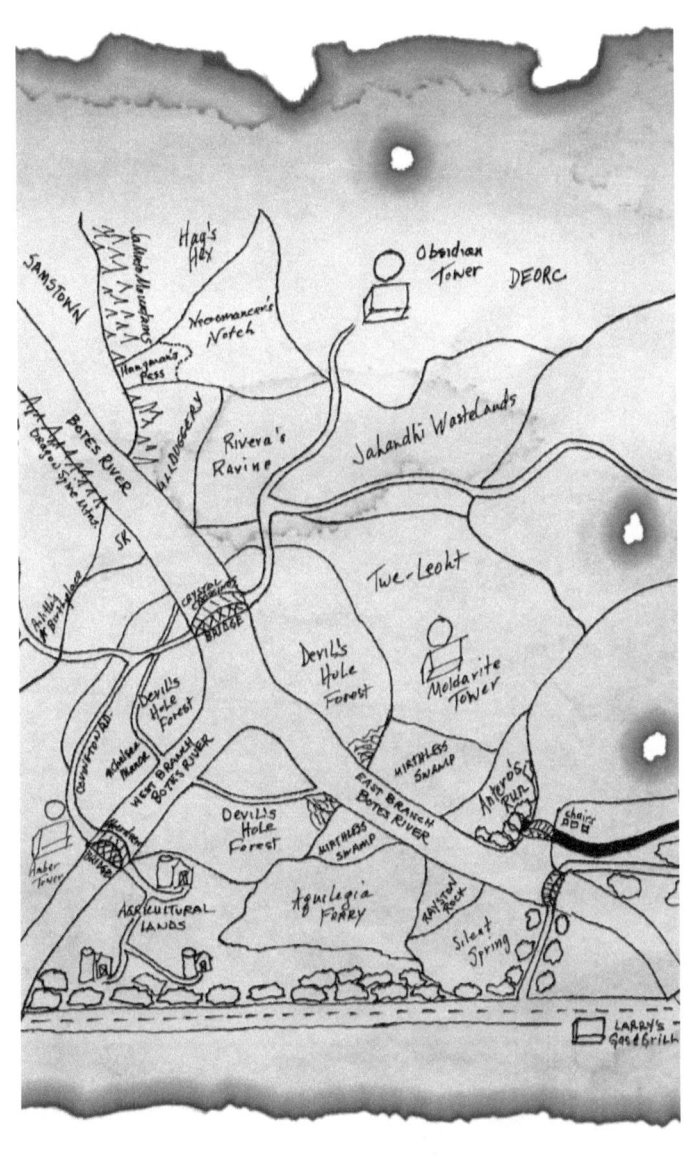

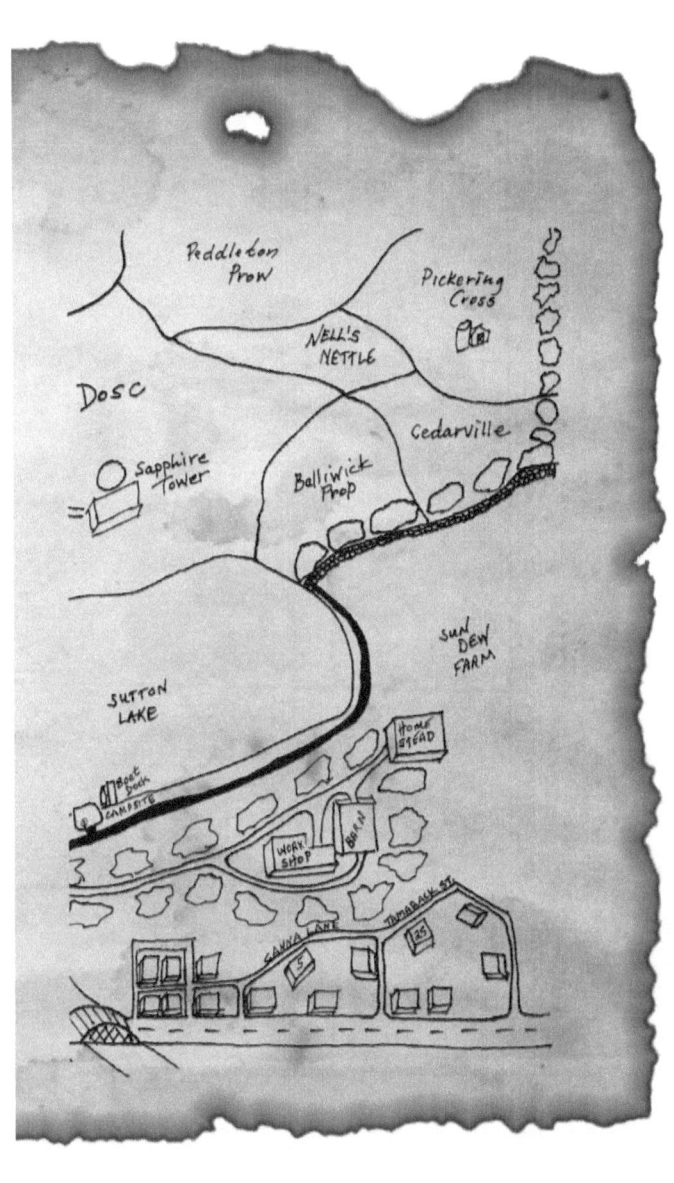

List of Characters

Outerworld — Pine Woods

Alex and Lucy Tipton: Will Tipton's parents

Ashley Parker: married to Bernie Parker; mother to Emily, Madeline, and Michael

Ben Sutton: married to Pearl Sutton, step-grandfather to Nate Sutton, originally from Devil's Hole, has a past yet to be revealed

Bernie Parker: married to Ashley; father to Emily, Madeline, and Michael

Emily Parker: second child of Bernie and Ashley Parker, powerful wizard

Fletcher: Nate Sutton's black Labrador retriever

Gordon Silversmith: best friends with Nate Sutton, step-son of Morgan Triebrecher

Jacob Daggerstein: friend of the Suttons, war hero, finds himself drawn into this new world against his will

Madeline Parker: youngest daughter of Bernie and Ashley Parker, member of the Gardener's Guild, polyhybrid

Michael Parker: eldest child of Bernie and Ashley Parker, Ailith's rider, powerful wizard

Morgan Triebrecher: step-father of Gordon Silversmith, real estate developer

Nate Sutton: grandson of King Arisaema and Pearl Sutton, friends with Gordon Silversmith and Will Tipton

Pearl Sutton: married to Ben Sutton, grandmother to Nate Sutton, mother of Belac, twin sister of Lorelei Lorelinda, original immigrant from the alien world of Sandari, immortal, shape-shifter

Dr. Willard Wombat: teacher at Walter Treaton School of Mystery, Magic, and Mayhem; lives under the Parker's willow tree

Will Tipton: friends with Nate Sutton and Gordon Silversmith, lives in Whispering Bluff with his parents Alex and Lucy Tipton

Innerworld — Innes

Amethyst Tower of Dagung

Ailith: Thryth's daughter, dragon of the defunct Amethyst Tower

Arisaema: dead King of the defunct Amethyst Tower and the lands of Dagung

Beastly Hadley: bull mastiff, retired brigand, best friend of Crooksey Snively

Crooksey Snively: orange tom-cat, retired brigand, best friend of Beastly Hadley

Dieter and Greta: Ben's brother and sister-in-law, own and operate the vineyards in Dagung

Dipsacus: Head of the King of the Amethyst Tower of Dagung's personal guard

Jonah Hobken: eldest of the Hobken brothers, Michael Parker's friend and guide

Thryth: Amethyst dragon, Ailith's mother

Sapphire Tower of Dosk

Arion: Nate's white war-horse, was originally Nicolas Heldring's horse

Byron Pettiman: High Official of Dosk, allied with Belac and the Obsidian Tower

Caleb Hobken: twin of Gaelen Hobken, sentenced to the dungeons of Dosk

Cereus Heldring: Queen of the Sapphire Tower and the lands of Dosk, married to Nicolas Heldring

Elizabeth Heldring: Princess of the Sapphire Tower, daughter of Nicolas and Cereus Heldring

Fiona Dunne: sister of John Dunne, rider of Onager

Gaelen Hobken: twin of Caleb Hobken, sentenced to the dungeons of Dosk

Gorgos: slave, Captain of the Guard and head jailor in the dungeons of Dosk, famed torturer, rider of Naptha

Nicolas Heldring: long-dead King of the Sapphire Tower and the lands of Dosk, married to Cereus Heldring

Onager: dragon of the Sapphire Tower

Ted McShane: finder of Lost Objects

Serpentia: ancient serpent that guarded the enchanted island where Arion slept

Moldavite Tower of Twe-Leoht

Drakken Aruhl: Lorelei's former warder and lover

Lorelei Lorlinda: twin sister of Pearl Sutton, Lady of the Woods, Gaia image of Innes, immortal, alien immigrant from the planet Sandari, Queen of the Moldavite Tower

Wynn: Dragon of the Moldavite Tower

Amber Tower of Leoht

Calthexis: King of the Dragons, dragon of the Amber Tower

Cymbidium: married to Daedulus, Queen of the Amber Tower and the lands of Leoht

Daedulus the Inventor: King of the Amber Tower and the lands of Leoht

Dan Farnell: Sargeant Major of the King's military; friend and confidante to King Daedulus

Dimitri: Gordon's owl and animal totem

Elinor: Princess of the Amber Tower, daughter to Daedulus, rider of Calthexis

Ing: sprite who lives in the Garden District of Kuhnston Derry

Ira Pufflehump: owner of Chelsea Manor, overseer of the Pufflemals, married to Maize Niblet

Jolly Hobken: youngest of the Hobken brothers, Gordon Silversmith's friend and guide

Leo Gentlefoot: animal caretaker at the circus, shape shifts into a lion

Maize Niblet: married to Ira Pufflehump, leader of the Gardener's Guild

Rho Dora: member of the Gardener's Guild, friends of Madeline Parker

Iris Cristata: member of the Gardener's Guild, singer, Maize Niblet's best friend

Obsidian Tower of Deorc

Belac & Mortifera: monarchs of the Obsidian Tower, wraith-like Dream Stealers

Bhodi Hobken: brother of Gaelen & Caleb

Draedon: assassin, right hand of Belac

John Dunne: brother of Fiona Dunne

Naptha: dragon of the Obsidian Tower

Fairy Clans:
Checkerspots	Lacewings
Monarchs	Morpho
Painted Ladies	Paper Kite
Red Admirals	Metalmarks
Ringlets	Swallowtails

Prologue

"I have to take responsibility for much of the demise of Dosk," she countered. "After your death and the death of our daughter, Abigail, I was empty. I didn't realize it until your return that I have been praying for death for nearly seven hundred years. You have no idea what that can do to an individual."

He laughed, "It's ironic, but for nearly seven hundred years I've been praying for life." Silence hung in the air between them. "What ever happened to the young man who married our daughter?", he asked.

"I'm not really sure," she said. "I suppose he's dead by now. That was a long time ago."

"And yet, very recent for me," he said.

— Excerpt from a private discussion between Cereus and Nicolas Heldring during their reunion in the Sapphire Tower

1: Promises Made

Heldring dismounted from Windwalker, took reigns in hand, and started up the narrow cobblestone street. It had been some eight hundred years since he'd last set foot in this back alleyway. He wondered if the old smithy was still alive. He'd temporarily given his hardware to Nate and needed a new blade. He could ill-afford to be seen with his old sword so early in the game. He stopped in front of the forge and looked the place over before entering. He would have recognized both the blade maker and the place anywhere; they had changed so little over the last eight centuries. He noticed a bull of a young man hammering a large shield then dipping it in a water bath where it made a loud swooshing noise. Heldring returned his attention to the elder gentleman seated in front of a large work bench laden with all sorts of hand tools including: screwdrivers, hammers, and wrenches.

"Good sir, I wish to purchase a blade. Preferably one made by your own hands," said Heldring.

"Huh, sorry, I didn't hear what you said," said the old man. He grabbed a well-used metallic horn and placed it near his ear.

"I said, I want to purchase a blade … made by your own hands."

"Oh, a blade," he said. "We don't have many left, what with this infernal war going on and all."

"I see," said Heldring. "Tell me old man, what news of the war have you heard?"

"No news is good as far as I can tell," as he spat the juice from the wad of tobacco lodged in his cheek.

"That High Official Pettiman has ruined the likes of this fine city what with his cheating and stealing. And can you believe that he had the nerve to lock the Queen herself in the dungeons — not more than a fortnight ago. Heldring would have never stood for this, but alas, our fair King is long dead." He paused, looked Heldring up and down, and then cleared his throat. "What did you say your name was? We don't get many single buyers around these parts anymore, just them that loads the swords and shields onto their carts for the front. You can see my great, great-grandson Olaf is banging out a shield as we speak. He'll work well into the night and still not make enough shields. The demand is so great."

"I can pay," said Heldring.

"A blade like the one you're asking for will cost you plenty. What'd you say your name was?"

"I didn't," said Heldring. "But I am looking for a special blade. One that has a blade of elven and dragon steel and a handle of burnished ironwood." The smithy was taken aback. His hard, grey eyes shrewdly reassessed this stranger before replying.

"There hasn't been a blade like that around these parts for hundreds of years. Once upon a time, a fellow came in and asked me for a similar blade, but he never came to pick it up. Funny thing too, an expensive blade like that, 'cause it was all paid for. What'd you say your name was?", asked the smithy.

"I didn't," replied Heldring. "Do you still have the blade?"

"Well, that was a long time ago," the smithy said, "in case I forgot to tell you that." "You made it clear. Do you have the blade?", asked Heldring again.

"A blade that special has to be tended to, regular like, you know what I mean," said the smithy. He walked to a ceiling-high wooden closet located at the other side of the room. He pulled a small stool from the corner and placed it in front of the open door. He leapt on top of the stool like a man in his youth. Heldring could hear him shuffling papers and items that had been collecting dust these last long years. He slowly emerged with a small hand-carved wooden box and brought it back to the work bench. He opened the lid and carefully handed the velvet-lined box to Heldring.

"It's miraculous," said Heldring. "You, my good sir are truly gifted." He removed the knife from the box, turned it from side to side. The deepest blue sapphires were inlaid into the burnished ironwood handle. Platinum gilding wrapped vine-like around the handle to add beauty and security to the handle but little in the way of weight. The twelve-inch blade itself cast an ethereal silver-blue glow, a result of the folding of the two metal types. The smithy removed the matching sheath, which had the finest engravings etched by the smithy's own hand.

"How much will you sell this fine blade for?", asked Heldring.

"I'm not sure I should sell it. I mean I did make it for someone else. Not that they'll claim it, I guess."

"Please, fine sir, I'm in earnest. What do you want for this blade?"

"Tell me your name. And not the name you're travelling under. I want to know it's really you. Although ...," he paused. "I couldn't really tell you how it's possible. But, I must know that I'm right and that there is hope for us all." Heldring looked upon this man who was once his chief armorer and good friend. They'd fought side by side on many battle fields, and, truth be told, he was one of only a few of Heldring's trustworthy friends. He was glad that he was still alive these many centuries later.

"Bring the blade, and let's retire to your rooms, up-stairs. That is, if you still keep those rooms."

The smithy smiled as he grabbed the box, "I'll be back in a while, Olaf. I don't want to be disturbed. Is that understood? Take your supper when you're ready. I'll find food when I'm hungry." Olaf shrugged and went back to his work.

"He's not a bad boy, a little daft maybe, but good at heart." Heldring followed the smithy up the narrow staircase and into a well-furnished room. He set the box on the side table next to his heavily-stuffed arm chair. He grabbed two glasses from a cabinet in the next room and returned with a dusty bottle of spirits. The smith handed him a tumbler filled with a delicious full-bodied whisky, clinked his glass to Heldring's, and plopped into his chair. He took a large swallow and then placed his glass on the side table next to the box. Heldring watched the long-remembered routine of his friend. He knew the smithy wasn't settled until he was puffing on his pipe.

Heldring hesitated, "What are the current affairs of state?" The smithy made no bones about his feelings for the current regime and twice spat the names of Belac and Mortifera as if they left a bad taste on the tip of his tongue.

"So it's true then, old friend." Heldring stood and walked to the window overlooking the forge. He could see Olaf slowly working the fine metal as only a well-trained smith could. Heldring was the son of a metallurgist. His father was a man who could smell the differences in the ore used for all sorts of purposes. Heldring, himself, had learned the art from the time of a small boy. He could feel the depth of a perfectly made sword or knife as only the smithy, who had loved and crafted the blade, could feel. Heldring removed the box from the side table and placed it upon his lap as he reseated himself across from his friend.

"You still haven't given me a price," he said to the

smith.

"You still haven't revealed your true name," countered the smith.

Heldring chucked, "You always were a tough old bird." He leaned forward in his chair, "I don't think I need to tell you the result of a loose tongue, do I?"

The smith leaned forward in his chair, "If my tongue was loose, you would have cut it out eight hundred years ago."

"This is truth, but people change, and I've been absent for a long time," said Heldring as he leaned back in the battered chair.

"That it has, that it has. However, like the day we met, I am still a simple smith who leads a simple life."

Heldring turned the blade in his hands, "You are hardly a simple smith," he said. "Only a true master could make a blade as fine as this."

"So, are you going after her?", the smith asked rather pointedly.

"You already know the answer to that question," countered Heldring.

"Have you given any thought as to how you'll get into the castle?", asked the smith.

"I thought I'd get myself caught for drunken disorderly, and they'd throw me in the dungeons," Heldring laughed.

"Sounds like a good plan," the smith agreed. "There's only one problem with that."

"What?", said the suddenly-serious Heldring.

"Olaf told me that the main jailor, Gorgos, had silently moved her outside of the castle walls. They are good friends, you know. Well, as good of friends as you can be with someone like Gorgos. I guess they're more like drinking buddies and they were out carousing the other night. Olaf came back in quite a state, I must say. He was rambling on about how Gorgos had a deal with the Queen and how he'd moved her to his own house, and how afterwards his wife had been taken away into the southlands. He just kept talking up a storm about how Gorgos was gonna kill Pettiman and such."

"I see," said Heldring. "This information does change things somewhat." He sat in silence for many minutes before he spoke again. "Can your grandson take me to Gorgos or at least to his house?"

"Stay the night tonight, as my guest. I have plenty of room and a comfortable bed for you. We'll see what information we can extract from Olaf after work tonight."

"Thank you, I'd like that," replied Heldring. He returned the knife to its velvet-lined container and delicately closed the lid. "I'm glad that you're still alive after all these years," said Heldring.

"I'm glad to see you as well," the smith replied. "But, I think you have some explaining to do. Where have you been for the last eight hundred years and why do you look so different?" The two friends talked late into the night, long after Olaf came up from the forge and they loosed his brain of information about Gorgos and his part in the grand scheme. At last they parted ways for the night, each retiring to their own realm of nighttime dreams. In the wee hours of the morning, Heldring gathered the box and its contents. He wrote a short note, grabbed the box, and silently slipped through the doorway to the street.

The smith read the note aloud several hours later: "I will pay for the blade with his blood once she is safe. Of that you have my promise. Signed, 'Heldring'."

+   +   +   +

Gordon noticed a pungent odor in the air as he stopped
to have a quick snack to calm his nerves and fill his
always hungry belly. He'd never noticed it before. He
sniffed at the air again; it kind of smelled musky, like a
wet dog. He didn't see anything, so he finished his
snack and drew his doorway. He stepped through and
closed the door before he saw the animal that had been
watching him. He stepped out of the doorway into a
back alley below the castle keep. The stench of
slaughtered animals and raw sewerage brought the taste
of bile to his mouth.

"Maybe I shouldn't have eaten," he thought. He
covered his golden-brown hair with the wool cloak's
hood.

"Hello Father," said a passerby. He must have
looked like a monk doing service work in the poor
neighborhood – so much the better. He followed the
map he'd drawn in his mind to the little house at the
end of the street: the one with the yellow shutters. He
knocked once, as he had been instructed, and walked
into the house. The room was poorly lit, so he couldn't
see the man who spoke to him from the shadows of the
room.

"You'll takes the packages to Leoht as arranged?"

"Yes," said Gordon who wasn't sure how big his
packages were going to be.

"No questions asked?"

"That's correct." He brought the packages from the
next room.

"Go! Now!", he whispered harshly. "I'll finds you
when I can." A middle-aged woman of medium build
and a tall, lithe woman with long black hair stepped
into the few rays of light in the cottage.

"Cover your heads," said Gordon. He collected
payment, a pen and ink well, turned to the women and
bluntly said "Let's go." They wound their way towards

the outskirts of the castle. He drew their escape door and then stepped through to the Devil's Hole Forest. Once the door had closed completely, Gordon started to walk towards the Covington Road. His mind raced to fill the silence that existed among the three travellers. Who were these women? What made them so special? Were they a piece of the puzzle? His orders were to take them to a small farm over the Aberdeen Bridge.

He'd never been to the farm country. It'd be a nice change. Before their emergence onto the main road, Gordon stopped for lunch. Cook had packed meat pies for the three of them. They were absolutely delicious. The middle-aged woman spoke for the first time.

"You're very lucky to have such a wonderful chef. They're few and far between. What's her name?"

"I don't know," answered Gordon truthfully. "I only know her as Cook."

"Offer her my appreciation when you next see her." There were several minutes of silence before she asked, "What can I call you?"

"No names, remember?"

"Oh, right. Well, you can call me B." The other woman held her silence like a tightly wrapped shroud. Gordon looked at the middle-aged woman sidelong for a few minutes.

"That's not breaking the rules," she said. "I just picked a letter from the alphabet."

"I guess that's okay," replied Gordon. "You can call me Z." He always wanted to be called Zane, after his favorite cowboy author Pearl Zane Grey. "We should go," said Gordon. "We still have a long distance. If we're lucky, we'll be able to hitch a ride on a farmer's wagon." That did happen but not for several hours after their emergence onto Covington Road. By nightfall, they had arrived at their destination: a small farm on the boundary of Leoht and Aquilegia Ferry.

Gordon handed B the key to their new home. He followed them into the house to make sure nothing was amiss. He set the bag with the few items they'd taken with them on the kitchen table.

"Everything looks just fine," he said. "Be happy in your new home."

"Thank you Z, and I hope to see you again and repay the favor. Maybe I'll bake a meat pie for you." Gordon looked to the other woman who stood in front of the long kitchen window staring at the endless rolling hills.

"That'd be just fine," he said. "Until that time." He turned and walked away. He needed to get home and soon. He was getting that prickly feeling that he'd been getting of late. It wouldn't do to get that feeling with another man's wife regardless of how he felt, especially not when he had the interest of two women at home. The doorway closed with a fizzle.

+ + + +

Gorgos slowly removed the rockslide that inhibited his forward motion through this newest of his exploratory tunnels. He'd never been down this passageway and yearned to see what was beyond this rather large impasse. He'd been working for days removing the rocks, a very tedious job, as he had to carry them, one by one, back to the previous cavern. The passageways were so narrow that he could only put one rock next to the other to make a row lining the entire passageway back to the cavern. He'd spent so many years in the underground that he found old tunnels, like this one, partially blocked from years of cave-ins, soothing to his soul.

He was close to the Obsidian Tower, he was sure of that and none too pleased about it, but he'd become emboldened over the years of seeing no one deep within the bowels of the earth. Gorgos stretched his aching back muscles; he was made for the underground. He loved the smell of the damp earth and the claustrophobic passageways — passageways that were built by dwarves, for dwarves, many centuries ago. He was sure that if he looked far enough, he would find a labyrinth of tunnels under the entirety of Innes.

When he was underground, he felt safe. Maybe he, Gorgos himself, had dwarf blood in his family lineage. There were many months that the dungeons of Dosk sat empty and his skills were not needed. It was during these periods that he would explore the caverns and narrow passageways that barely allowed his large, well-muscled body to pass.

He knew from experience that this underground network was rarely used. He'd been derelict from his duty for over two weeks. Since Pettiman occasionally removed the soldiers from the Sapphire Tower, Gorgos had spent his time between the luxuries of the Tower and the tunnels of the underground. Pettiman was so consumed with his war effort that he paid little attention to his own living room, so to speak.

He'd easily conquered Twe-Leoht – although Gorgos had his own thoughts on that subject. In his mind the old hag, Lorelei, had been vanquished too easily. He didn't believe the stories of her demise, no, not for one minute. He had had the women safely removed from Dosk. It had been costly, but it was worth it; besides, he'd found a small cache in the underground that he'd slowly been carrying out of the darkness, which easily covered the expense.

What did he need with an old pen and ink set? He couldn't read or write, and didn't really want to learn. For the first time in over twenty years, he was free to do as he pleased. He removed the last rock from the impasse and decided to rest before moving on. He measured his water into his drinking cup and then removed from his rucksack a pre-portioned meal – a meager offering for a man of his size. He removed a pair of lightening bugs from their packaging and fastened them into place. The lamp cast a soft, slightly bluish glow. He carefully repacked his belongings and then carried the bag in front of him as he stepped past the rockslide.

He could feel the tunnel's slight descent and changing wall texture – becoming smoother, the deeper he crept. He could feel a sudden onset of heat as he walked down the slightly sloping passageway. He detected an unusual odor, one that was quite distinct from the damp rock walls. He could see the end of the passageway was low and decided to slow his descent. He was glad that he had because the tunnel ended suddenly, leaving one of his feet hanging in mid-air. He looked down on a huge cavern backlit by a glow of slow moving lava. In the middle of the lava atoll was more gold than Gorgos had ever seen. He knew immediately that he'd stumbled into a dragon's lair. He'd heard of such stories as a child, but stories they had remained.

How was he to get down there, and, once he was there, how would he get back out again? The top of the lode was at least twenty feet below him. He'd brought a length of rope with him, but even if he found somewhere to attach the one end, the other end would dangle precariously close to the lava flow. He sat down for a few minutes to take stock of his gear and the situation.

He noticed another passageway opening lower down on the opposite side. He saw other openings as well, but they had been overtaken with lava. There has to be other ways in and out of here, he thought. The worm that lived here needed to hunt. Speaking of which, where was the resident dragon? Suddenly the ground began to shake and several of the rocks broke loose from the impasse. He swung his body aside just in time, as they came thundering past him and into the lava.

He thought it would be nice to know the depth of the lava channel. He'd dislodged hundreds of rocks. If he could just push them into the channel, it might give him an opportunity. He had nothing to lose. He started dislodging those rocks closest to the entranceway. The smaller ones just puffed into smoke while the larger ones gradually disappeared into the flow. He continued with his labor, in no particular hurry, not really sure if this would be successful. He worked the boulders slowly and carefully to the end of the passageway. He kept one boulder back, as an anchor to tie the end of his rope; the others were pushed into the channel. Unbelievably, he could see the top of one boulder. It was all the edge he needed. He pushed rock after rock into the lava until he saw a pathway develop that was high enough to serve as a dam, and to allow his passage.

He knew he'd have to move quickly. He doubted the thick soles of his boots would tolerate the heat for long. He secured his pack and double checked the rope.

"Here goes nothing," he said aloud. He sparked his adrenalin and jumped. He rappelled the first ten to fifteen feet. He could feel the heat lick at his thick skin. The rope jerked to a stop and he began to untie himself when he felt the rope move. Looking up, he saw the remaining boulder onto, which he was tied, slip off of the cliff's edge. He roared into action, flying across the rock tops, his feet barely touching the tops. He tore at the rope trying to loosen the tightened knot. He freed the rope from his waist just as the boulder hit the stone dam. The molten lava was released, and prevented any possibility of his return in that direction.

He panted as the sweat poured from his horny brow. He could feel the hairs singed from his arms and eyebrows. His heart pounded at the close call. He moved away from the lava towards the center of the mound. He poured himself a double ration of water, sprawled onto the flat rock's surface, and closed his eyes until his heart returned to its normal beat. He got up and slowly surveyed his surroundings. It would do no good to be fabulously rich if he couldn't find his way out of here.

The cavern was immense – the biggest he'd seen by far. There was enough gold to finance the war effort, he thought. He could pay many a good soldier, become a general of his own army, rather than a slave — or, he could keep it all for himself. He climbed atop the burgeoning mound of gold, in part, to get away from the heat, in part, to see what was in the chamber.

He surveyed three-hundred sixty degrees and spotted a tunnel he hadn't seen from the upper passageway. He figured to scan the tunnel in hopes of a way out of the chamber. The worm must come in and out from somewhere, he thought. Although he hadn't really heard of any recent dragon activity, he still assumed that the resident dragon was alive and well. They were magical after all. Gorgos slowly made his way down from the top of the gold horde. He stopped every couple of minutes to put a gold coin in some secret compartment of his clothing, just in case, he thought. He walked across what appeared to be a stone bridge, and made his way into the passageway. The light of his little lantern was lost in the darkness of the space he'd just entered. He found a wall and started to follow it.

Fortunately, he found several torches that were still

viable. He lit them and placed them around the room, making a complete circuit along the outer wall. What he saw stunned him more than the gold-filled room had. Standing in the middle of the floor, behind four glass-like enclosures was a dragon. But this was not just any dragon – Gorgos knew better. This was the Obsidian Dragon of Deorc. But why was he locked behind these walls, unmoving – like he was frozen in time? He stood with his hand opened against the glass with a longing he'd never known in his life. He hated seeing this magnificent creature caged.

Suddenly, a spark of an idea lit up his brain, and, for an instant, time itself stood still. He decided in the one moment that he was going to free the dragon from its icy embrace and take it away from these horrible wraiths. How could they be so cruel? He'd been accused of cruelty before, in his dealings with Dosk prisoners. But here, behind these four walls, he saw into the depths of Wraith malice. In his mind, this cruelty was far worse than any he'd meted out and he was appalled.

He walked around the enclosure looking for any breaks or seams in the cold wall. He could find none. He thought for many minutes as the dragon's fate crowded his mind. He couldn't … no he wouldn't leave the dragon encased in this icy tomb. He didn't know if the dragon was dead or alive. No matter — freeing the dragon was his only concern. When he started to reach a frenzied panic, the idea of the lava sprang from his mind. The lava, bring the lava into this room and let it melt the ice or whatever material entombed his prize. The next problem was how to move the lava? If he could only get a small amount of the lava into the room, he could at least test his theory. He returned to the lava chamber. Not gold, he thought – that will melt. He thought about the few items he carried in his pack, none of which seemed to solve his problem.

Then he looked at the flowing channels of lava. Of course, how obvious the answer had been. If only he could harness the lava to warm the ice and release the creature. And then, as if in answer to his problem, the ground shook. At first it was only a minor tremor, which shook some of the gold mound into the lava flow. He could see that small cracks had appeared in the flooring of the chamber, but not enough to solve his problem. A few moments later, the ground shook as if hell itself had come to the surface of the planet. Gorgos was knocked from his feet. He curled into a ball and covered his head for protection from the falling debris. When the ground quieted, he returned to his feet, and, as if his greatest wish was granted, a channel opened and lava flowed immediately under the chamber behind where the dragon was encased. Multiple aftershocks cemented the work of the major earthquake.

Gorgos inspected the dragon's cell where cracks started to appear. He looked at the horned beast, the way a father looks at his newborn son. He wanted so badly to touch the dragon's iridescent underbelly, stroke the curved horns on his head and feel the power of the beast, as they launched themselves to the skies.

"What is your name?", Gorgos asked the silent beast. He realized that the cell was only slowly diminishing, so he sat back against the closest wall and shut his eyes. Fatigue tugged at every muscle, and, within moments, Gorgos was fast asleep. Many hours later Gorgos awoke to a large head with flaming-red eyes staring not more than a foot from his own. He reached his large sinewy arms to encircle the dragon's head in a loving embrace.

"You must be starving," he said as he reached into his pack and pulled out two pieces of elfin-whey bread. "I knows it's not much, but it's the best I can offers right now. But I promise you, when we gets out of here, I knows where the best sheep and cows are pastured." He rubbed the dragon's nose and placed a piece of the whey-bread on his tongue. He could feel the dragon perk up, as the magical qualities of the sweetbread were released as it melted on his tongue. He gave the dragon several more pieces of the elfin bread.

"What is your name?", he asked again.

"Naphtha," whispered the dragon.

"Naphtha, reborn from the infernos of hell," he said. "Let's rests and then finds a way out of this damnable place." The dragon rested its large head on Gorgos' legs, like his old dog Otto used to do. His thickly calloused hand rubbed the heavily scaled skin of his new friend. Gorgos could feel the hypnotic effects of the binding, making them more than friends. He knew with absolute certainty that he would die for this creature. Of this, he had no doubt.

+ + + +

The front door of the blacksmith's shop closed quietly onto an empty street. Heldring stepped onto the cobblestones, breathed deeply, and turned toward the Sapphire Tower. He'd made a promise to release Jacob and his gnome. He meant to fulfill that promise before his rescue of Cereus. He could smell incense emanating from the temple several blocks away. He was glad to see that the residents of Dosk were still able to worship if they were so inclined. He'd seen no signs of religious persecution since his return, at least no other signs than the Way of Wraith. Heldring had heard of this, although he was not privy to the teachings. He'd been long in the vaults when Belac began to convert other Innesians to the Dark Teachings.

The cool, late-winter air felt good on his face. He thanked the Pillars of Flame and proceeded to walk to the not-too-distant Tower. He figured he'd find Jacob hidden behind the secret passageway door. The real question was how to get into the kitchen without being seen by the soldiers that Heldring knew guarded the castle. He quickly stepped into a café; the smell of fresh baked bread overwhelmed his sense of urgency. But it was the sound of footsteps – many of them – that finalized his decision. He looked from the darkened doorway as an entire brigade of foot soldiers tromped on their way to the frontlines of Pettiman's war.

He ordered bacon, eggs, and black coffee. The waitress, a pretty young girl, watered his glass and placed small bowls of baked beans, butter, and marmalade on the red-checkered tablecloth. He thanked her and asked of news. She pardoned herself to her many duties and left Heldring to his own devices. He listened to the conversations of the people at the surrounding tables. Tidings were the same. This terrible war, that none of the Doskian people wanted. And why did the Queen allow Pettiman, "to get away with it?" These were the words whispered by most of the patron's lips. Each of the women sitting at the table behind him had a husband or brother who was at the front or on their way to the front.

He considered his plan as he ate his sunny-side eggs and wheat toast heavily slathered with butter and marmalade. He knew of one way he could enter the tower without getting caught, but it would require a great deal of luck on his part. He could hear a reckless voice chattering in his head, but Heldring didn't like to leave plans up to luck, unless he could stack the deck, in his favor of course. He didn't have time to enter the underground in the Jahandi Wastelands. There were few who knew the castle as well as he did. It was his architects who added secret passageways to connect different portions of the castle. Not that Heldring ever expected a coup d'etat, but it was better to be prepared. He stood at the corner bistro where he and Nate and Tom had stopped several days before their capture and exposure to Cereus. He would have preferred an alternate meeting, but one didn't always have control of future events.

He walked to the gatehouse. For some reason, there was only one guard on duty and he'd fallen asleep at his post. Heldring could smell sweat and the musty smell of the soldier's leather gherkin, long overdue for washing. He quietly walked to the farthest wall behind the soldier's station, and carefully began to look for the release that would allow him to slip through the curtain wall and into the lower bailey undetected. He was concerned about rust after all these years, and hoped that the release would silently dislodge. Ah — there it is, he thought. He tickled the catch — it released as if it had been oiled yesterday. He silently slid behind the wall, as the soldier roused from his nap. He felt the catch slide into place as he pushed the wall closed behind him. He found a torch hanging on the wall and lit it.

"Cobwebs!", he gasped. How he loathed spiders. He removed his new dagger from the sheath at his belt, climbed ten steps, and proceeded through the fifteen-foot wall to the lower bailey. This part was easy. What was tricky was emerging from the wall undetected. He stood alongside the wall and slid his fingers lightly along the brick, while looking for the plug that hid the eye hole from all but the closest inspection. "Ah, here we go," he whispered aloud as he removed the plug from its hole. He released the latch and slid the door open onto the lower bailey. He smiled and decided he owed his old friend, the smithy, a draught. What foresight made him keep these locks oiled all of these years; besides, how did he accomplish it? He chuckled at his friend's resourcefulness as he slid along the wall toward the Sapphire Tower.

He had to cross the bailey proper to the Tower entrance, about a hundred feet from his position. "Out in the open," he murmured, "I better look like I belong." An urgent message should help me gain entrance, he thought. He removed a scrap of paper from his vest, an obvious message, and walked to the main entrance. He grasped the heavily- weighted iron knocker, an ornate sigil of the house of Heldring, and banged on the heavy oak door. He was surprised to be confronted by an old man. The same old man that attended to Cereus — what luck. Again, he could hear an unknown voice nattering in his head. He stopped to laugh for a second — who was he, Nicolas Heldring, calling this fine gentleman old, when he himself was a thousand years old. The irony was not lost on him, and he chuckled to himself again. Jacob didn't recognize this newcomer and wasn't feeling very welcoming.

"What's so funny?", he asked.

"Nothing," said the newcomer. He paused a few moments, "Can I come in?"

"How did you get past the guards?"

"I have an important message, one that I needed to deliver myself," said Heldring.

"What is your message,", asked Jacob.

"Please, I'd like to come in," replied Heldring who ducked below Jacob's arm that was holding the door ajar. Heldring walked around the vestibule, while peaking his head into each of the adjoining rooms.

"What are you looking for?", asked Jacob who'd had enough of debauchery and moral turpitude.

"Are we alone?", asked Heldring.

"Yes," said Jacob. "Why? What is your message?"

"You don't recognize me?", asked Heldring.

"No, should I?", replied Jacob.

Moments later a gnome came walking into the waiting area, eyed Jacob, and said to Heldring, "Please, come with me." He put his finger to his lips to shush any response Heldring might utter and turned towards the kitchen. Jacob grunted and shrugged his arms. The gnome always seemed to know what was happening. He wished he'd share some of his information, at least once in a while. Caleb dismissed the cook after she put the kettle on and laid out a few snacks. Heldring was grateful, his belly rumbling loudly in response. It had been several hours since his last meal.

"How is it that you are in the tower with no guard?", asked Jacob.

Heldring responded with a cat-like smile, "Would you like to hear my message?", he asked. Both men nodded their heads in agreement.

"I'd like to know how it is that neither of you are under guard because when I left here the last time, an entire regiment was banging down the door."

"Who ARE you?", demanded Jacob.

Caleb smiled, "The last time I saw you, you were in Lorelei's rose gardens. But that was when you were Drakken Aruhl, if I'm not mistaken."

"You are a sly one," laughed Heldring, along with the other voice in his head.

"What is going ...," said Jacob as he finally realized what was happening. He gasped: "Your Highness ... I didn't know."

"Of course you didn't know. Stand up. I've come to understand some of the aches and pains that you must feel every time you have to kneel and stand back up." Again he chuckled. Just as they were about to partake of their snacks, there was an uproar in the vestibule. Jacob and Caleb looked at one another.

"Hurry, we must go. The soldiers have returned." Caleb opened the hidden door that Heldring had used to escape the last time. Jacob grabbed the food tray and kettle and off they went through the doorway. Heldring closed the door silently behind them just as the soldiers entered the kitchen.

"There's no one in here," they could hear one of them yell. The three men sat in silence for many minutes after they heard the last soldier rooting through the kitchen. The cook would be angry at the disturbance. She didn't like interlopers in her kitchen. But then, this was the first time in history that interlopers had forced themselves into her space.

Heldring sat back on his heels, "I can see I'm none too soon. I've come to rescue the two of you, and I mean to do just that. I made a promise to Nate, and I mean to keep that promise."

"So Nate is safe?", asked Jacob.

"Yes he is, at least for now. But Pettiman's soldiers are very near Lorelei's lands, so we must act quickly."

"How are we going to get out?", asked Caleb. "The paths out of these catacombs could take days."

"I've left Windwalker with a trusted friend. We just need to slip out the way I came in. Then you two take Windwalker out of the city through the crypts and I'll be on my way."

"Where are we going? Where are you going? How are we getting out of the Tower?", the questions poured forth from Jacob.

Heldring chuckled: "Have faith my friend. I have a plan."

"Are you going for Cereus?", asked Caleb.

"Of course," said Heldring.

"My brother, Gaelen, was here yesterday. He said that Cereus is no longer in the dungeons and that Gorgos has disappeared into the caves he was exploring, dead by all accounts. Pettiman is furious." Gaelen told us, "Pettiman put a huge price on Gorgos's head. The Pillars of Flame have pity on his soul if he is still alive. Every low-down cutthroat will be after him," said Caleb.

"That makes our task even more urgent," said Heldring. "Was there any news as to where Cereus was taken?"

"Not that we've heard," said Jacob. Heldring could hear the voice rankling in his head again. Maybe the former occupant's being didn't entirely leave when the wards were broken. It appeared that way, at least in his situation. He paced in the secret passageway behind the stoves in the kitchen of the Sapphire Tower; minutes had turned into hours and then a full day.

"We can't stay penned up like sheep," he ranted. It had only been a day since his return to the tower, but he'd not had a good morning. Adapting to this new body hadn't been easy, and sleeping on the stone floor had aggravated every joint ache and old scar pain. He could feel the remnants of Lorelei's rage and how it had tempered this entity akin to forged steel. He didn't mind that part at all.

It's better than the other option, he thought. He shivered at the thought of returning to centuries of being banished from all whom you loved, all that you knew, all that you were, until you are nothing but a shred of your former self, with only a glimmer of hope that someday, someone will come along and rescue you from an eternity of suffering and shame. But he did like the feel of youth, and Nate's body had been strong and supple. He missed that.

"Will you please sit down for a minute," hissed Jacob. "I know you're ready to go and fight. But take a minute, be reasonable. We're outnumbered."

"Why are the soldiers still hanging around?", Caleb

wondered. "Usually they don't stay around this long."

"At least Gorgos released Cereus from the dungeons," chuckled Nicolas. "It just goes to show that Pettiman is not as almighty as he thinks he is."

"She said she had a plan. She knew that Pettiman would arrest her eventually. She would say that he thinks I'm without resources or power. Or else he just doesn't care. She was not sure which answer was correct, but she hedged her bets knowing that, either way, he would come for her on some trumped up charges," said Jacob. "When you showed up with Arion, it was inevitable."

"I'm sorry to cause so much trouble," said Nicolas. "I had no idea that events had gotten so out of control."

Heldring paced for a few more minutes, "Jacob, I want you and Caleb to take Windwalker through the crypts and go on to Twe-Leoht."

"I couldn't manage the crypts," said Jacob. "I have no idea where I'm going."

"That's the easy part. Windwalker will remember. Don't forget he is a magical horse," said Heldring.

"You must meet up with Nate and Ted within the next couple of days. It's urgent."

"But what about you, Your Majesty,", asked Jacob.

"I'm going to stay hidden for another day or so. I agree, the soldiers will pull out soon and then I can leave. I have enough food and water to last. You've seen to that," he laughed.

"Why don't you come with us?", offered Jacob.

"I have other matters to attend to before I can leave Dosk. Promises have been made."

2: Happy Birthday Emily

"I know it's been several weeks since you've received a luncheon invitation Emily," said Bhodi, "but you need to snap out of this mood. It's not healthy for either one of us."

"I'm sorry if I don't make you happy, Bhodi. It's not like I asked for any of this to happen."

"I know. But you have to make the best of the situation. Sulking and crying all day isn't going to change your circumstances. The masters are trying to break you ... take away your will ... your individuality. Mold you into their image."

"Isn't that what they've done to you," she sneered – "Made you their pet."

"You have no idea what they've done to me," he replied sadly as he sat down on his cot, face in hands. It was true, she didn't. She'd been so self-involved that she never really asked him anything about himself. She was always so willing to accept his generosity without returning anything of herself. She was selfish and vain; she knew that. She had always been that way. She sat on the edge of her cot. It was obvious that no one paid her any mind. She could scream out the cell doors as long and as loud as she wanted, but it would do no good.

"Bhodi," she said, "I'm sorry. I know I'm not very nice. I don't want to be mean or say mean words. Sometimes I can't help it. It's like I have this other personality that takes over my brain and makes me do and say things I don't really mean to say and do. What can I do?"

"I don't know, Emily. I just wish you wouldn't take your frustrations out on me. If you notice, I'm in the cell with you, not sipping tea with the master and mistress."

"I know. Again, I'm really sorry." She came and sat down next to him on the cot.

"I know you like the pretty dresses and the good food they served you. But you must know; they're playing you: plying you with the best items money can buy. How little or how much will it take to bend you to do their bidding? Why do you think they're doing it?"

"It's just that I've been here for so long. I liked the way I felt when they brought me a new dress, instead of leaving me to rot away in this dark hole."

"I know Emily. Don't you see? That's their game?"

"I guess I do. Thanks Bhodi," she said as she hugged him. As if in response to her acceptance, Miss Van opened the cell door and the processional of porters and maids followed with linens and scents for her bath. Emily's heart skipped a beat in response. What could this possibly mean? Her mind raced with the possibilities. She repeated the daily process of those previous months; only this time, her black hair was piled high on her head and her skin was powdered white. Miss Van laced her into a black satin bodice with a long, sweeping, black satin skirt. Black ballet-type slippers were laced onto her feet by the handmaids.

The powdery whiteness of her skin contrasted with the darkness of her eye makeup and the blood-red lipstick painted on her lips. Emily looked to Bhodi as she was escorted from the jail cell like so many times before. She was taken to a room she had never visited before and was told to sit on a dark-colored upholstered plush divan. A fire crackled in a huge fireplace, but it barely diminished the chill that lingered in the air. She looked around the room, noticing a medium-sized table set with luncheon china and two chairs. The large room had floor-to-ceiling windows, which were covered by heavy brocaded drapes. What little light brightened the room came from gas-lit sconces hanging from the walls and ceiling. In addition to the divan where Emily sat, the room was furnished with matching, upholstered, plush chairs and two sofas. The room had a slight citrusy odor mixed with wood from the fireplace.

Her stomach started to growl. She wondered when they would serve lunch and she'd be allowed to move. She'd decided she would play their game, if only to get her released from her jail cell every day. Just when she started to get fidgety, a tall spidery thin man in a tuxedo walked through the door. His translucent skin glowed, a silvery color in the lamp light of the room.

"Please stand for the mistress of the Obsidian Tower. That would be you, young lady." Emily was frozen where she sat. For so many months, she'd been brought to some room, watched (she was sure), then fed, and sent back to her jail cell. When the man offered his instruction, she was unprepared.

"Stand up, miss," he instructed again. Emily rose to her feet. She could feel her body trembling from head to toe. Images of the last meeting with one of these creatures flashed through her mind, sobering her initial anxiety. She wouldn't make the same mistake twice. A tall, lithe figure with black hair entered the room behind the butler. Emily lowered her eyes and curtseyed as the woman stood before her.

"Look at me," said the woman to Emily. "Such lovely green eyes," she sighed.

"My name is Mortifera," she said as she extended her hand towards Emily. "I hope you haven't been too inconvenienced, but my husband and I had to leave the tower for a few days. I hope you'll accept my apologies."

Emily's eyes met Mortifera's deep black eyes as she stuttered, "Yes ma'am, thank you ma'am." She noticed the thin circle of red that surrounded the black irises, the long black lashes, and pale translucent skin. Emily noticed Mortifera's heavy, black eye makeup, almost Egyptian. She's beautiful, thought Emily.

Mortifera laughed, "I was thinking the same of you, dear. You're quite spectacular yourself." Emily blushed and then realized that neither woman had spoken aloud.

Emily looked at Mortifera, "You can hear my thoughts?"

"Yes dear, I can hear your thoughts."

"But how can I hear yours?"

"We've evolved beyond the need to speak. We can speak when we need to, of course, but most of the time, we don't need to. You could try to block me, but I think you found out how unpleasant the experience is when you were in the council chambers." Emily nodded her body taut with anxiety.

"Good. Now, why don't you join me for lunch, I was just about to eat." Emily agreed. The butler seated Emily, a different servant poured a glass of water, an iced tea, and two others brought her a soup, salad, and a sandwich.

"I hope you find the fare satisfactory," said Mortifera.

"May I ask if you're also eating," asked Emily.

"Oh no dear, we don't eat. At least, not like humans," she replied, as the butler placed a carafe filled with something red and a brandy snifter in front of her. A different servant, the footman, she thought, poured the thick viscous liquid into the snifter and tasted it.

Mortifera looked at Emily and picked up the snifter, swirled the liquid in the glass, and said, "There are circumstances I'd like to discuss with you – mainly your future." Her cheeks flushed a light pink color, within moments of taking a taste of the nectar.

"Please Emily. Eat. I noticed you haven't tasted a morsel. You're going to make me feel like a bad hostess."

"I'm sorry, Mortifera. You're a wonderful hostess. I'm still just a little bit nervous." Emily ladled the soup into her mouth. It did have a wonderful taste, and her appetite soon took over her feelings of uncertainty. Emily felt flushed, and her senses heightened after eating the delicious soup. She was going to ask for more but didn't want to seem piggish, as she still had a salad and sandwich in front of her.

She ate the balance of the food provided even though her bodice was stretching at the seams. The tightening of the bodice prevented Emily from slouching, a habit she had, and made her more apt to sit with her back and shoulders straight. By sitting in just the right manner, she felt relief from the pinching bodice. Next time, she'd have to eat a little less, so she wasn't so uncomfortable.

Just as Emily was finishing her food, Mortifera's butler came to her side and whispered something into her ear.

Mortifera smiled and said, "Emily, we'll have to continue our conversation tomorrow. I have unexpected company that I must receive immediately. You understand, dear, don't you?"

Emily nodded and was led out the door she had entered and returned to the little cell she shared with her gnome friend Bhodi Hobken. She changed back into her regular clothes and took care to hang the others on a small hook by her bed. Bhodi said nothing as he watched her stare out their little window. Emily retired early that evening, with no words spoken. And so it went, day after day.

After the tenth day, Bhodi noticed that the hand maidens didn't need to apply the white powder to Emily's face and hands. After fifteen days, the blue veins could be seen through her increasingly translucent skin. By the seventeenth day, Emily could no longer stomach the food that had kept her strong and vital. In its stead, the hand maidens brought carafes of the red viscous liquid she'd seen Mortifera drink during their first luncheon.

After twenty days, Emily's emerald green eyes changed to black and red. By the end of the month, the change was complete. Emily had become one of them. She never complained, never argued, never cried over the painful changes to her body. After three and a half months of forced imprisonment, she was surviving in the best way she knew how. Bhodi couldn't fault her. She'd made the best decision based on the available information. There was no way she could know the outcome. There was no way any of them could know the future. Affairs in Innes were changing; there was no doubt about it. He sat next to her on her little cot and handed her a small box wrapped with a lime green bow.

"Happy birthday, Emily." She eyed him carefully.

"Have you forgotten? Today is your eighteenth birthday." She took his gift and started to cry.

$+ + + +$

Draedon returned to The Boiling Cauldron around midnight. He knew the innkeeper well and knew she'd have a hot meal awaiting his return. He wasn't disappointed. He'd shared her bed off and on for over five years, returning as often as his trips to Dosk allowed. He found her skilled enough and fun enough to be with – not as demanding as his romps with Cereus. He loved her long golden locks and womanly curves. She was the complete opposite of Cereus's tall, willowy stature and jet black hair. Lily provided the playfulness that Cereus lacked.

He'd gotten the feeling that something had changed with Cereus. He wasn't prone to conjecture or fantasy. Rather, he liked facts. But he had this nagging feeling about Cereus. He'd have to tuck it away for now, as he was too far away to find out for himself. He needed to get to Deorc. Returning to Dosk was out of the question. He couldn't send his new charge. Will lacked training, and Draedon still wasn't sure he trusted him. He would send Lily to collect the balance of his money. He'd sent her in the past with success. Maybe she could poke around and pick up threads of news while in and around the tower.

He'd expected more problems, and, other than that pesky dog, Lorelei's execution was rather simple. It nagged at him that the dog didn't die with everything else in Twe-Leoht, but Lily's warm embrace helped him to forget. Yet, Draedon didn't like loose ends, and the dog was a loose end. Loose ends had a tendency to come back to bite him in the end. He didn't know how or when, but this loose end would surely haunt him in the future. Sleep didn't come easy, and his thoughts turned to Will: asset or liability. His usefulness was still unclear. But Draedon was a gambler and would see his bet through to the end.

3: Loyalty

Nate and Ted went back into the tower, swept up the remains of Lorelei and Olivia, took the ashes to the once profitable gardens and then released them into the gentle breeze. They used the remainder of the day to survey the rest of the tower. They collected items that seemed of value and placed them in a common area. They would hide them later. Nate had no intention of leaving heirlooms for the soldiers to loot. They just had to figure out a really good spot. Day two found Nate within a few feet of entering the Devil's Hole Forest. He stuck a long piece of grass in his teeth, sat down, and stared into the forest. He'd never been here, and yet, there was some sort of familiarity, a feeling of déjà vu.

He looked at the forest as he contemplated their next move. He'd heard magical stories of the Amber Tower since his arrival in Innes as well as other not so magical stories of the Obsidian Tower. He'd been in two of the five towers. Neither of them could hold a candle to his beloved Sun Dew Farm. He was thrilled for Fletcher and gave the sleeping dog a scratch on the butt.

It was some kind of luck to find him in the hundreds of miles of woods that made up Monkshood Forest. He saw it as a good omen. They'd found a series of caves about two hundred yards into the forest. Tomorrow was day three. He would finish stashing the items to be preserved from the Moldavite Tower. He was glad they'd gotten as much done today as they had. It made the day go by quicker; besides, he was pretty sure he smelled snow in the air. He hoped the good weather would hold for a few more days.

Ted had left a couple of hours earlier, saying he "wanted to survey the landscape."

Nate figured he wanted to see if any of Pettiman's soldiers were close at hand or maybe he just wanted to leave the devastation. It was a sobering reminder that the thousand year fabric, which held Innes together, was being shredded. Life as these folks knew it was ending, whether they were consciously aware of it or not. From everything they could find, it looked as though all life in the entire county of Twe-Loeht had ended abruptly. Then he looked at Fletcher.

"Why didn't you die? Somehow being from outerworld prevented your death." He would have to think more on this issue. Darkness had almost enclosed the landscape as Nate entered the tower. After making a light supper in the kitchen, he climbed to Lorelei's rooms.

He couldn't possibly imagine – what it meant to live a thousand years and what it meant to be the mother of Innes. He walked around her rooms for the second night, trying to find out what kind of woman she was. He sat on the edge of her bed, pulled off his boots, and relaxed atop her thick down comforter with Fletcher next to him. Both were soon fast asleep. After an early breakfast, Nate went back to his task of preserving Twe-Leoht history.

Ted rode into the castle sometime close to lunchtime. "Pettiman's soldiers have entered into the Jahandhi Wastelands," he said.

"How many soldiers?", asked Nate.

"I counted seven divisions. They haven't moved into Twe-Leoht yet. But it's only a matter time before someone does."

"Let's get this finished and get the opening well-hidden." Ted added items from his own personal collection as well.

"Did you go home?", asked Nate.

"There were a few things I wanted from the place. I figured I'd never see my house again, or at least not for a long time, and there were items I didn't want poached. I also grabbed more stingers and some other little nasty armaments I like to keep close by." Nate shivered at the thought. He'd been on the receiving end of one of those nasty little items, not too long ago himself. Fletcher's sniffed the dead chickens that Tom removed from his bag and the half a dozen or so eggs.

"We can boil these up; they'll stay longer. I let my cows go and brought my other horse. We'll need a pack horse at the least, even with all the items we stashed in the woods." The well-fed men and dog passed a dreamless night. The snow started somewhere around noon into day four of their vigil. Nate was glad they'd finished their task of preserving as many items of value as they could. There was little else to do, but wait. He and Fletcher took a walk around what had been Lorelei's flower gardens.

"These gardens must have been a sight to see," he said to the dog. Fletcher looked up at Nate and then trotted ahead. The thin blanket of snow covered the scarred landscape, giving the illusion of beauty. The full moon shone onto the ice crystals, adding to the magical qualities that the landscape seemed to be undergoing. He walked towards a small cottage he had just noticed, hidden in a dense thicket. He would have walked right by the cottage had it not been for the moonlight and the snowfall lighting the pathway.

There was no response when he knocked at the front door. He opened the door and stepped inside. Fletcher had somehow beaten him into the cottage, and was lying at the feet of an impossibly old woman who sat in a rocking chair next to the fireplace.

Nate cleared his throat, "I'm sorry ma'am. I didn't know anyone was at home. Please excuse my rudeness, it's just that ...."

"Please come in grandnephew, I've been waiting for you."

"Grandnephew?", he asked.

"I guess she never told you?"

"I'm sorry, I don't understand. What are you saying to me?", he replied.

"No I guess you wouldn't," she countered.

"Well, allow me to introduce myself. I'm Lorelei Lorlinda, the twin sister to your grandmother, Pearl Sutton. That makes you my grandnephew."

"But, ... you're dead. Everything in Twe-Leoht is dead."

"It's true, I am old, but I'm not dead, not yet anyway. I know that fool Draedon thinks so. Come over here," she said. Nate walked closer to his grandaunt.

"It's imperative that everyone think I'm dead. Do you understand me?"

"But why aren't you? Everything else is in a shambles – dead and dried up. Who were those ashes that we scattered in the gardens?"

"Nate you have so many questions. Slow down, will you? I am an old woman after all," she said. As she laughed at her own statement, she transformed into a beautiful woman who looked just like his grandmother.

"I knew he was coming of course. I released Drakken from his warder's responsibility and placed his obligation upon this trusty animal."

"On Fletcher?"

"Is that your name? Thank you, Nate. It's a good

strong name, straight to the point. I see you know each other."

"Well, yeah, he's my dog, my friend."

"I can tell. He's torn between the two of us right now."

"Why would you make a dog your warder?"

"Because no one would think of it, and we are at war. I'm just an old lady with a dog in a broken-down cottage. Who'd think differently of me?", she said, as she transformed back into the old lady he'd seen upon his arrival.

"It makes sense, I guess. So when I leave tomorrow, Fletcher will need to stay with you?"

"If it's okay with you?", she asked. "I know it's a tough decision to leave such a trustworthy friend to do an old woman's bidding but your dog is now bound to me. If you insist I can release him from his duty, but he'll always try to return to me. Dogs are very loyal as I'm sure you know. Besides, didn't Nicolas take my warder's body? A fair trade, if you ask me."

"You know about that?"

"Of course I do. Why do you think I released Drakken from my service and put him square in your path? I know Nicolas Heldring; I couldn't have him running around in my nephew's mind, indefinitely."

Nate laughed heartily at that thought. "I see what you mean. Thanks." She tilted her head in agreement.

"I still don't understand why you didn't die when everything, when everything else is dead."

"I had to lay everything in Twe-Leoht to waste, when Draedon killed the individual he thought was me. I had to return to the source of my power, here in this cottage, until it was over, all of it gone, including those I loved."

"You did this?", asked Nate. "How could you?"

"I will have to live with the results of my decision, the ramifications of which are far greater than you can know, Nate. But I'm afraid many more will die before all is said and done." Nate shook his head in disgust.

"It's important that you listen carefully, Nate. I have been able to rewrite a portion of the Book of Dreams without detection. I run the risk of discovery if I make any more changes and I can't allow that as the rest of Innes is in jeopardy. Tomorrow, two people will be joining your party. Heldring will not return."

"What is the Book of Dreams, and why isn't Heldring coming back?", asked Nate.

"Take heart, you will be reunited with Heldring when and where you least expect him. He has much to do before you can be reunited. He has, however, sent Cereus's servant and his gnome to you. Do not tell them I am alive. No one must know. It's a great burden I know, but you are from strong stock and can bear the weight. Where were you and your party headed?"

"Leoht."

"That's a good idea. Take the route through the Mirthless Swamp; then skirt the edge of the Devil's Hole Forest. By going through the swamp you will miss most of the snowfall. It will not be an easy trek. Make sure you go through my closets and find adequate dry gear. Take the wool clothing. When you get to the Botes River, ask for the boatman named Hans. He will want money, but he will also want something personal from you and each member of your party. Give him your watch or take one of mine, I have several. It is annoying I know, but he is reliable, and no friend to Pettiman or the Black Tower.

Once you have cleared the swamp, pass quietly through Aquilegia Falls and then skirt the Devil's Hole

Forest. You should be safe to cross the Aberdeen Bridge and then on to the Amber Tower."

Nate was quiet for several minutes after Lorelei finished speaking. "How will we recognize the proper route through the swamp?"

"It is marked by small, floral-shaped pink tags. Look carefully. They're spaced every twenty feet or so. The tags are a little closer together as you reach the interior of the swamp."

"Okay," Nate agreed. "But what about you; we can't leave you here? Pettiman's soldiers will certainly kill you."

"You need not worry about me. I will send for you when I need you again. Until that time, you are Daedalus's concern. Your other party members will be here before breakfast. Feed them, and then leave. Do NOT wait any longer." Nate bent over to rub Fletcher's head.

"You stay here with Aunt Lorelei. Okay? Make sure you keep her safe. I'll be back soon enough." Fletcher's tail wagged.

"I love you, boy." Fletcher's tail banged the floor in agreement. With his goodbyes said, Nate left the cottage and returned to the tower. He was grateful that Ted had already gone to bed. He didn't want to offer any explanations tonight. He climbed onto Lorelei's four–poster bed. He figured this to be his last night of comfort for a long time. He wanted to make the most of it. He assumed travel through the Mirthless Swamp would be without joy. He was glad of the snow since it would slow Pettiman's soldiers considerably, giving them some time. Although they might not have to trudge through the snow, he suspected there would be other nightmarish hazards to cross their paths.

"Tomorrow," he thought, as he drifted to sleep. The morning brought Jacob and Caleb, just as Lorelei had said. Nate welcomed them into the castle for a warm, fulfilling breakfast. He chose appropriate clothing for everyone and repacked their horses. He knew Jacob and Caleb were hoping for a night under roof, but Lorelei had specifically said they were to leave today. So they would. He was glad Heldring had given Windwalker to Jacob and Caleb. He knew Nicolas could find good horses in Dosk, but few were Windwalker's equal. The travellers were back on the trail by lunch.

They passed through Lorelei's ruined gardens in the south, passed the now concealed cottage, down the hill, and onto the path leading into the Mirthless Swamp. They made their way single file, Nate first in line, Jacob and Caleb on Windwalker in second place, while Ted and the pack horse took the rear position. Nate followed the markers, which were placed about every twenty feet, just as Lorelei had said.

The warmth and humidity made snow accumulations impossible within the swamp. Nate was grateful for that, to say the least. Yet, travel was difficult. Clumps of sod grass gave the appearance of sturdy ground, but were inconsistent and left these unwary travellers struggling to extricate themselves from some nasty-smelling bottom muck, as Nate quickly found out. They did the best when they travelled a narrow path of solid ground that cut through grey murky pools of standing water. Nights were worse; it was like the swamp came alive with every creepy crawly that took up residence.

The first two nights, they slept in their saddles. No one wanted to stop, neither for sleep nor food. On the third day the travellers found a piece of solid ground, an oasis in this floating world. They decided to make camp, the horses needed rest and so did the party. Jacob got an idea to dig a small trench to encircle them, and in that trench build a fire. It would prevent snakes and other crawlies from entering their campsite.

"Each of us will maintain one part of the circle," said Jacob. Fuel was found in abundance, and, after a light lunch, the exhausted party fell into a deep sleep. Nate awoke shortly after midnight. The rest of the party was awake and rebuilding the flagging fire or readying food for the cook pot. The horses seemed to fare well enough, although they still seemed skittish.

"What can I do?", asked Nate.

"You can chop these carrots," said Jacob.

"Nate, I want to thank you for sending Heldring back for us. Cereus was arrested for treason and taken to the oubliette, and we were next. The soldiers looked everywhere for Caleb and I, but we'd hid behind the kitchen wall. We holed up there every time the soldiers returned to the tower. I spent more than six months in the Dosc dungeons; they'd have to kill me before I'd go back."

Nate nodded. "I was hoping he wasn't too late."

"I think she'll be okay; she has some arrangement worked out with that monster Gorgos."

Caleb put his hand on Jacob's shoulder, "He is what Pettiman has made him. Try not to be too hard on him. Like many of us, he's done what he's had to do in order to survive a bad situation."

"He seems to take delight in his work," retorted Jacob.

"It's true, I'll grant you that, but for those who don't make his life more difficult, I've almost seen kindness. He would add an extra crust of bread or fresh fruit or vegetables that his missus grew in her garden for those inmates. Where do you think the extras came from on your plates? Not from the kitchens. They'd serve gruel to the prisoners if Gorgos allowed it. But they're afraid of him too and wouldn't dare cross him."

Ted listened to Caleb's explanation. "As the Finder of Lost Objects, I myself have had a couple of face-to-face meetings with Pettiman. He is loathsome and foul – a disgusting human being whose greed and wickedness have been the final nail in the Sapphire Tower's proverbial coffin. I can easily understand how a man like Gorgos could be corrupted. A servant has little recourse when he doesn't like his job. A slave has none."

Nate had said little as he listened to his friends' conversation. He tossed the chopped carrots in the pot on the hot embers. "How will Heldring find Cereus?"

"It's no secret she was arrested and taken as a prisoner. I think she knew it was coming and had some sort of a back-up plan. You don't live a thousand years without learning some things, most notably your enemies," replied Jacob. "Now I have a question for you. Why would you choose to traverse this infernal swamp?"

"It was either the Mirthless Swamp, or Devil's Hole Forest. I kind of hoped the swamp wouldn't have accumulated snowfall, and we could make better time. We still have to pass through the forest, and, by all accounts I've heard, you might be better back in the Dosk dungeons. But I do admit I'm starting to second guess my choice."

"You've made the right choice, Nate," replied Ted.

"But if it's all the same to you folks, I'd like to rest one more day here on solid ground. There's no telling when we'll have another chance." All agreed to another night within their fire ring.

Caleb looked at Nate, "When you got into Twe-Leoht, what exactly did you find?"

"Everything was dead. We found nothing alive," answered Nate. "It was like a fire had scorched the earth and taken every living thing with it."

"You found no one alive?"

"No one," said Nate.

"How did Drakken Aruhl survive?"

"We found him sitting on a rock in the Dosk Wastelands. When we tried to ask him some questions, he didn't seem to know who he was or how he'd gotten to Dosk. It was like he was an empty body, if you get my meaning."

"I do. I just don't understand how Lorelei could be destroyed so easily. It just doesn't make any sense."

"If you ask me, none of this makes any sense. My being in Innes doesn't make any sense. But here I am, sitting in the middle of some god-forsaken swamp running away from people who I don't even know. Now, that doesn't make any sense."

Caleb said, "I suppose you're right. Sorry to go on about it; it just doesn't fit." Nate shrugged his shoulders and got up to stir the stew pot. The men returned to sleep after a filling supper. Sometime after one o'clock, the full moon shone on their campsite. With the moon, came night noises: shrieks, screams, and loud hisses. The horses became increasingly restless, until a crescendo was reached and then total silence – completely and instantaneously, as if someone turned off a switch. The tension grew – the air heavily charged with electricity. Blue sparks erupted from the tree tops and relentlessly rained down on the travellers. The smell of burnt clothing and hair permeated the already stifling humid air. Suddenly, there were small bodies with wings swooping and diving into the fire circle.

They seemed harmless, like gigantic mosquitoes, except that the blue light emitted from their electrically-charged wands were shredding limbs and uprooting small trees. Sparks continued to rain on the travellers, burning their clothing and skin. Jacob and Caleb tamped out the small fires erupting around the camp. Ted was trying to shield the horses from the sparks as they burned their manes and tails.

Nate stood in the center of the circle and, with a depth he didn't know he commanded, roared, "That's enough!" The fairies halted in their tracks; all their attentions were now on Nate. The hundreds of little bodies advanced on the solitary figure. He held his ground, despite the threat of incineration.

The largest male, about four inches in length, flew to about a foot in front of Nate's nose and asked, "Who are you to give orders?"

"Well, I'm no one, really," replied Nate. "But you were scaring the horses and burning our hair and clothes with your sparks."

"What are you doing in our fairy ring?"

"Yes, what are you doing here?", Nate could hear the entire group whisper in unison. "Did you ask permission to be here?" Again the group whisper.

"Will you please stop that," said Nate. "I heard him just fine, the first time."

"Ooh, isn't he the bossy one?", the fairies all said at once. "Yeah he's a bossy, bossy one."

"Hey, wait a minute," said a white-haired fairy. "I recognize you. You killed Serpentia. Look – there's the white horse!" A hush went through the fairy horde.

"Is that true? You killed Serpentia?", asked the fairy leader.

"Yes, I did. To free my horse, Arion," said Nate. "And I'm glad for it. She was a foul, loathsome creature." Another hush went through the crowd.

"We're members of the Metalmark Clan, and my name is Sidney."

"Hi Sidney, I'm Nathaniel Sutton. My friends call me Nate."

"Hi Nate," said the white-haired fairy who also

called himself Sidney.

"Are you father and son?", asked Nate.

"Oh no," said Sidney white hair. "Why do you ask?"

"You're both named Sidney," explained Nate.

"Oh you're so silly. All the men are named Sidney and all the women are named Cindy."

"How do you tell yourselves apart," asked Nate.

"We just know who is who."

"Well, how do I tell you apart, or let you know what Sidney or Cindy I'm talking to?"

"You could call me Cindy red-stripes," said one of the female Metalmarks.

"And I can be Sidney, broad-chest," said the largest Sidney, as he puffed out his chest. And so it went, until all three hundred or so Sidneys and Cindys identified themselves.

"We'll call you Nate, the Liberator. When you freed your horse, you freed us as well. We were ousted from the Devil's Hole Forest, for crimes against the forest. We like to battle, as I'm sure you've seen, and we accidentally burned down a portion of the eastern forest. The trees were in an uproar and wanted justice. So we were cast out of the forest and into the Mirthless Swamp. The other clans figured we couldn't do as much harm with all of the surrounding water. Most of the swamp residents like us being here; it livens things up a bit. The lack of laughter around here will drive any fairy insane. So we whoop it up every couple of days. The bullfrogs had three to one odds on us."

"I thought the box turtles gave better odds," said Sidney white hair.

"Now tell us, what are you doing here?"

"We're on our way to Aquilegia Falls," said Nate.

"What's in Aquilegia Falls, besides the waterfalls?", asked Sidney broad-chest.

"I don't know," said Nate. "We're just passing through, on our way to Leoht."

"The others can pass freely," said Sidney broad-chest. "But you, Nate, cannot leave. You must stay."

"What?"

"Serpentia's slayer must stand trial. It is decreed."

"Why? I thought I helped your clan to escape," asked Nate.

"You did. That's why you are to stand trial, for freeing the exiled ones. As you've admitted to her slaying, there won't be much of a trial. It'll be more of a sentencing, I suspect," said Sidney white-hair.

Jacob stood to his feet, "Now wait a minute, here. You can't just take him away like this. It's most urgent that we get to Leoht. The dark ones are coming, can't you see?"

"We said you were free to pass. You may stay the rest of the night, but be gone by morning. Nate, we'll give you one hour to set your affairs straight with these men."

"Can you at least tell us where you're taking him for sentencing?"

"Sure, we're taking him to the Morpho Clan's Ring. It's their ruling. They are the judges and juries in all the fairy lands," said Sidney white- hair.

"We'll return in one hour," said Sidney broad-chest.

"You may send one individual as his representative, for that is his right. He'll be tried immediately upon arrival at the Morpho ring. Sorry, but that is the best we can do. We love Nate the Serpent Slayer, but he's a criminal now, just like us." With that, the fairies blinked out of sight.

"This is a bunch of bologna," said Jacob. "Nate doesn't fall under fairy law. He's human."

"Actually, that's not completely true," said Caleb.

"Nate is Innesian, and, by the treaties signed a

thousand years ago, he's definitely liable to fairy law."

"But we can't let them take him," said Jacob.

"I don't see any way around it," said Ted. "Caleb is right — Innesians are subject to fairy law."

"Listen, we don't have much time and I have a lot to tell you. Otherwise, I'm not so sure you'll get out of here alive. I've been sworn to secrecy, so please don't ask me how I know what I'm about to tell you. You'll force me to lie, and I don't want to. To be free of the swamp, follow the pink markers in the trees. You'll see them about every twenty feet or so. Then he showed Ted what to look for in the tree. When you get to the Botes River ..." and on Nate explained everything that Lorelei had told him to do.

"When you get to Leoht, tell King Daedalus that Jacob is an outlander, and offer your stories especially where his soldiers were when you left Dosk. I'll follow when I can. Don't worry about me," he said as he put his hand on Jacob's shoulder. "Since being in Innes, I've discovered I end up exactly where and when I should."

One last thing," he said as he removed his Innesian star, "please give this to Daedalus and ask him to hold it until I come for it." He finished hugging the members of his party just as his fairy jailors blinked Nate, Arion, and themselves out of the fairy ring.

"This isn't right," said Jacob. "I didn't get a chance to thank him for saving my life once again."

"Don't worry, my friend. I don't think we've seen the end of Nate Sutton," said Caleb.

"I hope not," said Ted. "I was really getting to like him. Maybe we should change our path and follow him to the Morpho ring?"

"He wanted us to find Daedalus," said Caleb. "I think we should stick to our course, at least until we're out of the swamp. Maybe we could split up then. You are, after all, The Finder of Lost Objects. You found him once, I'm sure you can find him again."

"You're right, I like that plan. Then you and Jacob could go ahead to the Amber Tower. It's really the two of you that the king will want to speak with," replied Ted.

"That's settled. Let's get the few remaining hours of shut eye and then get out of this crazy swamp."

++++

The soldiers were finally quiet. Heldring could hear their bawdy songs of women and war as they partied long into the night. Now was as good a time as any, he thought as he slid the secret doorway open. Fortunately, the kitchen was empty, so he grabbed a few items and shoved them into his pockets. He peered into the great room and saw men and women lying willy-nilly on the floor, on the tables, asleep in his and Cereus's chairs. Cereus would not be happy if she saw the degree of denigration that had occurred under her roof. He left the men to sleep it off, made his way to the vestibule, and pushed the heavy wooden door silently closed behind him.

He retraced his original path, hoping that the guard was in the same condition as his compatriots. He silently thanked his old friend, the smithy, once again for his diligence with the locking mechanisms. He slipped through the gatehouse and onto the cobblestone street. He crossed the street, making his way to the cathedral. It was a good place to order his thoughts and his plan. If Cereus had truly left the city, then his tenure here was unnecessary. He needed to be certain. If only he could find this Gorgos fellow.

He walked briskly to the cathedral, and found a place to sit in the balcony. He hadn't thought about his timing and whether there would be a service in progress. The choir covered the sounds of his footsteps as he snuck into a seat. It had been hundreds of years since his last time in a church and he had forgotten about the experience. The smell of incense tickled his long forgotten memories. He painfully remembered Cereus's love of music and art. His insides ached with the knowledge of how much he'd missed while locked away in the tomb. He wiped a tear from the corner of his eye. No time for sentiment, he thought.

The choir was finishing its hymn, when a large processional walked down the center aisle. The main feature was a large doughy man who was being carried in a litter. He'd grown so corpulent that he was unable to stand, let alone walk to his seat. The archbishop began anew, once the group was settled into their designated areas in the front of the chapel. Heldring couldn't believe his eyes. He figured that he'd have to go through all kinds of obstacles to get to Pettiman. But no, here he was, in the flesh, seated no more than a short arrow away. If only …, he thought. The service ended and Pettiman's entourage removed him from the diocese.

Heldring found himself a room for a couple of days in a non-descript inn called the Quaking Cat, ordered food to be brought to his room and dropped his head on the first pillow in a week.

He awoke several hours later to a knock on his door; a groom presented him with a tray filled with fine smelling food. Heldring ate his fill, smoked his pipe, and returned to a restful night. His bones thanked him for the fine choice in mattress. The morning would offer better insight into his next move, or so he hoped.

++++

"How will we gets out of here?", asked Gorgos as he viewed the terrain and the lava flows that had taken over most of the available exits. The well-timed earthquake had freed his new friend but had put the pile of gold in jeopardy. Gorgos assessed the bookbag-like satchel that he carried around his shoulders and a small leather coin purse in his left breast pocket. Not nearly enough space to save even the smallest of portions of the treasure. "Where would I puts it, even if I could rescues all of it?", he muttered aloud. Naptha had remained quiet through Gorgos's thought process.

"May I interrupt you, Gorgos?", asked Naptha.

"Of course, anythings for you," replied Gorgos.

"We should get some sacks and then return to gather the loot," he said.

"We can do that? You don't mind?", asked Gorgos.

"Of course not," replied Naptha casually. "I don't want to leave all this gold behind either. It's taken many years to amass so much wealth. Besides I don't want any chance of the blood suckers getting this much cash."

"I sees what you mean," said Gorgos.

"Where can we stash it?", asked Naptha. "It's been many years since I've been on the surface. I'm not sure what to expect."

"Well, I knows one thing you can expect," said Gorgos. "Big fat sheeps and cows and goats to your heart's content," he laughed and patted the dragon's horned-head. His statement was followed by a deep rumbling.

"Is that another earthquake?", asked the startled Gorgos.

"No, that was my stomach," replied Naptha. The companions laughed long and hard.

"Let me thinks about a safe place to hides our loot," said Gorgos. The huge dragon moved closer to Gorgos, returned his head to his lap, and closed his eyes for another nap. Gorgos thought long into the night before he saw a possible solution. He closed his eyes, satisfied to put his plan into action the following morning. He knew they needed to leave the cavern soon, his own rumbling stomach confirming his thoughts.

4: The Wintering Caves

Michael waited several days for Jonah to return, before
packing his gear and striking out on his own. He'd
figured Jonah would get caught up and would not return
on time. That's why he stayed longer than they had
arranged.   Michael didn't really like the idea of
wandering around the Devil's Hole Forest by himself.
He knew Chelsea Manor lay to the west and Twe-Leoht
to the east. The question was, "which way should he
go?" After careful consideration, he chose Twe-Leoht,
their original destination. He had a couple of problems:
for one, he'd noticed it starting to get cool at night.

Fall must be close at hand and he was not dressed
for cold weather. Secondly, his dragon had grown to a
degree that made flying through the trees difficult, and
she was already too big to carry. For now, he'd wear
the extra clothing at night. Ailith was another matter.
They'd travel for as long as possible; he didn't see them
making it to Twe-Leoht before they'd have to stop and
make a more permanent camp: preferably at or near a
fairy ring, so she could have easy access to the skies.
That was his plan anyway. She'd told him she needed a
few more months of growth before she could carry him.

They gingerly picked their way through the dense
forest. Their first day was tough going; the forest
canopy was so dense that little light broke the
claustrophobia and the isolation that Michael felt.
Fortunately, Jonah had shown Michael how to make a

snare, and the forest seemed to be an abundant source of rabbits and squirrels. He'd caught several each day, keeping one for himself and giving the others to Ailith, who seemed embarrassed not to be catching her own supper. They'd travelled for several days and found no fairy rings, and thus no easy way for Ailith to leave the forest to hunt. The land continued to slope downward, but Michael tried to keep them on the highest points, hoping to find a fairy ring or a vantage point. On the seventh day of travel, they had a bit of luck. They came across a series of possible refuges — some were just rock outcroppings, but others were caves that appeared to be fairly deep.

Michael tied a length of rope around his mid-section. The other end he tied to a large tree. With his wand in front of him he said, "Illuminatus". The tip of his wand glowed, a brilliant silver-blue color. He cautioned Ailith, and then stepped into the dark mouth of the cave. It took a few moments for his eyes to adjust to his surroundings. He stayed close to the rock wall of the cave, his memory of the galraug still burning brightly. The first two rooms were nothing special, small and non-descript, like a reception room. The third room, however, was something to behold. There was a huge fireplace on the far wall, unlit of course, but piled high with logs as if in waiting for an imminent night of cold. Pots and pans hung from a rack on one wall over a large cabinet or butcher-block table. In the middle of the room was a long oak table and matching chairs, sixteen he counted, with three candelabras evenly spaced on the table.

Unlike most caves, these three rooms were warm and dry and had only the slightest smell of organic decay. The three inches of dust made him believe there were no current occupants, so he decided that he and Ailith would stay here for a couple of nights. He returned to the cave's entrance, removed the length of rope, and set several snares for their morning meal. He created a small fire in the front room and set his pots to boiling. He sat with his back against the wall and opened one of the packs Ailith had been carrying. It was Jonah's pack.

He was going to stop looking through his friend's bag, feeling like he was intruding on his friend's privacy, when he realized he may never see his friend again; besides, there may be useful items contained within the pack. He picked up a little mirror and looked at his reflection. He hadn't seen himself in a mirror in over five months and was surprised by what he saw. His darkened reddish-brown hair was past shoulder length. His usually scraggly patch of beard was about five inches long – thick and full.

He'd occasionally touched his hair and beard, so he knew it had become rather unruly, but there was something about seeing how unkempt he was that came as a total surprise. He found Jonah's long pipe and tobacco. He tried it for the first time when he finished his supper. Somehow he found it calmed him, probably because it reminded him of his friend. He placed the pipe back in the satchel, stretched out on his bedroll, and was soon fast asleep.

He and Ailith decided to stay in the caves for a few days. The weather had turned rainy and damp; the cold aggravated an old injury to his knee and made it ache unbearably. Food and water were plentiful — a long rest might be what they both needed. Ailith was about the size of a pony at this point. Michael realized that the few squirrels and rabbits he was collecting were not going to be enough sustenance for her.

He hoped they found a fairy ring soon. The next day he thought about striking out for a day trip, using the caves as a home port and travelling a few hours

Baby Ailith

every day in each direction. Ailith would have to stay back, as he travelled faster without her at this point. She might not mind because she seemed to want to rest a lot right now. Maybe leaving her by the fire for a few days would be better. He could explore and she could rest. He ran his proposal by her after lunch. She was perfectly content as long as he didn't wander beyond their hearing distance.

"Okay, that's settled," he replied. "I'll start exploring tomorrow." He spent the rest of the day practicing magical incantations.

Michael had breakfast on the fire early the next morning. He had a newfound purpose. He knew he had to find a way for Ailith to leave the forest for food. It occurred to him that she was sleeping a lot in an attempt to conserve energy. All of her energy reserves were being used for growth. There wasn't much left for wandering around in this silly forest. He gave Ailith a pat on the nose, left her three squirrels, and started on this day's adventure.

He decided to stay along that line for a few hours, and then return in time for lunch. He continued to walk along the top of the hillside until almost midday. When he realized the time, he turned around to backtrack. He'd found nothing out of the ordinary, just more trees and dense canopy. They had been staying uphill to maintain a vantage point if possible. He marked his trail, so he would know he'd already travelled in this direction. Tomorrow, he'd go over the caves to the top of the hill. He hoped for better luck.

By the fifteenth day of marking trails and living in the caves, Michael began to panic. Ailith had grown larger and had also become more withdrawn. He knew she would starve to death if he didn't find her a way out soon. Today, it was downhill. He'd been reluctant to go down the hill, thinking that he may not be able to return to his spot of relative comfort. His comfort wasn't important: Ailith's life was. He'd find her a way out.

He awoke to a cold crisp morning with a light snow. He moved around the back of the caves in search of some heavier clothing. He found several smaller rooms he'd overlooked during his first search of the cave. Luckily he found a dusty but rugged purple wool overcoat that hung to his mid-calf, and a matching hat that he pulled tightly over his ears. He would put more time into these back rooms when he returned from today's journey. He moved to the front cave and stoked the fire to help warm Ailith and set out on his journey.

He opted to carry his breakfast with him, munching on nuts and a swizzled carrot as he carefully marked his way down the hill. The overcoat and hat were an excellent find, and he hoped for more treasures, possibly boots and gloves. He walked for an hour before seeing what he thought to be a clearing in the forest. He slowed his pace as a precautionary measure.

He came to the end of the line of trees and a river bank. He walked upriver for a few hundred yards and reversed his path to the same distance downriver. There were no signs of civilization in either direction. He'd found the answer to Ailith's problem and she could at least hunt now. Once she was stronger, the distance between the cave and water's edge wouldn't be so daunting. He'd forgotten his reptile physiology. This cold has probably helped to slow her metabolic processes down. It just occurred to him they may have to pass the winter in the caves. He found his way up the hill and back to their cave without incident.

"Ailith, I have some good news. I've found a way out of the forest, at least temporarily, so you can hunt."

"That's good news," she weakly replied, "but I'm so cold."

"It's snowing," he replied. "Can you get yourself around to follow me down the hill so you can hunt?"

"I'll try," she said.

"Come on, love, you can do it. Go catch yourself a nice sheep or deer. You have to get your strength up. I've brought you three squirrels. Here – open wide." He stuck the first squirrel in her mouth. She flipped the squirrel in the right direction and swallowed.

"Thank you, Michael. That was very nice."

"Here, I have two more." She accepted the meager offering. "Let's go. We have plenty of daylight left." She slowly followed him to the river's edge and took flight.

"Michael, go back to the caves. I'll return when I'm finished."

"But don't you want me to wait for you?" He was crushed.

"No," she said. "I won't be long."

"All right," he reluctantly agreed, and started back up the hillside towards their winter retreat. Michael was almost at the crest of the hill when he heard voices. He hunkered down and tried to slow his breathing so he could hear the intruders. What if they were the original occupants, and he was the intruder, he thought. He searched his pockets to determine his assets: wand, nuts, a scrap of paper, but nothing else. It seemed like meager possessions to fight off, who knew, how many intruders. He inched his way closer to the mouth of the cave. He could hear snippets of conversation, but nothing more. He sat back against the embankment for what seemed like an eternity, trying to decide what to do.

Finally, against all good judgment, he climbed the rest of the way up the hill and emerged at the cave opening. He had his hand on his wand, which was hidden deep within his right-hand pocket. No one seemed to notice him at first. Rather, they continued with their conversation around his fire. He could see two men, humans it appeared, with their backs to him.

The one had long reddish-brown hair, the other grizzled grey. He saw an unbelievable sight sitting opposite them: the largest dog Michael had ever seen, and a gnarly orange tomcat chatting away as if they did this sort of thing every day. Michael gasped, and in the following second, Beastly had Michael pinned to the wall, three feet off the floor.

He growled in his thick Scottish burr, "Who are yi? What are yi doing here? Answer me before I rip your bleeding head off!" Beastly's threat took Michael by surprise. But, he figured out the reality of the type of beating this creature could give him.

In spite of the danger, he stammered, "You're in my shelter. I should be asking you the same thing. Who are you? And why have you assaulted me?" Michael saw the man who had been seated closest to the large dog stand up and face him. Michael couldn't believe his eyes.

"It can't be!" Michael rubbed his eyes with his free hand.

"What's the meaning o' this?", asked Beastly.

"Father?", Michael weakly asked. "I must be dreaming." He squeezed his eyes shut a few times, wondering if the prolonged isolation had left him hallucinating — yearning to see his father again.

"You know this guy, Bernie?", asked Beastly.

"He's my son," he replied. Beastly set the young man on his feet.

"Sorry mate, I didna know."

"No harm done," Michael said as he walked to face his father. They looked at each other another minute and then embraced for several minutes. When they released their grips, they both had tears of joy in their eyes.

"Let me introduce my friends," said Bernie. "You already know Ben Sutton."

"Michael, how good to see you," said Ben. As he held his hand out to shake hands, Michael hugged him as well.

"This is Crooksey Snively, and you've already met Beastly Hadley."

"My pleasure," said Michael as he shook the paws of his new friends. All of a sudden the cave shook as if an earthquake had hit. Streams of dirt poured from the ceiling. The members of the party scrambled to find shelter. Michael remained standing and laughed as a hearty laugh as he had in many months. The others looked on cautiously in a half-crouched position.

"What was that?", asked Bernie.

Michael chuckled again. "It sounds like Ailith's home."

"Ailith? Who's Ailith?", he asked.

"Hang on a second; she's almost at the opening. Please don't be frightened; she's afraid that you'll not like her. She's terribly sensitive and still very young."

With that, the beautiful yellowish-green female dragon stepped through the cave opening. The entourage fell into a hushed silence.

"They don't like me, Michael, I can tell."

"Oh don't be silly," he replied aloud. "They like you just fine. They're just a little overwhelmed. It's not every day that one can see such an amazing dragon as you, my dear. And by the way, how did you land on the roof? I didn't see a clearing when I hiked in that direction."

"I landed in a fairy ring," she replied.

"How could I have missed it when I was exploring?", he asked.

"It's hard to see through the heavily-treed forest,

Michael. I had a better vantage point," she said.

"I wonder which clan it belongs to?"

"It belongs to the Morpho clan," replied Crooksey. Michael had almost forgotten the others were with him. It'd been so long since he'd had company other than Ailith.

"This cave network is one of our hideouts from our thieving days. It's a little off the beaten path, as you've seen, so we don't use it that much." Crooksey came forward towards the dragon.

"Excuse my terrible manners, my lady," he said as he bowed, "I'm Crooksey Snively. My friend is Beastly Hadley." Upon mention of his name, Beastly bowed in a stately manner, as if meeting royalty.

"Well, Michael, you must have some kind of story to tell us," said his father as he came to Michael's side and introduced himself to Ailith. Ben bowed and offered his services to the young dragonette.

"Michael, I'm very cold." Michael led Ailith to the still blazing fire. She sat with her backside closest to the fire. He sat next to her. She laid her head in his lap, and he laid his arm across her body until she fell asleep. Michael spent most of the evening recounting his tales of his disappearance from the king's stateroom to Thryth's passing and the hatching of Ailith. When he came to Ailith's rescue of Pearl, he slowed the telling of his story and allowed Ben to ask ample questions.

"I can't believe that it was Ailith that scooped her out of the water. We thought for sure it was a raptor of some sort. I'll have to thank her properly when she awakens."

"She's awake now, Mr. Sutton. She just told me she's feeling much better; she wanted to thank everyone for sharing their fire with her."

"Ailith? Can she hear me? ... Michael?"

"Yes, she hears you just fine."

"Ailith, thank you for bringing Pearl to your friend Jonah, thank you from the bottom of my heart." The hope that Pearl might still be alive had left Ben Sutton weeks ago. He'd resigned himself to her death. This new information stabbed deeply at freshly healing wounds. He didn't want to hope too much, as he figured if she had survived the trip to Chelsea Manor with Jonah, she was still in bad shape from the galraug venom.

"You're welcome, Ben Sutton," she replied. Ben's eyes became wide as she continued. "The twin had to be saved, if possible." Michael watched Ben as Ailith answered his questions.

"It takes some getting used to," Michael said. What was the strangest phenomenon was that all of the travelling party heard Ailith's reply, directly in their heads.

"Hey, I didn't know you could do that, Ailith," said Michael.

"Neither did I … until just now," she chuckled and a little puff of smoke came out of her nostrils. At that the group laughed a hearty laugh. It'd been the first time in many weeks they felt untroubled and at peace.

Unfortunately, the peace wouldn't last, and after seven days, Ben was anxious to start anew towards Chelsea Manor. Michael couldn't blame him, really. He was surprised that Ben was able to contain himself for a week. Michael suspected the renewed hope that Pearl was still alive had given his spirit the opportunity to rest. The other members of the party obviously agreed, as they began to repack their gear.

"Michael, why aren't you packing?", asked his father.

"I can't leave father," he replied. "Ailith can't travel yet."

"But she's hunting and growing like crazy," replied

his dad.

"Yes, that's true, but if we get into an area where she can't take wing, she'll freeze to death. You must understand, Father, I can't take the chance."

Bernie nodded his head. "I do understand, Michael. But I'm your father, and I can't leave you again. Not since we've just found each other."

Michael hesitated some moments before speaking. Each member of the travelling party listened to their discussion before offering their input. It was decided that Beastly and Bernie would stay back with Michael until Ailith was able to travel. Ben and Crooksey would go ahead.

Finally Michael came to a decision. "I've come to care about each of you in this short time, and Father, you know I love you. But you must keep your promise and continue your quest. If Ailith were full grown, we could fly to Chelsea Manor in a matter of hours, but alas she isn't." Michael held up his hand to stop Bernie's next statement.

"We can't be separated for more than a few hours; the binding has made our lives permanently intertwined, for better or for worse." Michael stopped and turned his head in the direction of Ailith.

"She says to tell you that the Manor is only about a hundred miles from here. If you travel well, you should be there within two weeks. When you get there, you'll need to ask for Jonah Hobken. He can make your introductions easier. Once you've made your connection with the Guild, Father, you can ask Jonah to translocate back here with you. Crooksey, can you provide Jonah with the exact coordinates to the caves?"

"Near enough to get back to the river bank anyway," he replied.

"Good. Don't you see, Father? Then you don't have to break your promise and we'll see each again soon."

"I agree to this arrangement, but under protest," he finally said.

"You must trust me, Father. It's what's best for all." It was Ben who came forward this time. He'd been silent throughout the entire dialogue.

"Michael, you're a fine young man. I hope Nate has fared half as well as you. Thank you," he said as he held out his hand for a handshake. Everyone in the group let out a sigh. They'd been so determined in their path; they'd forgotten that Ben's grandson was still lost to him, somewhere in Innes.

"We'll be back for you, son. Please don't leave the caves until we return. And Michael...."

"Yes, Father...."

"Please be careful, the both of you. Ailith is my first grandchild, take good care of her." He hugged Michael and walked out of the caves, pack in hand.

"Oh Michael," he said as he fished in his pants pocket. "I forgot to give this to you. It came in the mail from your sister, addressed to you from Maystonery. I've been carrying it around for months." He handed Michael the small golden dragon talisman.

"How could she have known?" Michael's father shook his head, gave him one more hug, and walked off after the others. Beastly was the last to leave the cave.

"We'll be back for yi kid, don't yi worry none," he laughed, and then clapped him on the back as he left the sanctuary. Michael walked with them until he couldn't hear Ailith's thoughts anymore.

"This is as far as I can go," he said. He watched as they departed into the darkness of the densely treed forest. He returned to the caves as Ailith was moving her body position towards the fire.

"Well kiddo, it's just you and me."

"Are you okay, Michael?"

"Yeah, why?"

"I know it was difficult for you to see your father and friends leave."

"That's true," he agreed, "but not so difficult that I'm willing to risk your life."

"Thank you, Michael."

"You're welcome," he laughed. "But save your energy and go back to sleep." Ailith agreed and lightly snored to show her consent. Michael stoked the fire a little higher. The extra hands had made sure he was well stocked with firewood. They'd also showed him the secret way into the storehouse. With a few fresh rabbits, he'd have plenty of supplies to last him indefinitely.

Removing Jonah's pipe from his pack, he lit the tobacco from a small stick that was burning at the edge of the fire pit. Michael leaned back against the cave wall and watched Ailith sleep. He watched the drama of the rainbows dance off her skin in the light of the fire. It had started to snow again, and he didn't relish travelling in this weather. Hoping his father's party was safe and making rapid headway, he slipped into an afternoon sleep that lasted well into nightfall.

He awoke at somewhere around midnight, or so he thought. Ailith had changed her positioning again, probably in response to the fading embers. Michael stoked the fire once again and went outside the cave to relieve himself. He could see that they had gotten about eight inches of new snow. He thought about his father's travelling party. It would make for some tough going. He could see the full moonlight glancing off the newly fallen pristine snow. He walked away from the cave entrance in an effort to loosen the tightness in his legs. The cold invigorated him. He wasn't really dressed properly, so he didn't wander too far from the cave opening. But it was just far enough that he could see what looked like electric blue lights flashing against a silvery-white background. He climbed to the top of the cave to watch the light show within the fairy ring.

It was his first time meeting this clan, and they were playing in the snow. Unlike the Monarchs, they didn't appear to sing. But the light show was candy for his eyes. He'd never seen such a sight. There were hundreds of fairies – dipping, diving, and burrowing in the snow. He could see that the girl fairies closest to him were dressed in blue overcoats and leggings trimmed in white fur with matching cone-shaped hats and mufflers. The boy fairies were dressed in matching blue pants and shirts with white fur trim, matching conical hats and gloves. Their golden, almond-shaped eyes sparkled with obvious delight.

Michael stepped forward into the melee and found himself pelted with hundreds of tiny snowballs, as if they were awaiting his arrival. The fairies streaked by him, giving the appearance of trails of blue and white lights. All of a sudden the commotion stopped, and a blue frog with a gold crown hopped into the center of the fairies. He was also wearing the same cerulean blue winter outfit as the fairies.

"Hello Michael," he croaked in the common tongue, so Michael could understand him.

"Hello, Your Highness," replied Michael, who hadn't a clue how to properly address the frog.

"How's your dragon?", the frog king asked.

"She's doing much better now. Thank you for asking."

"May we speak with her?", he asked.

"Certainly, I'm sure she'd love to have company. Can you come into the cave and sit by the fire for a bit?"

There was some chatter amongst the fairies, and the King resumed, "Is she unable to meet us in the circle?"

"I'm afraid, Your Highness, that she is very near to hibernation right now. She's growing so fast, and, with the added pressure of the cold, she can barely keep up with her dietary needs. She's explained to me that she can hear and speak with anyone, but movement is only for hunting and re-arranging her body to the fire."

There was some additional chatter, until the King announced, "It's most unusual to leave the circle, but circumstances are such that we'll have to. Fortunately, the caves are under the circle, so technically, we'll still be within the circle, even if vertically. Michael, can you carry me to your cave? I'd be most obliged."

"Certainly," said Michael as he lifted the frog king and carried him down the hill and into the cave to the highest point facing Ailith. Hundreds of fairies filled the cavern, from top to bottom, all wanting to see and hear the newest-born dragon.

The frog king explained to the little fairies: "It's been hundreds of years since the last dragon birth, but unfortunately, he was killed by a slayer's sword. Four of the towers have a dragon as most of you know. But what you may not know is that Ailith is the only free dragon. She's not been imprisoned in ice, as is the obsidian dragon of Doerc; she's not embedded in amber, as is the golden dragon of Leoht; and she's not been mistreated, abused, bound and cast to the swamps, as was the sapphire dragon of Dosk.

You, my fey family, are witnesses to the new world and the return of wizards and dragons to their rightful place within the natural order. These woods have housed our kind for thousands of years, far longer than our Innesian neighbors. We cannot allow these aggressors to end our way of life, no matter the cost."

"Michael?"

"Yes, Ailith."

"Please tell the King I'll speak to him now. Do you

have any little snacks I might gnosh on whilst I'm awake?"

"Yes, Ailith. I caught a couple of rabbits for you.

Your Highness, I'm sorry to interrupt you, but Ailith is awake and can speak with you now." Michael walked to the back of the cave to collect the rabbits he'd caught earlier in the day. All eyes were upon him as he deftly put the rabbits in her mouth.

"Thank you, Michael, that's much better."

"Please, Your Majesty, she's ready now."

"Thank you, Michael," he said, and turned his attention back to the dragon.

"Ailith the Free, Dragon Heir to Dagung, we the Morpho Clan would like to welcome you to the world and offer our services to you in whatever capacity we can." At the King's last statement, the entire Morpho Clan flashed their electric blue lights. Michael's thoughts were of fireflies blinking on a summer night. The disturbance from all of the fairies flapping their electric blue wings at once was like a cool summer's night breeze.

Michael's attention trailed off as his thoughts turned to summer at Silver Birches. He was stricken with pangs of homesickness. Throughout his entire time in Innes, he hadn't thought about his ability to return to his home. He couldn't be without Ailith, but he didn't know if Ailith could cross into his world. He felt a few moments of loss at the thought of never returning home. His attention came back to Ailith and the fairies. At that moment, he knew it didn't matter whether he could return home or not. She was his life now, to the end.

The Morpho frog king had resumed speaking, "We know you've been exploring a bit, and just wanted to give you a head's up. The Red Admirals live about ten miles to the southwest of our territory. They're okay chaps, a little militant for us Morphos, but they shouldn't bother you if you cross into their territory. They're certainly no friends of the Obsidian Tower. Just be careful. Not all that lives in the forest is good."

"The Monarchs told us the same thing."

"The Monarchs are wise, you should heed their warnings. You'll be relatively safe as long as you stay within our territory; after that, we won't be able to help you. The fey folk are territorial. It's only a couple times a year for festivals and such that borders are freely crossed. There are certain places that are designated free zones for all, particularly along the water ways. We all need access to the water, but that's it." The frog king turned to go, "Oh, and one more thing Michael, you have our leave to allow other clans to access our fairy ring. News of your dragon is spreading, and other clans will be asking permission to meet her soon."

"Thank you Highness, but I didn't think other clans could cross into foreign clans' rings without an invitation."

"Yes, that's true, but right now you're living under our ring. It'd be impolite for us to hold Ailith for our own. She's free, and we'd be no better than the others who've imprisoned their dragons if we denied them access to her." Michael nodded his understanding.

"She's more important to the fey folk than you know, Michael. We've not been able to reproduce for hundreds of years, mostly due to human/Innesian development of the Monkshood Forest and the killing or capturing of dragons."

"Why would someone kill a dragon?", asked Michael. "They're amazing."

"They were killed for sport or for money. Great prizes were put on the heads of the largest and fiercest dragons. Loss of the dragons has resulted in the extinction of some clans. The Xerces Blues Clan, for example, was lost to us many years ago."

"I still don't understand how dragons are involved in fairy reproduction," Michael said.

"I'm sure you know by now that dragons are magical. They process their food differently than other creatures. When they've finished digesting, their excrement contains the magical properties that are needed to fertilize our fairy pods or seeds you might say. Depending on what the dragon eats, these seeds grow into different varieties of flowers, each variety specific to each clan. When the flowers produce their pollen, they also produce a type of nectar that is an aphrodisiac wine for us. We deliver the pollen packets from flower to flower, tending our gardens for future generations. But it's the nectar from each flower variety that allows us to reproduce. So you can see, without the dragons, no flowers, and, without the flowers, there is no nectar and no baby fairies."

"When was the last baby fairy born," asked Michael. The frog king thought for some minutes.

"That would be Bunny, born five hundred years ago – at least for the Morpho clan," he replied.

A tiny fairy came forward. "I'm Bunny," she said. "I'm the youngest of my clan. May I touch your dragon?"

"Hi Bunny," replied Michael. "You can ask her yourself, she's awake and listening to the conversation."

With that, all the fairies asked, "Michael, may we touch your dragon? May we please?"

Michael laughed, "I'm sure she won't mind." Michael sat back against the cave wall, lit his pipe, and watched the interactions of the Morpho Clan and Ailith. It really was a sight. His thoughts wandered to home. He hadn't seen his sisters or his mother in almost a year. He hoped they were faring okay. He looked outside the cave. It had started to snow again. His father's group was going to have a difficult time walking in this weather.

Crooksey had told him they had another hideout about twenty miles downriver. Their plan was to make haste to that shelter, recuperate, and then travel into the interior of the forest to find Chelsea Manor. Under the best of circumstances, they figured two to three weeks of travel would find them at their destination. I don't think they counted on snow. And from what Michael could see, it didn't look like this was going to pass any time soon.

"Ahem," said the frog king, "Ahem." Michael turned his attention back to the frog king.

"I'm sorry Highness, I was thinking about my family. I didn't mean to be rude."

"It's alright. I was going to ask for a lift back up to the clan's ring. The snow makes travel a bit difficult for me."

"Of course," replied Michael, who scooped the King into his arms and carried him to the middle of the ring.

"Please visit again soon. It gets lonely for me, especially now that Ailith is sleeping so much."

"Glad to," replied the King. "I'd like to hear more about your world and your family." With that the king turned into the circle and disappeared.

"Good night," said Michael as he returned to the warmth of the fire in the cave. He sat down next to Ailith and put his hand on her side.

"Sleep well," he said. Sitting back, he puffed on his pipe, and stared deeply into the flames.

5: Hidden in Mauch Chunk

Ira Pufflehump walked though his pufflemal menagerie, taking care to check each of the residents. The aftershocks resulting from the fall of Twe-Leoht shook the foundation of Chelsea Manor, even with it being hundreds of miles away. His household was in total disarray. The central question was, "Who was so brazen to cut the heart out of Innes? And why?" Lorelei Lorlinda held the central role in maintaining the Innesian illusion and in masking Monkshood Forest from the outer world. Belac must have had something to do with it. He had Dagung razed, and his own father, Arisaema, killed. Why not their Innesian mother as well? Gordon knocked at the door.

"Gordon, my boy, please come in. I could use your help."

"I was hoping there was something I could do," replied Gordon. "Since the King decided to leave me at Chelsea Manor, I feel so useless."

"Glad to have you, my boy, glad to have you. Don't let the King's reticence about taking you immediately to Leoht worry you. He's looking out for your best interests and he feels that would be better served at Chelsea Manor.

Come, I'm checking each animal by hand to make sure they're intact, even if a little shaken. Check their enclosures as well; we wouldn't want any escapees in the night." Gordon started with the pufflepigs. He'd never seen pink and lavender pigs, but then again, he'd never seen a three-inch pig until six months ago. He picked up the pink polka-dotted pig first; they knew each other well. She was wearing a little name tag that read 'Clara'.

"Well hello, Clara," Gordon said as he picked her out of her enclosure and scratched her back, much to her delight. He gave her a tiny pig treat and then checked each of the residents and their enclosure. Upon completion, he moved on to the next enclosure. He didn't see anything moving at first, but he could hear a gentle rustle in the leaves. He looked around this new enclosure and spotted an odd looking pair of glasses. He donned the glasses and then peered into the enclosure. There were several trees in the glass-enclosed structure, and, from each of these trees, Gordon could see hundreds of little bats hanging upside down. They looked like little dark-brown chihuahuas with wings.

Ira stood next to him, "I see you've found my chihuahuabats. We'll let them out in about an hour or so. They're really important to the forest, as they can eat their weight in bugs, every night."

"Wow!" was all Gordon could think to respond. Their little bodies made no sound when they were released some two hours later. Gordon's next surprise came about four enclosures later when he discovered a pen with two adult dodo birds and three baby dodos.

"I thought these birds were extinct."

"These are the only known individuals in existence. There are several species I've collected that exist only here in my pufflection. It's a gene bank you might say, something akin to your Noah's ark. I've selectively bred them to be small so I can fit more animals into a smaller space. But they're genetically identical to their larger cousins. I've been knocking around for some time, Gordon, and have seen the detriment of man's hand to our animal brethren. A few species that you've seen are my creation, such as the chihuahuabats. They also function as messengers here at Chelsea Manor. That's why we knew that Twe-Leoht had fallen before the King's messengers could send word."

"How did you start doing this, with all of the animals?", asked Gordon.

"Well my friend, that's an old tale whose beginnings start with the death of my last living relative, my grandfather. My mother died in childbirth, my father a few years later in a coal mine explosion. You see, Gordon, I'm from outerworld like you."

"You're human?"

"Yes, just like you."

"But when were you born?"

"By outerworld standards, I was born a few centuries ago in a little coal town called Mauch Chunk. My father worked in the mines, my grandfather worked on the trains. My grandfather died when I was eighteen and I was on my own. I joined a travelling caravan, a circus to you, and learned about animals from a good friend whom you'll meet in the next few days. He's been away from the Manor for about a year and is due any day now. Even after my return to the family estate in Innes, I travelled with the caravan for many years.

I liked the open road, and, over the years, I've seen amazing things, Gordon, from snow-covered mountains that reached well into the clouds to my fey friends, whom you've also not yet met. I don't travel as much any more and have chosen to spend all of my time in Innes these days working with my pufflection. You see it's become obvious to me that many of these species don't stand a chance if someone doesn't intervene on their behalf. That's the role I've chosen for myself."

"Do you miss outerworld?", Gordon asked.

"I do, at times. Sometimes my world shrinks here at the Manor. But I can always go outside if I choose. I possess an access point that bypasses the trees; only two other individuals know about it. That's why the King left you behind Gordon. You're being sent home, well at least to my starting point, what was once my home. I've had new clothes made for you, something appropriate to the present day and your new size." At that, Ira chuckled. Gordon wondered about his size. His Nikes no longer fit him, and, when his clothing seemed too tight, new ones were tucked into his dresser drawers. His hands had hardened with thick calluses from the long hours of sword-fighting practice. It was true on, most days, he ate like a horse.

"Why?", asked Gordon. "Why send me back? Did I do something wrong?" Uncertainty had left a bitter taste in Gordon's mouth.

Ira looked hard at Gordon, "Do you think you're being punished?"

"Yes," replied Gordon, "but I don't know why."

"Gordon, you're not being punished. In fact ..." Ira hesitated, and sighed. "This mission is dangerous; you may not survive it."

"What do you mean?", asked Gordon.

"You're being sent because you are trusted, not because you're being punished, although some may disagree."

"I'll do whatever you want, Ira, for you and the King."

"Let's take a little walk, shall we? I don't want to stress the pufflemals any more than need be." The two men walked to the gardens where two months earlier Pearl Sutton was brought to the Manor.

"Has there been any change in Gran's condition?", asked Gordon. Ira had come to understand the connection between the shapeshifter and this young man. He knew her condition was difficult for Gordon, who spent long hours into the night reading to her at her bedside.

"I'm sorry, Gordon, but there hasn't." Gordon nodded.

"So what am I supposed to do? And when?"

"Day after tomorrow, after supper. I don't want anyone to see you go. No one can know that you've found any of these items I'm sending you to retrieve. I'll give you all the items you need to complete this journey. It'll be your tenacity, however, that'll help you survive."

"How will I know where to look?"

"I'll give you a map; once there, you must destroy it. Memorize your way back, though. A metal box was installed within a blue-colored vortex at the top of the mountain, above the waterfall within a thicket of spruce. It can only be seen once a year, and the time is upon us. You must retrieve the contents of the box and return here within two days. And Gordon, you must do this alone. No one – and I mean no one – can know of your presence in outerworld. Don't contact your parents. They're being watched." Gordon's surprise was obvious.

"Is my mom okay?"

"Yes, they'll leave her alone as long as you stay away. Fortunately, she's with that Triebrecher fellow. That offers her some leverage, even if she's not aware of it." Gordon scoffed at that statement.

"Gordon, whether you like him or not, she's better off with him right now. Belac has plans for him." Gordon had heard that name over the last few months. He still didn't really know who he was other than he was causing all of the discord within Innes and something about Dream Stealers and nightmares seeping out of the Innesian world and into his. He was sure he'd find out more as time went on, since he was in Daedalus's personal escort. I guess that didn't pan out either. He didn't see what was so dangerous about getting some junk from a box in Mauch Chunk; he'd been camping there a few years back. A nice enough town, nothing to be afraid of that's for sure. Ira could see Gordon's unhappiness at his request.

"Gordon, do you trust me?", asked Ira.

"Yes," he responded without hesitation.

"Then please, do this for me. Look at it as a special request from me, one friend to another."

"Of course Ira, I'd do whatever you asked of me."

"Be careful with that offer, Gordon. I may ask." Gordon looked at Ira, a new expression, maybe a new understanding, Ira wasn't sure.

"Come on, Gordon," Ira lightened the mood, "let's see what kind of pie Cook has left for us tonight." Gordon's face lit up. He sure loved Cook's pies.

The next day found the morning favorable for travel. A cold wind out of the north brought news of a later day snowstorm.

"Listen Gordon, you can't be seen. I know it sounds like a simple task to retrieve the box. But I assure you, it won't be as easy as it sounds."

"I've been to Mauch Chunk. It's not a scary town."

"Well of course not. It's what's watching the town that is scary." Gordon looked at Ira for a long moment.

"You must climb to the top of the waterfalls and look for five spruce trees in a group. You'll find these trees about 150 yards back from the top of the waterfalls. Be careful Gordon, this is a difficult and dangerous climb. Look for the spruce with the notching; I.P. + M.N. in a heart. Sit directly underneath the etching and wait until the full moon is directly overhead. You'll see, if you don't feel it first, a small eddying shape, and inside this vortex is a metal box. In order to retrieve the box, you must say the following words: 'I need to see the dreams, hidden deep within the book. I need to see my dreams, please let me take a look.' You should be able to remove the box from the vortex. If it refuses to leave, you must trick it into wanting to come with you. I can't help you with that. You'll have to use your best techniques, I can assure you."

"I don't get it," said Gordon.

"What don't you get?"

"What do you mean "trick the box"? Like the box will know if I'm talking to it?"

"Well, of course it will. Tell it a story or something about yourself. Make the box want to leave with you. Oh, and Gordon, make sure you introduce yourself. That should help."

"Okay," said Gordon not comprehending fully.

"Once you have the glasses, return to the caravan immediately. The last part is very important – remove the glasses from the box, wrap them in this cotton cloth, and return the box to the vortex."

"Return the box?"

"Yes, I don't want anyone knowing we've got the jump on them. If they think the box is still there, they'll think the glasses are safe inside."

"That's pretty sneaky," said Gordon.

"That's pretty smart," returned Ira. "And don't think for one minute they'll make the same mistake twice. Belac means to bring darkness to all of us, Gordon. Make sure – I can't repeat this often enough – make sure you lock the forest entry door whenever you're coming or going."

"When do I leave?"

"Now, I've packed a few sandwiches and some assorted sundries you may find yourself in need of. Good luck my boy, and do not dawdle, I smell snow in the air." With that, Gordon bent down and gave Ira a father-son hug and set off into the Devil's Hole Forest to find the caravan.

Gordon chose not to carry a sword. He wanted to travel with few belongings, opting for his elfin chain mail and knife, and little else. Ira gave him directions to the caravan, but the forest was so dense and dark it was not easy to navigate. Ira told him to walk for about a half day to the southeast. That would get him to the caravan. The caravan, however, could only transport to receptor sites. Once at the receptor, the traveller would still have to navigate to his destination.

For Gordon, this meant that once he was in Mauch Chunk, he'd have another half day's walk to the bottom of the trail head. Gordon figured he'd shortcut the process by hitch hiking a ride once he got to the receptor. He knew there were several companies that took people biking, hiking, and rafting; he'd catch a ride with one of them.

As long as he didn't get caught in snow, he figured he'd be okay. He thought Ira was right though, he could smell snow in the air. He was glad to be unencumbered; it felt good to move at a fast pace through the trees. In the months he lived at Chelsea Manor, he came to appreciate the beauty and grandeur of the old forest. It no longer intimidated him as it once did. He was not so foolish as to underestimate the forest or some of its denizens.

Surprisingly, he found his destination rather easily. He decided to enjoy one of the bountiful sandwiches packed for his lunch. He sat with his back against a hundred-year maple tree and started to eat a wonderful chicken sandwich. He shared the ten-foot clearing with the brightly-colored caravan. Ira told him he could change his destination by rearranging the settings of latitude and longitude within the caravan. The correct coordinates would land him in Mauch Chunk. He only needed to step through the back door of the caravan to enter this new place. It was a crazy idea because the caravan never left the woods or this circle. Gordon really only cared that it worked.

He was about to take a bite from the other half of his sandwich, when a black, red and white-winged fairy landed on his wrist. It startled him into dropping his sandwich on his lap. Several other fairies landed on his legs, boot tips, and laces. Gordon picked his sandwich from his lap and placed it back into the original wrapper. Another, slightly larger fairy hovered about twelve inches from Gordon's nose.

"Who are you?", the fairy demanded.

"I'm Gordon Silversmith," he replied.

"What are you doing here, Gordon Silversmith? Who gave you leave to loiter in our fairy ring?"

"I'm sorry if I'm loitering. I wanted to have lunch before entering the caravan."

"What! You're entering the caravan? Upon whose leave? Sergeant! Sergeant Vellum!"

"Yes sir," replied Sergeant Vellum.

"Did you give this stranger leave to enter the caravan?"

"No sir."

"On whose authority were you entering the caravan young man?"

"Ira Pufflehump, sir."

"Harrumph, so you say."

"I have the key to prove it." Gordon removed the golden skeleton key from his pocket. It wasn't so much the key, but the old military insignia the key was attached to that seemed to impress the fairy.

"Where did you get this?"

"I told you, from Ira Pufflehump. I live with him and his wife at Chelsea Manor."

"But you're an outsider. I can smell it on you."

"This is true and my destination is outerworld."

"Will you be coming back?"

"Yes sir, in a day or two."

"Next time, ask for our leave first."

"Sir, may I ask your name, please?" Gordon had never served in the military, so he wasn't sure how to ask his question properly.

"I'm Rear Admiral Silk of the Red Admiral Clan."

"It's a pleasure to meet you, Admiral Silk," said Gordon. "And this is your clan's fairy ring?"

"Yes it is." Gordon couldn't figure out why Ira didn't tell him about the keepers of the ring and that it might be problematic accessing the caravan.

"Well sir, if it's okay with you, I'd like to continue on my journey."

"What is your name again?"

"Gordon. Gordon Silversmith."

"Okay Gordon, we don't want to keep you from your mission. But remember, next time ask for permission, with any fairy ring. Trespassers are not looked upon kindly. Not all fairies guard such a unique and vital object, but their rings are sacred nonetheless."

"Thank you," said Gordon. "I won't make that mistake again." With that, Gordon pulled the keys from his pocket and entered the caravan. He walked to the wall and changed the compass as Ira told him to do. Then he put the key into the lock and turned the doorknob. He didn't really know what to expect. He half figured this to be a joke, and balloons or cameras would come from behind and they'd have a good laugh about how they duped him.

He really wasn't prepared to walk through the library doorway onto the main street in downtown Mauch Chunk. He could smell car exhaust and hear the train whistle as the train pulled from the Victorian-era depot. He was home, or near enough. He breathed deeply the pollution of modern technology and set about his path. He found a bunch of picnic tables in a grove of trees near the train station. He hadn't finished his lunch and decided that a few minutes more wouldn't hurt. He reached into the bag to remove his sandwich and found a wad of money stuffed towards the bottom of the bag. Gordon laughed; Ira thought of everything.

There was a street vendor selling hotdogs and chips. He ordered a cola and a bag of sour cream and onion chips, and sat at one of the picnic tables. He was in heaven or the nearest thing to heaven, he thought. He hadn't realized how much he missed his world until this minute. He finished his lunch and found a fellow who was transporting a group of tourists for a bike trip.

Gordon thought it was a little cold for such a trip, but they appeared to be hardy enough folks. He seemed to have missed any snow, which was good news. Ira said this hike up the mountain was treacherous enough without adding snow. The bus driver dropped Gordon off at the parking lot in the Glen Onoko. Gordon gave him a nice tip, shook hands, and thanked him. Maybe their paths would cross again. Gordon doubted it, but who knew. Life had a funny way about it. Gordon crossed over the railroad tracks and started up the mountain. It was fairly easygoing in the beginning of the trip and very scenic as well.

The mountain stream had cut a path about ten-feet wide, making for a lovely series of riffles and pools. The stream was heavily covered by the canopy of the trees, and, when Gordon put his fingers in the water, he found it almost painfully cold. It was, by all accounts, the end of November, but he suspected the water heated very little even in the hottest months of the summer. He took a sip from the bottle of water he'd stashed in his bag and returned to his climb.

At about the half-way point, he had to climb with both hands and feet, since the hill had gotten so steep –

until he found himself at the bottom of the waterfalls.

How to get to the top? He started to his right and found a narrow pathway that wound itself farther up the hill away from the waterfalls and then backtracked on itself over a rocky ledge. The damp moss on the rocks made the climb treacherous. He snaked his way until he emerged at the top of the waterfalls. Fortunately, there hadn't been rain recently and he was able to walk onto the level, granite tabletop-like stone at the summit of the waterfalls. He looked down to the bottom, at least a fifty-foot drop. His stomach rolled a bit. He wasn't afraid of heights, well not generally anyway. He walked up the stream bed in search of his destination. He found the spruce trees and sat himself down below the inscribed tree.

He hoped Ira packed him something warm. It was going to be a long, cold night. He found a thin blanket, which was surprisingly warm, and a hat and gloves. He removed his second meal from the bag. He knew it was his second because Cook had marked each one in their order to be eaten. When he removed the wrapping, the food was still warm: roast beef, mashed potatoes and gravy, green beans, and a big wedge of apple pie. He loved that woman.

He rolled the packaging into a tight bundle and stuck it in the bottom of his bag. Carry it in, carry it out. He was taught to appreciate the beauty and not leave his garbage lying around behind him. The meal was so satisfying he couldn't keep his eyes open for another minute. He comfortably napped until the moon was full in the sky. He could see the outline of the vortex as the moon started to peek through the trees.

He suspected the trees had grown considerably since Ira placed the box here. The box came into full view for a few moments only. Gordon had to work quickly. He hoped he didn't have to entice the box from the vortex, such a strange idea.

Fortunately, the box wasn't in the game playing mood. Maybe it too knew it was being hunted by unsavory characters and wanted to ensure its own safety — who knows. When he reached inside the vortex, the box easily slid from its hiding place. He removed the glasses and put them into the cotton bag and secured it with the string. He placed the bag into the bottom of the travelling pack. He put the empty box back into the vortex and sat under the marked tree. He pulled the travelling blanket from his pack and covered himself up to wait out the balance of the night. At about 4:30 am, he awoke to something making noise in the underbrush but immediately dismissed it as a deer or fox. At 5:30, the sun started to peek over the horizon. Gordon stretched, packed his blanket and started his way back down the path.

A thin layer of ice made his descent from the mountaintop even more treacherous as he slipped and slid his way down the steepest part of the trail. He returned to the place where he'd previously rested. He relaxed next to the streambed as he took his breakfast from his travel bag. Once again, Cook outdid herself. She packed him a steaming hot bowl of blueberry oatmeal and two egg and bacon sandwiches. How she was able to keep the food warm, he didn't know, but it was a great secret to have. He'd take her some chocolates from the candy store a couple of doors away from the library.

He finished his morning meal and started back down the path. He got the distinctive feeling that there was at least one pair of eyes on him. He turned to look several times, but saw no one around. He continued over the railroad tracks and emerged onto the road leading out of the Glen Onoko. He started a light jog hoping to cover the two miles or so back into town more quickly. He ran about a half a mile, when he saw three guys lingering by the side of the road. His mind started to race. He was only mildly winded from his exertion. The crisp air did make his mind sharp, although he wasn't sure he could take three guys on by himself. Maybe they were just hanging out. He'd wait and see. He was within one hundred yards of them when they started to fan out.

There, he thought – they've made their move. He decided he'd take the biggest guy out first. When Gordon left outerworld so many months ago, he was a lanky guy, maybe 5-feet-nine inches, a hundred forty-five pounds. He was that guy, no more.

He hit the brute with all six-foot-two inches and a hundred ninety-five pounds of pure muscle. Gordon hit the first ruffian so hard and fast, he flipped his opponent several feet into the air. Gordon spun a hundred-eighty degrees to his left, right arm fully extended at shoulder level, and he struck the second guy in the windpipe. He fell to his knees, breathless.

The third guy, not as big as the others, pulled a knife from his pocket and came at Gordon as fast as a mongoose. Gordon swirled away from the knife point and picked up a hefty stick that was lying by the side of the road. The third ruffian rebounded and came after Gordon, trying viscously to stab him.

The guy sliced Gordon before he countered by striking the guy behind the knees with the stick. When the guy fell, he spun around and smashed the guy on the back of the neck with the stick. Gordon could hear his neck snap as he fell onto the roadway.

Gordon winged the stick over the embankment into the streambed and checked for car keys. He found a cloth in the bottom of his bag, wrapped his sliced forearm, and pulled the long sleeve over the makeshift bandage.

He left the three bodies lying where they'd dropped and drove the criminals' car into town. He wiped the steering wheel and anything else he might have touched and locked the keys in the car. He remembered the chocolates for Cook, grabbed a few colas, walked through the library door and back into the caravan in the Devil's Hole Forest.

He locked the door, changed the latitude/longitude settings for good measure, thanked the Red Admirals and said he'd visit with them again. Then he proceeded towards Chelsea Manor. He got within sight of the manor, sat down on a large rock, and started to cry. He'd never killed anything before, and today he'd killed three men. Granted it was in self defense. But still, he had taken three lives. Somehow Ira knew where he was, walked up, and sat down alongside him on the rock. Ira placed his hand around his shoulder.

"What happened?", he asked.

"I killed three men in self-defense," replied Gordon.

"You did what you had to do. Come on, no sense sitting here when we could be enjoying the gardens." Gordon allowed himself to be led to the gardens where Madeline was sitting. She helped to soothe the lines in his face and heal the knife wounds on his chest and forearm. After a few minutes, Gordon sobered and remembered the chocolates and colas. He handed Ira the bag and the balance of its contents.

"Ira, I hope you don't mind, I spent a few dollars. The rest is in the bag."

Ira laughed, "That's why I put it in there, Gordon. What did you buy?"

"Chocolates for Cook and three colas," he replied, as he handed one to Madeline and one to Ira. Ira was thrilled.

"There are a few things I miss from home," he said.

"This is one of them." Madeline's eyes lit up as

well.

"It's been so long," she said, as she placed the can on the ground and stuck her toe in the opening. Gordon just couldn't get used to her doing that. She ate like normal. Why not drink like normal. He figured it was her way of being different. He didn't mind, not really.

When they had finished their colas, Ira said, "Gordon, come to my Pufflection Room after you've had dinner. There are measures we need to discuss." Gordon agreed.

Rho Dora stood at the doorway watching the threesome in the garden. She tried not to be jealous of the time Gordon and Madeline spent together. She understood they grew up together; besides, Madeline was perfect. She couldn't fault Gordon for finding her attractive, but sometimes she couldn't stop the angry feelings that bubbled below the surface when she saw them together.

She also found Gordon very attractive, and, if it weren't for her attraction to Madeline, she might make a play for him. She was so confused and angry, yet loved Madeline and Gordon too. She didn't know what she should do. She passed Ira as she walked into the garden.

"Hello young lady," he said.

"Hi Ira," she replied.

"Please excuse me," he said. "I have to look in on my little beasties." She nodded and walked to Gordon and Madeline.

"Hi Rho," Gordon blushed.

"Hi Gordon," she replied.

"Hi Madeline," she said.

"Hi Rho," Madeline replied. "I'm glad you came to the gardens; it's such a lovely evening, too beautiful to be cooped up.

The weight of the day's events tensed his muscles.

He found himself longing for a hot shower. Gordon sat and talked to Rho and Madeline for a little while longer and then excused himself to his rooms.

"Thank you ladies; it's time for me to retire." He started to walk away, then turned and said, "You're both as lovely as a sunrise that makes my heart sing." He blushed and hurried away.

"What has gotten into me?", he muttered under his breath. "You make my heart sing. Yuck!" He could hear them giggling and whispering behind him. He accelerated his pace as he looked for the anonymity his rooms would offer.

6: An Overdue Kiss

Draedon followed the butler into Mortifera's receiving room.

"Ah, Mortifera, my Queen, it's good to see you again," he said as he bowed to the mistress of the Obsidian Tower.

"Welcome home, Draedon; it's good to see you too. What news of your travels do you bring to your Queen?"

"Pettiman's soldiers have begun their advance on Leoht. Unfortunately, snow has hindered their march."

"Pettiman is a bumbling fool. His troops were supposed to have left weeks ago. What else?"

"Lorelei Lorlinda is dead."

"Now that is good news. I wouldn't suppose you knew how, or by whose hand she met her demise?"

"Yes M'lady, I do know." He handed her Lorelei's ring, "A gift to the Queen of the Obsidian Tower."

"Oh, you are a naughty man," said the Queen, her eyes ablaze with delight.

"And what of the young man in the outer hall?", she asked.

"He's my new protégé."

"I would like to meet this protégé, if I might."

"Your Highness, I'd be delighted to show him off. I would love to know what you think of him." She clapped her hands, and Will was shown into the parlor.

Draedon walked to meet Will, and whispered into his ear, "Don't embarrass me, kid." He walked him to meet the Queen.

"Come here, young man. Turn around, and let me

look at you," said the Queen. "You didn't tell me he was from outerworld, Draedon. How could you keep such a secret?", she asked, a dangerous tone in her voice.

"Honestly, ma'am, I wasn't sure. He keeps talking about Pine Woods and camping and such. But I didn't know for certain, until this minute."

"I see," she said. She beckoned to the butler, "Take this young man ... what is your name?"

"Will Tipton, ma'am."

"Take Mr. Tipton to the Mahogany Room. Have him readied for tonight's dinner. I'd like for him to meet my own new protégé. Draedon, shall we say seven o'clock?"

"Yes, fine ma'am, I'll be here. Are you sure you want the burden of him staying here? I was going to take him home with me."

"Oh, don't be silly. It's no burden at all. I'm delighted that you'd care," she said as her eyes blackened and her cheeks blushed. "Until this evening," she said as she retreated to her inner rooms. Draedon left the tower.

"Damn. I just lost my protégé," he softly muttered. "At least I brought her a new toy. I hope I gain some points with this new acquisition." He couldn't read Mortifera, as he could everyone else. Thus, she unnerved him in a way that no others did. Even Belac, as dangerous as he was, didn't provoke fear in him the way she did.

He was to sup with her tonight; only Belac himself could sever that date. He walked to his rooms. He really hadn't expected Mortifera to take so much interest in his prize. It irked him more than he'd originally thought. Maybe her interest was only temporary but he doubted it. She had something up her sleeve. He normally spent his evening at the pub around the corner from his house. He would forgo that tonight. He needed to be on his game — no mistakes. He was their adopted prodigal son; but that claim could end quickly. He was under no illusions.

Nevertheless, he decided to go for a walk, since it had been some time since he was last at home. The neighborhood had changed little. The regular players still touted their goods or services: meat and produce, cheese, candle, bread, and basket merchants invited the shoppers in to purchase their wares. He noticed a new shop with a dark front at the end of the street. A small sign indicated a mystic had taken up residence in what was once a fancy cheese shop.

He entered the small, poorly lit room and waited for a grey-haired, overweight woman to engage the mystic's services. He was unceremoniously seated at a small kitchen table, told the fee, and asked to wait momentarily. Within a few minutes, the mystic joined Draedon at the table. He sat as a blank slate, not giving her any information she might use to create a fictitious future. He noticed that as she stared at him, her consciousness seemed to slip away. Her eyes started to flicker, her breathing keeping pace. She rocked back and forth on the little chair so fast he was sure she'd fall at any moment.

Suddenly she stopped, her eyes veiled with a white membrane, and growled, "There are few with a blacker soul than yours. But beware, new friends, they will betray even themselves in the end. There is one who loves her and wants her for himself and will not allow you to have her. Even now, he walks into darkness, prepared in ways that he doesn't yet understand.

Unlike you, he has given himself to the darkness, a conscious choice. You had no choice; you were born to it. But you do have the choice to remain. You can be saved, leave here, now, find the one you call Lily, build your house, and have a happy life." She sat back in her chair, breathless and nearly lifeless. The housemaid came into the kitchen and helped the mystic to a room separated by a curtain. Draedon thought about what she had said, rose from his chair, and followed them into her living quarters.

"You shouldn't be in here," said the maid. "I'll be along to collect her fee in a minute."

He pushed the maid out of the way and roughly grabbed the mystic by the throat, "What is this nonsense you're spewing?"

The mystic recovered her energy enough to answer,

"I have no control over what I see. This is your story — you must answer for it. You'll be given one chance at redemption to have the life you've always dreamed."

"What a bunch of crap," roared Draedon as he snapped the mystic's neck. The maid came at him with a fire poker, which he deftly dodged. He countered and broke her neck, as if snapping a stick for the fire. He locked the door as he left the mystic's house.

"What a bunch of crap," he repeated angrily. "But if it was such crap, why'd I kill them? It's easier that way; no loose ends." Draedon found himself whistling as he walked the streets to his own apartments. He was hungry already. He hoped Mortifera was serving something scrumptious.

Will felt uneasy being separated from Draedon. He'd come to like him in a strange sort of way, like an older brother. He didn't really mind that Draedon killed people. Will was no real fan of people anyway. He found them to be generally stupid and crass. He did remember his friends, Gordon and Nate, with fondness. But it already seemed like such a long time ago, so much had happened. Besides, he would never see them again anyway. Somehow he'd been whisked into this strange land, and, try as he might, he couldn't seem to find his way home. He followed Mortifera's butler up three flights of stairs, down a long, rather dark hall and into a large heavily paneled room. He could understand why it was called the mahogany room.

The butler set his bag on the chair and then opened the wardrobe. There was a lone black suit. Will assumed correctly that it was for dinner tonight.

"Tomorrow the tailor will take your measurements. Be ready by seven o'clock. You'll be escorted to dinner at that time. Do not – I repeat – do NOT be late."

"Okay," said Will. The butler shut the door and left Will to his own devices. He walked to the double French glass doors, which opened out onto a small terrace. He could see the inner city from his vantage point. Strange aromas wafted to his nose; men on horseback rode quickly through the streets on some important errand. It was peculiar though. By his watch, it should have been three o'clock in the afternoon, and yet it was completely dark. The streets were lit with gas lamps. He'd noticed when he was finally released from the dungeons of Dosk that the light always looked like it was dusk. The lighting never changed, and, when they entered this land, Deorc, they entered into complete darkness.

"It's a crazy place," he said aloud. He'd wait to see what happened; go with the flow as his father used to say. He thought kindly of his parents and, like his friends, didn't expect to see them again. He'd held strong to their faces while imprisoned, but their images were slipping from his mind these last months, like fading memories. He'd wanted to go home in the worst possible way. He realized now that he was home — a new home. The wraith were his new family. He was amazed at the beauty of their skin, translucent and pale.

Their black eyes drew the listener into their depths like a wakeful dream. He found solace in their darkness. He'd been looking for these people, his new family, since he was fourteen. First, they appeared in his dreams, a little over time, revealing their beauty in the darkness. He'd heard the way other folks spoke of the Innesians of Deorc; the Dream Stealers they were called. He disagreed; they were the grantors of dreams. They were his salvation. He turned from the light and willingly embraced the darkness and everything that lurked within its depths. Little by little, day by day, he would accept whatever scraps were given him.

"I will learn to master this world and make it my own." The butler came for him at 6:45. He was glad he'd prepared himself early. Tonight was his debut, and he wanted a knock-out performance. He was shown into a different room than the one he'd been in earlier in the day and asked to remain seated until his mistress entered the room. He slowly scanned the large ornate room. One slightly irregular feature he did notice was the absence of mirrors. He hadn't seen a mirror since he'd entered the tower. No difference to him. They were a wasteful item anyway. These people were so beautiful, they didn't need to fix themselves in a mirror.

Draedon was shown into the room at seven o'clock. The two men shook hands and then waited for the mistress to arrive. Will sat on the couch as he was told to do; Draedon paced. About fifteen minutes later, Mortifera walked into the room. She was marvelously clad in a floor-length black-silk dress, her long black hair adorned with several marcasite-laden combs. Her translucent white skin cast a silvery glow against the intricate spider-like design of the dress. She was followed very closely by a young woman, whom Draedon didn't know. He was immediately stricken by her stunning beauty; her long, curly, flowing black hair was left loose against her pale bare shoulders. She wore a black satin collar with a long flowing satin dress and matching bodice. She was tall, but not Innesian. Human, thought Draedon. Changed to wraith? This sight was an unusual one to behold indeed. Rarely did they make new wraiths, especially not from humans. Humans were food to the wraiths; that was all. Even he, Draedon, wasn't wraith. He suddenly felt oddly out of place. He felt himself an inconvenience at this little soiree. He looked at Will, who was openly staring at Mortifera's charge. Mortifera had obviously gauged the outlander's reaction correctly.

"Please be seated," announced the butler. He placed Will across the table from Emily, to Mortifera's left. Draedon sat next to Will.

"Gentlemen, allow me to introduce my new daughter, Emily."

"Your daughter?", asked Draedon.

"Well, of course, silly, I made her."

All of a sudden, the quiet, transfixed Will blurted, "Can you make me too?"

Mortifera giggled. Another trait Draedon had never seen or heard before.

"Have patience, William. You've only been in Deorc a day. How can I be sure it's the correct path?"

"It is. I can assure you," he adamantly replied.

Without warning, a handsome middle-aged-looking wraith walked into the room. Surprisingly, he was Draedon's double, except greyer. The grey streaks in his hair made him look experienced and desperately handsome. Draedon stood and bowed as the man joined them at the table. With Draedon's prompting, Will stood and bowed as well. They remained standing until Belac sat.

"Darling, why didn't you tell me you were joining

us for dinner? I would have had a place set for you."

"Where's that infernal butler?"

"I'm here, sir," he replied as he placed a red cloth napkin and a chalice of a thick red liquid in front of the King of the Obsidian Tower.

"I was able to get away for a short time and wanted to see how my lovely Queen was amusing herself while I'm away." She giggled again.

"I'm having a dinner party," she gaily replied.

"I can see. Draedon, my son, we haven't seen much of you at court these last months."

"Yes, Sire, I've been away in Dosk on business. Did Mother show you her new ring?"

"Yes, and I must say, I'm very pleased with your accomplishment. Was it difficult?"

"Not really," he replied. "Everything withered and died, just as you said it would." He dismissed the image of the black dog that kept resurfacing in his mind.

"Well my aunt was never very good at keeping secrets." He snapped his fingers for the butler. "Have the scribe and a fast rider brought to me immediately. Mortifera, I don't think I know the other two guests at our table. Would you care to introduce us?"

"Certainly, darling. The young man is named William Tipton and is a friend of Draedon's. He has decided to join our family if we are willing to have him."

"We shall see with some time, young man," replied Belac. "Where do you come from?"

"I'm from Pine Woods and have come into your world by accident, I think."

"What do you mean into our world?", asked Belac.

"I'm from outerworld."

"Draedon, you befriended him? How?"

"I found him in the dungeons of Dosk. I had him

released and brought him home with me."

"I see. Now William, this is important. How did you come into Innes?"

"I'm not really sure," he replied. "I remember camping with my friends when a terrible thunderstorm ripped our tent away. The only other detail I remember is a tall, ghost-like man beckoning me into the woods."

"One of the council," he muttered. Why would they be interested in this boy? "Who were you camping with?"

"My two friends, Nate and Gordon, and Nate's dog, Fletcher."

"It still doesn't make any sense," said the King.

At the mention of the dog, Draedon asked, "What kind of dog?"

"A black lab," replied Bill.

"That was it." Draedon rubbed his forehead. Now he understood why the dog didn't die. He wasn't of this world. He wasn't connected or made from Twe-Leoht. He relaxed considerably upon figuring the mystery out. It wasn't a big deal anyway. He's just a stupid dog, Innesian or not. The conversation was interrupted when the scribe and rider came into the room.

"Take this message to High Official Pettiman."

> 'By order of the King of the Obisidan Tower, send two units of your best men to secure the Moldavite Tower. The King thanks you for your participation in the acquisition of said Tower. The lands of Twe-Leoht will be added to the holdings of Deorc immediately.'

"Get five hundred gold coins from the treasurer and give them to Pettiman along with my proclamation. Ride hard, ride fast," he said to the messenger.

"Darling, you're so generous. I wouldn't have sent him a single coin," said Mortifera.

"I'm just trying to keep on good terms. He's not to be underestimated, and I'm not done with him yet. So where were we?", Belac asked, as he took a long draught from his chalice.

"Ah, yes, William. You were about to tell me about your friends."

"They're just a couple of guys I grew up with. We just hang out and camp and fish and stuff," replied Will.

"I see. What did you say their names were?"

"Gordon and Nate," replied Will.

"Darling, don't you want to meet our other guest?", asked Mortifera.

"Certainly, my dear. William and I can finish our conversation later," he answered.

"What is your name, dear?" asked Belac.

"My name is Emily," she replied.

"Isn't she lovely, Belac? She's our new daughter. I made her last week."

"You made a human?", he asked in surprise.

"I made a wraith of the strongest magi to enter the Obsidian Tower in over five hundred years. Don't those fool council members tell you anything? I have half a mind to go into the chambers and remind them of their sovereign rulers. Our chairs have been empty too long in the council chambers. It's time to remind them of their fealty and their duties to their monarchs." Belac raised his hand to stop her tirade.

"I'll see to it, Mortifera. Please don't stress yourself so much. You know what the doctors have told you."

"They're a bunch of fools, too. There's nothing wrong with me. We're immortal."

"Emily, how did you find your way to our family?", asked Belac.

"I was abducted and brought to the dungeons," she

replied with no evident emotion.

"Belac, I invited our guest and made it possible for her to find her way to our home," replied Mortifera. "I knew of her birth and decided to offer her an alternate way prior to her eighteenth birthday. I believe I'm correct in assuming you're happy with your new life. Isn't that so Emily?"

"Yes, thank you, Mother," replied Emily.

"What of your previous life?", asked Belac. "Tell us a little about yourself before you came to the Obsidian Tower."

"I was born Emily Parker. My father was Bernie; my mother was Ashley. I had a brother and sister, a cat, a dog, and a parakeet. I went to the Walter Treaton School, and I was to enter my senior year of study in September."

"Mortifera, we'll have to make sure she gets her last year of high school. Get the best tutors in Deorc. I'll arrange for a diploma from the school," said Belac.

"Thank you," said Emily.

"Only the best for our children," he replied as he arose from the table. "I've been away too long. Those thieves will wipe my war chest clean." He walked around the table and kissed Mortifera on the cheek.

"Darling, you have kept my heart fluttering for more than five hundred years. Here's to five hundred more," he finished the drink in his chalice, rapidly set it on the table, and left the room in an instant.

"I think it's time to turn in. Sleep well, children." Mortifera rose and left the table.

The butler led William back to his quarters and Emily to her new quarters. She'd finally been released from the dungeons and this night would be her first sleeping in a real bed for many months. She lay down on her new bed, not even taking the time to look around the room. Thoughts raced through her mind. Was

Bhodi still in the dungeons? How did Will Tipton get to Innes? He mumbled some story of camping with Nate and Gordon. Were they in Innes, too? "I can't let anyone know we knew each other, not yet," she muttered and sighed, "I'd forgotten about the huge crush I had on him before he moved. I didn't think I'd ever see him again." Her heart started to race as she thought of him. Her cheeks flushed, as unexplained warmth spread throughout her body – warmth she only felt when she fed. She was startled out of her reverie by a knock at the door. She gathered herself together to receive her guest.

"Come in," she answered. It was Bhodi.

"When did they let you out of the dungeons?", she asked, still slightly breathless. "I was so worried about you."

"They brought me upstairs when you were at dinner. I have the adjoining room to yours." He showed her the door. "We can talk anytime we want," he said.

"I can't believe they let you out," she said. "I can't believe they let me out." She started to cry. Tears of blood ran down her translucent cheeks and onto the floor. Bhodi rushed to give her a handkerchief.

"You must be more careful," he said. "Carry a handkerchief with you from now on."

"I keep forgetting," she said. "Somehow I don't really feel any different, and, even though I've not seen a mirror, I know I must look different."

He sighed in resignation, "You're still beautiful Emily, but in another way." There was another knock at the door. Emily opened the door to Will Tipton standing in the hallway.

"May I come in?", he asked.

"Of course," she replied. "What are you doing here? Did the butler say it was okay?", she asked.

"I took the risk," he said. "Besides – no one is around; it's like a tomb on this floor. I didn't even see any servants," he said.

"Well be careful," she said. "I've been in the dungeons for too many months, and I don't want to go back."

"I can understand," he nodded. "I won't stay long. I just couldn't believe it was you. I thought I was the only one in Innes."

"I haven't seen you in, like, five years," replied Emily. "Where did you go? You were supposed to call me for a movie or something."

"I know," he said. "My parents moved us out of Pine Woods in like the middle of the night. It was so fast I only got to say goodbye to Nate and Gordon. I've only been allowed to see Nate a few times over the years. My parents didn't want me in Pine Woods, period. I guess I can understand why, now."

"How long have you been here?", Emily asked.

"I figured it's somewhere around six or seven months, but I could be wrong. I spent quite a few months in the dungeons of Dosk, so I know what you've been going through. I'd still be rotting in that jail if Draedon hadn't freed me. I owe him everything."

Bhodi stepped into the conversation, "Did you know my brothers, Caleb or Gaelen?"

"I knew Gaelen. He was your brother? Caleb, I'm sorry, I didn't know. Caleb was assigned to Jacob's cell."

"Jacob?", Emily asked.

"Yeah, Jacob Daggerstein, Nate's granddad's friend. It was crazy when we first found each other. I had Gaelen assigned to my cell. But I don't know what happened to him after I was released. He wasn't released with me, I'm sorry to say. I'd hoped they'd release him when they released Jacob. I guess no such luck."

"I can't believe you're here, Will," she said as she walked to the terrace doors. "I thought I'd never see anyone from home again. Ever." She paused a moment or two. "Look, it's starting to snow." Will and Bhodi joined her at the terrace watching the ever increasing snowfall.

"It's so beautiful," said Emily. "I'd forgotten what true beauty looked like." They both agreed.

"If you don't mind, I'd like to go to bed now. It's my first night in a proper bed in years, and I'm exhausted." Bhodi was the first to say good night and left them to go to his own room.

Will and Emily stood at the window watching the snow swirling through the streets. He put his arm around her shoulders as she leaned into his body for warmth that she no longer needed.

Will wasn't accustomed to drinking alcohol and he still felt light-headed from the wine at dinner. The feel of her chilled skin and the faint smell of her perfume made his pulse quicken. He pulled her closer to him — their eyes locked in an intense gaze. He kissed her lightly on the forehead, cheek, and neck. But before he could kiss her lips, a rapid knock at the door jarred them from their passion. Bhodi flew into the room.

"Will, you must leave now. Mortifera's coming to Emily's room. I heard her speaking on the lower landings. You must leave, now! She won't be pleased to find you here without her permission." Will left the room reluctantly, but as quietly as he'd entered. Emily opened the terrace doors and stepped outside. She needed to calm her emotions before her mother's arrival. There was a light tap at the door. Bhodi opened the door and Mortifera entered.

"Emily, what are you doing on the terrace?"

"Watching it snow, Mother," she replied.

"Very well, but come inside now. I want to speak with you."

"Yes, Mother."

"Bhodi, you're dismissed to your rooms. You won't be needed for the rest of the night."

"Thank you, Mistress," he said as he bowed and left the room.

"Emily, do you know the young man that Draedon brought with him?"

"Yes, Mother, I do. He used to live in our neighborhood."

"Are you friends?"

"We were ... a long time ago. I haven't seen him for about five years. His parents moved when we were thirteen."

"I see," she said, and then hesitated as if trying to discern something intangible. "I want you to limit your contact until I decide what to do with him. I don't want to send him away, as it would hurt my Draedon dearly."

"Yes, Mother," replied Emily. "I will do as you ask."

"I'll let you in on a little secret, if you promise not to tell. Promise?"

"I promise."

"Draedon will be permanently changed to wraith in the next few months. You're to be his bride by the vernal equinox – our gift of love to you both." Emily was noticeably shaken, and tears began to flow down her cheeks.

"It's okay, Emily. All brides are nervous before their wedding. He's a good man. You could do much worse, you know," she said in a tight voice.

"Yes, Mother, thank you. I don't mean to seem ungrateful. I just hadn't thought of myself as married for some time to come, or at least until I'd finished high school."

"Nonsense, you're a beautiful woman, and Draedon is a handsome and wealthy man. Besides, Belac has already decreed you'll continue your studies. We won't push for grandchildren until you finish your education."

"Thank you, Mother."

"Now, go to bed. You will start your lessons after breakfast. The kitchen will send your tray to you in the morning."

"Good night, Mother."

"Good night, child, and remember to allow the remover of dreams into your sleep. It'll be much easier for you that way."

"Yes, Mother, I will." When the door had closed and her footsteps were gone, Emily threw herself into her pillows and cried. She allowed darkness to enter her as she cried herself to sleep. She awoke around midnight to what sounded like someone crossing the floor of her room. She fell back into troubled dreams of marriage and children and Will Tipton.

She'd had a crush on him since they were twelve. She was devastated when he told her his parents were moving the family from Pine Woods. She cried herself to sleep every night for a week until she discovered his friend Nate. That was then, and this is now, and she was getting married to an unknown man in four months who didn't even know about it. She wondered how he'd feel about Mortifera's big plans. She thought about her real parents a lot when she was first kidnapped. Now it was too difficult to think about them. Now that she'd changed to wraith, they'd never know the truth. "I'm sorry," she mumbled as she slipped back into the protective darkness of sleep with no dreams.

7: Nate's Trial

Nate was surrounded by the Metalmark Clan as they made their way through the Mirthless Swamp. They stopped momentarily where Nate had lopped off Serpentia's head.

"It doesn't look anything like my dream," he thought. He could see brownies hanging out in the trees.

They threw pine cones and twigs and anything else they could find and shouted, "Our hero, killer of the beast, murderer, scourge of the universe, you set the Metalmarks free," and a bunch of other profane phrases. Nate could remember Heldring saying that brownies were known to use some rather foul language at times. This moment must have been one of those times. It was ironic being persecuted for what happened in a dream, and yet he sat high atop Arion as proof of his deed. He could see the island where Arion had been suspended in time. Arion whinnied in disdain of the place and thanked Nate once again for his release.

The brownies taunted, "He has Heldring's horse. He has Heldring's horse."

Nate patted Arion on the neck, "It's okay old friend. I wouldn't have left you there one more minute than necessary. I know Heldring left you as a last resort to protect you against Metazial."

"What's that, you say," said Sidney the white-haired. "Did you say Heldring?"

"Why do you ask?", replied Nate.

"I must be dreaming," said the Metalmark fairy.

"How could he possibly know Heldring? Why do those hateful brownies keep chanting 'you have Heldring's horse'?"

"What if I did know Heldring?", asked Nate.

The entire Metalmark Clan shouted, "All hail Heldring!"

"Heldring is our King," said Sidney broad-chest. "Our clan was cast out of The Sapphire Tower when Heldring died. All magical creatures were forbidden within the castle walls. The hag made it so."

"And what of Cereus?", asked Nate.

"She became hard and hateful. She killed innocents just for fun."

"We were cast into the Wastelands for hundreds of years until the Checkerspots and the Painted Ladies invited us into the Forest. We lived in the Forest peacefully enough for two hundred years. But the Sidneys got restless and played too rough. That's when we burned part of the forest. The rest of our history you know."

Nate dismounted from Arion. "I need to stretch my legs for a few minutes." He walked around the lake looking for something, anything familiar. He needed something to prove that he was in fact here at this spot and had done battle with the ancient serpent. He knew Arion to be real, but he could have walked from anywhere to their hiding place that restless night.

Cindy red-leg flew up to Nate's shoulder and whispered in his ear, "Do you know Heldring?"

"Yes," he whispered back to her.

"I knew it," she said. "I don't know how, but I can smell him on you."

"He hijacked my body in the Dosk Wastelands. I was Heldring until six days ago. I found a new body for him, an empty warder. He has returned to Dosk to rescue Cereus from the dungeons, and I'm here with you."

"Can you prove what you say? It will have a definite influence on your sentencing." Nate walked to Arion and pulled a long covered object from his saddle. He slowly uncovered the object for all to see. A hushed silence fell through the normally chatty Sidneys and Cindys.

Sidney white-hair flew to within a foot of Nate before exclaiming, "He has Heldring's sword."

A loud whisper sped through the fairy clan, "He has the Sword of Heldring."

"How can this be? Heldring is dead!", they shouted at once. It took several minutes for the chaos to diminish enough for Nate to speak.

"Heldring and I shared one body – mine. Now Heldring has his own body, and he's returned to his homelands of Dosk to free the Queen. I'm here with you."

"This sounds like a crazy tale, even for us Metalmarks. You must tell us something to make us certain that you shared a body with Heldring," said Sidney white-hair.

"He snores. I don't," suggested Nate.

"Too simple."

"He likes his coffee black. I like cream and sugar."

"More. Something more."

"He has seen the double red suns of Sundari. I haven't."

"Yes, yes, he really is alive," replied Cindy red-legs.

"Something more, one more thing," urged Sidney white-hair.

Nate looked directly at Sidney white-hair, "You were the Dosk ambassador for all of the fairy clans, appointed by Heldring himself."

"How could you know that?"

"From Heldring's memories. He has his own body now, but I still have his memories. It seems to be a side effect of the sharing. I don't know if it's permanent, and I'm not really sure there's anyone to ask about it."

"Heldring must live again."

"He does."

"All hail Heldring."

"But, you must keep this news a secret," said Nate. "He's in Dosk, and no one except for Cereus knows he's alive. It'd be terrible if anyone found out."

"But the Metalmarks must tell the Morpho for your sentencing," said Sidney green-eyes. "They must know, or else you'll be sentenced to death."

"Death?!", exclaimed Nate. "No one said anything about death."

"An eye for an eye, and all that junk," replied Sidney broad-chest.

"Can the Morpho keep a secret?", asked Nate. "At least until he gets Cereus out of Dosk." He'd grown to miss his counterpart, like an uncle, and actually worried for his safety. He'd have to take the risk. He certainly couldn't afford a death sentence right now, if ever. Nate mounted his horse, and the Metalmarks blinked out of the Mirthless Swamp and into the Devil's Hole Forest.

They expected their entrance to set off some sort of alarm. They weren't let down. Within ten minutes, they were under arrest, and the Red Admirals and the Swallowtails were escorting the Metalmark contingent to the Morpho Clan's ring. The snow was several feet deep; it was slow going for Arion and Nate. The clans didn't seem to mind. Nate was glad for the wool clothing he'd taken from the Moldavite Tower. He was underdressed and starting to feel the effects of the cold in his fingers and toes.

A few hours later the group was told to stop and

wait. The lead escorts from the Red Admiral and Swallowtail clans flew forward to what Nate assumed was the Morpho Ring. He was asked to dismount and step forward. Sidney white-hair took Arion's reigns. There was considerable tension in the air as he stepped into the Morpho Ring – none of it good. He was led to face a blue frog who was introduced as the King of the Morpho Clan. He could hear the Cindys trying to calm the restless Sidneys.

They were hollering in the background, "Let him tell his story."

"Silence," bellowed the fairy frog. There was more pushing and shoving amongst the other clans as they tried to silence the Sidneys. The frog king was about to read fairy legalese and describe the proceedings when from behind the King, a voice clearly said,

"Nate, Nate Sutton, is that you?" Out of the darkening woods walked Michael Parker.

"Michael?" Nate was shocked and amazed. "What the…?" Michael walked up to Nate and briskly shook his hand and then gave him a hug.

"You must be freezing. I have a fire in the caves below us. You can get warm and have some food."

Nate looked to the fairy king who had quietly watched the reunion of the two friends. There was another rush of talk through the fairy clans as they realized that Michael was the magi with the dragon.

"Who are these two strange humans?"

"Silence," the fairy king said once again. "I can see we've got more to this story, and your friend will freeze to death if we don't get him warmed. Michael, may we adjourn to your residence?"

"Certainly," said Michael, as he picked up the Morpho king and carried him down the hill. Michael held up one hand and said to the fairies, "Please take care when you enter the cave. Ailith knows you're here, but she's grown considerably and doesn't want to hurt anyone. Stay back from her until she's gotten used to where everyone is." He'd noticed as they walked from the Morpho ring that the Checkerspots and the Ringlets had shown up.

"I guess today is the day," he said. "Your Highness, I need to set you down until I can make a comfortable spot for you. Is that okay?"

"Certainly, I'd appreciate it." Michael took a thick piece of cloth and carefully laid it on the tall podium he'd made for the King. He set the King up high, as this was his clan's ring. Nate followed, walked over to the fire, and inhaled a deep breath as he saw Ailith warming herself on the other side of the fire. Michael put his hand on Nate's shoulder, "Don't be afraid."

Nate looked at Michael, "You didn't say she was a dragon."

"Sorry about that. It's just that we have quite an audience," he said as he turned and waved for the clans to enter his winter home. Nate noticed they sat in groups, their clans he figured. There were several new ones he had not seen before.

"They're the Anna Blues and the Paper Kites," said Michael. "It looks like we have twelve clans present. Excuse me, but I need to put out more places for them to sit." Nate helped him bring out several long benches and boards he used as shelves in other rooms. There were thousands of fairies in the cave, of all different colors and sizes. Arion had been led into the next room and given straw and oats. The Morpho King was the first to speak.

"Friends and clan members, we seem to have two purposes for gathering this evening – both for justice, in a manner of speaking. I would like to resolve the first issue, that of freeing the Metalmarks. We the Fey hold our laws to the highest degree. If a law has been broken and admission of breaking said law has been given freely, then all that is left is sentencing. However, it has come to my attention that this case is not as transparent as it might at first appear. I would like for the accused to stand and state his name and the details of his crime."

Nate stood and explained about his dream and his killing Serpentia to rescue his horse Arion. "I didn't know it would release the Metalmark Clan from their banishment. My only defense is that I didn't act alone – or at least by my own choice," he said as he finished his statement. There was a stir, as whispers sped around the room.

"Order," said the King.

"I find myself in a predicament beyond the sentence of death for slaying Serpentia," said Nate.

"What could be worse than death?", asked the King.

"Death?", asked Michael. "For slaying a monster?"

There was immediate silence in the room.

"It's okay, Michael," said Nate. "I'm going to answer the court's question. But be aware that my answer has far-reaching implications and affects everybody in this cave."

"Go on," said the King.

"When I first arrived in Innes, I travelled through the Dosk Wastelands. My travel companion and I were driven into the tombs to get out of the weather. We were driven into the last tomb where we spent several nights." Nate could feel the tension increasing. "The first night in residence I started to have strange dreams, the first dream about a woman I'd never met, the second dream about killing a monster I'd never seen. I'd been in and out of a fever for days. The first night my dreams included a waking dream where I acquired this," he said, as he slowly uncovered the sword from its cloth covering. It was like a wind had passed about

King Morpho

the room as the fairies flapped their wings and muttered their thoughts.

"In addition to the finding of this sword, I fought off some huge spiders, which apparently had been guarding the crypt, and then I acquired a crown, necklace, and a suit of armor. I was exhausted when I awoke in the morning, and I remembered the night before as if in a dream. The second night was equally disturbing, as that is the night I faced the fetid creature that my dream voice called Serpentia.

The voice kept going on about brownies and how he, for it was a male voice, hated brownies and needed to catch squirrels. He had me mix up a solution from Talus' bag while Talus was still under the effects of the spider venom. The next day I woke and found Arion in the crypt." Again chatter reigned through the cave.

"Silence, please. Go on Nate," said the King.

"This is the part I'm reluctant to tell," he continued, "because all of our lives are at stake." Another hush went around the room.

"Nicolas Heldring is alive." He waited until the chatter died down in the room.

"Lies," shouted several Checkerspots.

"It can't be the truth," shouted the Ringlets.

"Heldring has been dead to us these long centuries – by the witch's hand."

"He's telling the truth," yelled the Metalmarks. "He lies to escape his fate," shouted the Checkerspots. The cave erupted in shouts and name calling.

"SILENCE," shouted the Morpho King. "I will have silence, or else you'll all be asked to leave." The gallery reluctantly quieted, but the tension in the cave remained palpable.

"Please, Nate, continue telling your tale," said the King.

"Heldring initially borrowed my body, and I wasn't

sure he was going to give it back. But he knew that two strong consciousnesses couldn't remain in one mind. One of our tasks was to find him a new one, which we did. He has taken the body of Lorelei's warder, Drakken Aruhl." He could hear the crowd shifting again.

"You lie," shouted one of the Paper Kites.

"It's the truth," replied the Metalmarks vehemently.

"How can we know with any certainty?", sang one of the Monarchs. Shock and dismay ran through the twelve clans.

"Please, let him finish," the Morpho King said once again.

"He has gone to Dosk to rescue Cereus from the dungeons. Official Pettiman has had her arrested and incarcerated under the city. His troops march on Leoht and the Devil's Hole Forest as we speak.

"That's true, that's true," replied the Lacewings.

"We've seen his army across the river. Soon they'll be in our territory."

"We must try to help him, or at the very least, keep his existence silent. Pettiman doesn't know that Heldring has risen, so he has the element of surprise."

"Long live Heldring," shouted the Metalmarks.

"Soon they'll start to cut down the trees for firewood," said Nate.

"The trees won't like that," said the Checkerspots.

"We must make ready and protect our lands," shouted the Red Admirals.

"Order! Order in the court!", shouted the Morpho King. "We're still within court proceedings. How does the accused plead?"

"Guilty, Your Honor," replied Nate.

"It would appear that you're guilty with extenuating circumstances," he corrected. "I also have the distinct feeling there is more to your story than you're currently sharing. Be that as it may, the court finds you half guilty for the slaying of Serpentia and the subsequent release of the Metalmark Clan." Whispers swept through the cave.

"Will anyone stand for this man's character?"

"I will," said a voice as it entered the cave. All turned to see the new arrivals. Michael got a huge smile on his face as he saw the arrival of his father and Nate's grandfather.

"Granddad?", exclaimed Nate.

"Hi Nate," he said as he made his way through to the fire to hug his grandson. "I've missed you, son."

"Boy. Have I missed you too!", exclaimed Nate. Tiny fairy tears that sounded like little bells could be heard falling around the cave. Bernie hugged Michael.

"Please Your Honor, continue," said Ben.

"It is the judgment of the court that this man, Nathaniel Sutton, shall be sentenced to as many days as necessary to help with the reconciliation of the peace within Innes. It's obvious to me, and by all who are seated here, that like his forefathers, he has a way of bringing all forms of life together peaceably. This is my judgment. All in agreement say 'aye', all opposed.

The 'ayes' have it. It is the opinion of this judge and King of the Morpho Clan that one day you will make a fine ruler. I hope to be there when that happens." With the final verdict rendered, all hugs were given, tears cried, and forgiveness offered. The Metalmarks were given their old territory back with the condition that, when the Sidneys got rowdy, they move back to the swamp. After food and drink, which magically appeared, the King asked for silence once again.

"Now, for our second order of business. For the first time in five hundred years, we have all members of the remaining forest clans under one roof. Michael may we introduce Ailith now?"

"She's ready," he replied.

"To Residents of all the Fey Clans, Brethren of the Light, Residents of the Devil's Hole Forest, please allow me to introduce Ailith the Free, Daughter of Thryth, Late of Dagung." Shouts of "Ailith", clapping, whistling, hoots and hollers erupted from the tightly packed fairy assemblage. Michael held up a hand to stay the reverie.

"Please remember, she's still a baby. Be gentle with her." He placed a rabbit in her mouth and left several others as snacks.

"Will you be okay if I go outside for a bit to talk with my dad?"

"Yes Michael, I'll let you know when I've had enough." He turned to leave the cave. He noticed the fairies were already sitting on Ailith's tail and back and feet.

"Please, Ailith, tell us of your birth and your mother, your lineage and everything about you," the fairies chimed together. Michael ducked out of the cave to see the other men huddled together talking quietly amongst themselves.

"I can't believe that I'm here and that you're all here together as well," said Nate.

"We'll have plenty of time to talk about everything, Nate; for now, let's be happy we're together."

"Here, here," resounded a deep Scottish accent followed by the voice's owner Beastly Hadley and his partner Crooksey Snively.

They introduced themselves to Nate, who'd never seen such a large orange tom cat or as large a bull mastiff as those standing upright in front of him. He laughed as he shook paws with the two late comers.

In the distance, they could hear a wee voice yelling, "Hey you guys; wait for me. Couldn't you give me a lift?" Into the clearing burst Jonah Hobken, as Crooks and Beast had a laugh.

"Oh, ha ha," he scoffed. "Laugh it up! Michael, it's good to see you again!" The reunited friends shared a hug and had a good laugh together.

"Michael, do you think we can squeeze through the throng to the back room? I could sure use a drink and some dry clothes," said Ben.

"I think so. Most of them are sitting on Ailith or as close as they can get." They quietly made their way to the back room, not wanting to disturb the thousands of fairies that were intent on hearing Ailith's story. Michael placed food and drink on the table as the travellers changed into dry clothing.

"Thanks again, Crooks and Beastly. The cave has been integral in providing a place for Ailith's growth. I don't think she would survive the winter if it weren't for the two of you."

"Our pleasure, we're glad it's been put to use for good for a change. And as our pirating days are over, we should make all our stash houses available for good use," said Crooksey. "What do you think of that, Beastly?"

"Fine with me," he answered in his thick Scottish burr.

8: A Love Triangle

Madeline looked out onto the courtyard from her bedroom window. Her mother and aunts had left early this morning. It was very difficult, but her father convinced her that someone needed to go home and look after the estate.

Ashley was emotionally distraught when Bernie and his party showed up at Chelsea Manor. The stress of her family being separated in unknown places for so long was more of a burden than she could bear. Madeline's father had left just a few hours ago to check on Michael. He told a story about Michael wanting to live in some cave out in the forest.

She looked at herself and thought better of judging what seemed like a crazy story and ... there was still no news of Emily. The King of Leoht had left several days ago: to better strategize the imminent war with Dosk. They felt little change at Chelsea Manor. The only occurrence that showed the state of affairs in Innes was the increased coming and going of messengers. Still she didn't know what her purpose was. She felt useless in these matters.

She spent most of her day loitering in the gardens. Every last piece of free dirt was covered by huge dahlias, peonies, echinacea, daisies, and countless other flower species. Unlike her counterparts, who were more specialized, she seemed to have multiple talents that she hadn't yet come close to mastering. She could touch a fence and think rose, and an entire rose bush would emanate from her fingertips. She could heal as well as Maize herself, although she wasn't nearly as practiced in diagnostics.

She wasn't really sure what else she could do, as most of the time she felt like a wall flower hanging around the estate waiting for something to happen. She spent most of her time with Rho Dora and Gordon, when he was around. Ira had taken to sending him on missions, after which he would seek her healing abilities for the many bruises, cuts, and scrapes he seemed to amass. She missed the lug-head when he wasn't around. She knew he cared for her a great deal; they'd been friends their whole lives. She knew he cared for Rho a lot, and she for him, and of course Rho and Madeline were inseparable.

As much as they loved each other, it was an uneasy triangle of friendship at times. There had been others who had asked to call on her or Rho. They both sidestepped the invitations with a happy, "thank you for asking." Madeline had overheard Iris and Maize talking about them. They didn't know what to expect from a polyhybrid. Apparently, there had only been one other in their history some thousand years ago, and she had recently died. Madeline didn't know much else other than she needed something to do, and soon. She loved spending the days with Rho. Their friendship had certainly deepened. She wasn't too sure of herself after their first kiss, but had found it easier with each additional experience. She had talked to her mother about it.

She said, "Madeline, you're newly made and still trying to find yourself. Take your time and explore your options. You still don't know the extent of your abilities and should spend the bulk of your time honing your skills."

"I know, Mother, but what about Gordon and Rho. What do I do about them?"

"Why do you have to do anything about them? They are both lovely individuals with their own special attractions. Follow your heart, it's a powerful compass. I trust your judgment." She loved them both, and they were both really good at kissing. There was no running away from the truth. She saw no reason why she had to choose between them. She'd followed her mother's advice and worked hard to embrace her talents and hone her skills. She'd find some sort of usefulness in Innes.

She thought of going home and probably could, if she remained sequestered on the estate. But her involvement with that local community was now over. The people in the town of Pine Woods would never accept her as she now looked. She'd like to finish her studies at the Treaton School. Or maybe some arrangement could be made for private tutoring. She would speak to Maize about the matter this evening.

Rho popped in, "Join me for dinner?" She walked to the window and put her arm around Madeline's waist.

"What ya looking at?", she asked.

"Nothing really," said Madeline. "I'm just thinking about my folks leaving."

"That must have been real hard for you," she said.

"Yeah, but I'm glad to have seen them. It got me to thinking, though."

"Oh yeah, about what?", asked Rho.

"I feel useless just hanging around the Manor. You have your studies, and Gordon is off on his missions, but I'm just hanging around doing nothing."

"I'll keep you busy," said Rho playfully as she kissed Madeline.

"I know, and I like that, but I need something of my own. Like you and Gordon have. I'm going to ask Maize if I can continue my studies."

"You'll leave the Manor and go back to school?"

"No, silly," she said, and lightly kissed the tip of

Rho's nose.

"A teacher from the school, maybe they could come here and tutor me."

"Oh ... that's a really good idea. Why didn't I think of that? I can't see why she would say no. You've certainly had enough rest. I would think so anyway. Come on, let's go have dinner and then talk to her about your studies. Maybe someone could be here by week's end."

After dinner and a resolution to Madeline's education problem was determined, Rho reluctantly excused herself to her room. She hadn't reported to her mistress and was overdue. She'd experienced the wrath of the Wraith Queen when she was made to watch a servant's beheading because he'd forgotten to bow to the Queen's guests.

"I'm sorry. Yes, I know I'm late. No, there isn't much to report – except a lot of messengers have been coming and going. Not much else. The King left yesterday. I'll call next week." She wished she didn't have to make these calls. She hated being a snitch, especially to the Queen of the Obsidian Tower, but her mother was her handmaiden. There was little she could do. She lied to protect Madeline and Gordon.

"But if the mistress ever found out...." There was a knock at her door. "Come in."

Madeline plopped down on her bed. "How's your headache?"

"A little better, especially since you're here." Madeline stroked Rho's hair until she was fast asleep; then curled up next to her and fell fast asleep herself. In the morning Madeline awoke to Gordon snoring in her ear. She didn't know when he'd come in.

Sandwiched between Gordon and Rho, she struggled to unfurl herself from the covers. She had to lift Gordon's hand from her waist and crawl over Rho before she could leave the bed. Gordon grunted and mumbled something unintelligible and pulled Rho closer to him in the bed. Dimitri sat on the window sill looking out over the courtyard looking for a tasty morsel. Madeline left Rho's room and sprinted for the bath a few doors down the hall.

She heard voices in the hall, "... and where do you think the three of them slept?"

"I didn't know it had gone so far, maybe we should say something to them."

That was all of the conversation she heard before quickly trotting back to her own room and climbing into bed. She didn't want to be a problem for anyone. She heard the knob turn on her door and then the door closed very quietly. An hour or so later her door opened again, but this time it was followed by someone crawling into her bed. Madeline rolled over to see Rho, who had blushed a deep purple, crawling under the covers with her.

"You left me alone with Gordon?"

"Yeah, I had to."

"Why?"

"I was in the bathroom and heard someone talking about the three of us, as if it were some kind of problem, and that they should talk to us. So, I slipped back into my own room. It's a good thing I did too, because someone looked into my room only moments after I crawled under the covers."

"Do you think they're mad?"

"I don't know why they would be. It's not like anything has happened, beyond kissing, that is. Right?" Rho hesitated. "Right?"

"Well ... not exactly."

"What do you mean? Have you and Gordon gone all the way?"

"Well no, not all the way. But, a lot of the way."

"What about me?", Madeline asked, truly hurt and slightly envious.

"What about you?", replied Rho, a little defensively. "You were tied up with your family, and Gordon and I had some extra time alone together. That's all. It's not like we don't still love you ... and ... want you, too."

"I feel so far behind now," Madeline complained.

"We have another hour before breakfast. Let's hurry and get caught up. I'll show you what we did, okay?" Madeline answered her by rolling her over and pinning her arms to the bed.

"Show me everything."

"Okay, okay," laughed Rho.

The breakfast bell rang as Madeline lay back on her pillows, out of breath.

"Madeline, look at all of these flowers." Her room was filled with hundreds of flowers that had appeared every time she placed her hand on the head board or night stand. Her ability to grow plants on objects she touched coupled with the energy of her first orgasm created enough flowers to fill twenty vases.

"I didn't know," she gasped.

"I didn't either," laughed Rho.

"You learned to do that with Gordon?"

"Well, we've been practicing quite a bit," confided Rho.

"But you haven't gone all the way?"

"No, not yet."

"Why?" Madeline asked.

"We were waiting for you," Rho replied, as she blushed a deep purple. "We're going to have to wait a little longer, though," she sighed.

"Why?", asked Madeline.

"Ira sent Gordon on another mission. He came for Gordon himself."

"Were you terribly embarrassed?"

"No, not really; we're just people experiencing love. If you ask me, we need more of this activity. Then we wouldn't be going to war. Everyone would live peacefully and blissfully."

"Do we have time for more?", asked Madeline.

"After breakfast," replied Rho. "Right now I could eat a horse."

9: Serendipity

"Gordon, are you awake enough? Gordon?"

"I'm sorry, Ira. I didn't get much sleep last night."

"You should go to your own room now and again," laughed Ira. "Those girls will tap all of your energy."

"Actually, I didn't get back to the Manor until after two. I got hung up, or should I say, a couple of fellas got hung up." He reached into his pocket and handed Ira a small gold book mark.

"It was exactly where you said it would be."

"Good, good. We're close to having all the parts. I keep hoping we can assemble all the parts before we make the final grab."

"What is the final grab?", asked Gordon.

"The less you know the better. When we have all of the components I'll show you why we're assembling our puzzle and how."

Gordon couldn't understand why he didn't grab everything at once, but this was Ira's show. He would follow along. His thoughts wandered to Rho's perfect body. She isn't a skinny little thing with no place for a man to hold onto. She isn't a beast either. She is just perfect for a man like me, he thought. Madeline's face came into his mind.

He wondered if Rho had told her about their explorations. He thought about Madeline's body, curvy and full. He didn't know if he could manage two women. His schedule was strenuous as it was. When would he sleep? He laughed to himself; if only that were the biggest of his problems.

125

"Gordon, Gordon! Do you know what you have to do and where you have to go?", asked Ira, who tried to snap Gordon out of his reverie.

"Yes, I'll bring the books back to the Manor. I'll be back in a flash," he said as he turned and ran deeper into the forest towards the caravan.

This next mission sounded more dangerous than the others. He quickened his pace. He wanted to complete this mission quickly and get back to his girls. This time his mission took him to Dagung. Ira had given him a small pointed rod, no bigger than a roll of dimes. He showed him how to use the pointed end in the air to draw a door. An electric blue light appeared where the lines were drawn, and once a knob or handle was placed on the door, it could be opened. The tricky part was to know where exactly the door opened. He'd practiced for several weeks now and could get to within a few yards of his destination.

He quickened his pace further. Ira explained he had to be at least a mile from the Manor and well within the Forest. Ira felt this was an important strategy in case of dark spies. There had been some chaos when that Doskian soldier was brought in with Nate's granddad. They'd taken care of the problem by shipping him off to the garrison at Leoht. They were better equipped to handle a spy, if that's what he was. He's probably right, he thought.

Gordon had grown accustomed to rigorous exercise and didn't mind the fluffy, knee-deep snow that was impeding his forward movement. He stopped when he thought he'd put enough distance between himself and the Manor. He readied the wand, drew the invisible doorway in the air, and put one foot into the passageway. He could hear the cry of wolves, almost feel their breath on the back of his neck. He turned for one last look to see them running on the ridge about a hundred meters from where he was about to vanish. He could hear the howls of distress as the doorway closed behind him, barring the huge animals from entering the space and acquiring their quarry.

He stepped into the vineyards at the base of the Amethyst Tower. It was difficult to comprehend the extent of the damage to the castle and the surrounding grounds. The once lush vineyards, known throughout the lands of Innes for the finest of wines, were scorched to ruin. He saw a rotund man sitting on a flat rock, no more than thirty yards from where Gordon stood. He decided to talk to this stranger, in spite of the apparent danger.

"Hi," said Gordon, as he approached the distraught man.

"It's all gone," he said. "My life's work, years of culturing, nurturing, blending the finest grapes, all gone," he repeated as he waved his arm over the vineyards to show the extent of the damage. "All gone," he repeated, placing his head in his hands.

Gordon sat down next to the man, removed two sandwiches from his pouch and offered one to the man. He looked unkempt and Gordon surmised, correctly, that he hadn't eaten for several days. The man gratefully accepted the kind gesture and gingerly unwrapped the sandwich like it was gold. Gordon was only too happy to share. Cook was always so generous with him, doted on him really, and packed far more than he would eat.

"My name is Gordon," he said and extended his hand to shake, as an honorable man would.

"I am Dieter," said the man, who was obviously feeling better having some food in his belly.

"I'm sorry about all of this," said Gordon.

"Thank you, but it wasn't your fault. It was that soul-sucking pair, Mortifera and Belac, who caused this damage. It wasn't good enough for him to kill the king, his father. He had to ruin everything else. My life's work, and my Greta, too, killed when a beam crashed onto her when the inn collapsed. I have nothing left," he said, and began to sob into his hands once again.

While this wasn't part of the program, Gordon threw the dice. "Do you want to come with me, Dieter? It'll be dangerous; probably more action that you've seen for a long time," he said quite seriously.

Dieter laughed at that and patted his robust belly. "Maybe I could use some action in my life," he said. He stood up and removed his shirt. Underneath was a metal and leather framework that created the illusion that Dieter had an immense belly. Gordon looked at him quizzically.

"People like robust innkeepers," replied Dieter. "Makes them think the food is better. Mark me, my Greta was an excellent cook, the Pillars of Flame rest her soul, but the customers didn't know that." He dropped the fake belly and walked onto the path. "So where are we headed," he asked.

Gordon laughed and nodded to the tower.

"Oh, you weren't kidding were you? A Sunday outing, a walk in the park, a dance in a fountain, easy as she goes," he said as he drew in his chest and started towards the darkened tower.

A light wind blew through the few white hairs on his head, making him look all the madder for the dirty and tattered clothing that were now way too big for his wiry frame. They quietly approached the south wall of the castle, most of which was missing due to cannon fire. The smell of burned wood and flesh wafted through the gray smoke that clogged their lungs and stung their eyes. Dieter ripped several strips from his once-white shirt and indicated that they should tie them over their mouths and noses. Neither man dared to speak for fear of reprisal, but only the ghosts seemed to remain. The interlopers had removed all of the items of value, including the women and children — the spoils of war.

Gordon hoped that his quarry still remained. He pointed to the doorway to enter the tower; it hung open, half off of its heavy wrought-iron hinges. They quietly entered the tower and started to climb the spiral stairs. Ira had been very explicit where his next acquisition should be found and Gordon easily located the library, his targeted location. Heavy volumes and ancient tomes littered the floor. The east wall had been completely destroyed, leaving the massive library open to the extremes of weather. Gordon made his way along the still-standing shelves.

"I'm looking for three volumes," he said. "I was told where they should be, but with all of this destruction I have my doubts."

"Let's start with where you were told to look," said Dieter.

"The Book of Innes, under history. The Magic of Walter Treaton, under magic. Dragons and their Fey Folk, under zoology," said Gordon.

The two men scanned the shelves. "Here's the Dragon book," whispered Dieter. Within minutes the other two books had been recovered, as well as a couple that Gordon decided no one would miss. He stashed them into his bag and they left the library, slowly making their way past the rotting bodies, all the while murmuring prayers of protection under their breath.

+ + + +

Gorgos and Naptha worked well into the night, removing their booty from the underground lair. This new hiding place would work temporarily, just until he could work out a more permanent arrangement. He hoped that his wife was safely stowed in their new home. He'd planned ahead, stashing all the extra gold pieces that he'd found or earned from his side jobs. With this new-found wealth, he could pay off the place and build a sweet place for Naptha to sleep plus he could buy his own sheep and cows to feed him. After some food and rest, they took to the skies. Gorgos steered Naptha to the perpetual darkness of Deorc.

"We shouldn't be spotted as easily," he reasoned.

"I agree," replied Naptha.

"Do you misses your wraith masters?", asked Gorgos.

"I hate them," roared Naptha. "It was Belac, himself, who tricked me into the cube. I thought he loved me. But I realize now, these blood-suckers love no one but themselves." They had flown far enough to the north that Gorgos figured no one to be around. He saw a small patch of dead trees.

"Lightem' up," he hollered, as the adrenalin heated his blood. Naptha swooped at steep angle, the wind whistled wildly in his ears. An arc of fire lit up the night sky as Naptha torched the dead trees and surrounding grasslands. He could smell the napalm, burnt wood, and charred animal flesh as they banked over the flaming ecosystem. One more pass made short work of anything that survived the first pass.

"I feel better," said Naptha as he burped a few more fire balls onto the sweltering landscape.

"I'm sure you do," laughed Gorgos as he patted Naptha's scaly neck. "Let's goes back to our hideout. We haves lots of planning to do. Promises haves been made and must be kept." Gorgos' voice roared across

Naptha

the night sky, "The binding has freed me, a lowly slave, and I will die before I return to the dungeons." They zoomed through the black skies of Deorc to the perpetually gray skies of Dosk in the wee hours of the morning. He was glad to see that their place hadn't been breeched. He thought they'd be safe in Pickering Cross for a short while, not much here but forests and fields and lots of sheep.

+ + + +

Heldring watched as the soldiers lit the house of the servant called Gorgos. He watched as the flames jumped from building to building, flushing the tenants like rats from a sinking ship. Pettimen wanted the entire neighborhood burned, in case someone had decided to hide the turncoat.

Heldring turned and sauntered up the cobblestone street. "What a waste," he muttered to himself. "As if these people don't have enough problems, what with the poverty their overseer allowed to fester. Now they're burned out of what little protection they had. What few items they may have owned."

Heldring's mind turned to Cereus. Had she perished in the fire? Or had she been moved as Olaf suggested. "How will I find her?" He stopped so quickly that the man who'd been following walked directly into his back.

Heldring felt something sharp pointed into his back as an unknown voice said, "Come with me. And no funny stuff else, I'll poke your guts out." Heldring acquiesced and allowed himself to be guided several blocks to the right and then into a narrow alleyway. The hooligan knocked a special code on a non-descript doorway, which opened into an even darker hallway.

It had been a long time since anyone has tried to

manhandle me, thought Heldring. "What is this all about," he asked. "Do you want my money? Is that what this is about?"

"The Boss wants to talk to you," said the ruffian.

"Who's your boss," countered Heldring.

"You'll find out soon enough," said the thug. "Now stop with the questions and let's get moving. The Boss don't like waiting, even for someone like you."

"What's that supposed to mean?", asked Heldring. But the hoodlum would say no more. Heldring wandered through several rooms, up and down stairs, out a door, in another door. He figured the guy was trying to mess up his inner compass. The thug had figured right. Heldring had no idea where he was or how much longer this charade would continue. Just as he was about to say something, they entered a poorly-lit room. He was pushed onto a chair.

"Put your hands behind your back," said the thug. The man tied his hands and feet and then left him alone. Heldring sat for an undetermined amount of time before a small entourage entered the room. At the rear of the overly large men followed an average size man and a badger in a red velvet outfit.

"What do you think, Gabriel?", asked the unknown man.

"It's definitely Drakken Aruhl's body. Who's in it remains to be seen, Boss," he replied.

"Who are you, and why have I been brought here against my will?", asked Heldring.

"I think we should be asking the first part of your question to you," said the badger. "You even sound like Drakken Aruhl."

"What makes you think I'm not?", asked Heldring.

"Aruhl should have died when Twe-Leoht went dark," said the badger. "And yet, here you sit, unharmed and looking quite fit. This creates a paradox because you can't be both alive and dead at the same time. Therefore, it stands to reason that you have hijacked Aruhl's body for your own personal ends. This is what we're here to discover."

"I doubt Drakken Aruhl was an unmannered thug like you obviously are. So what is it of your concern?", asked Heldring.

"He was very much our concern," said the Boss who'd remained unusually quiet. "I will ask you once again. Who are you and what are you doing with Aruhl's body?"

Heldring remained quiet for some time before asking, "May I have a glass of water?"

"Tell us who you are and maybe I'll untie you. If you are who we think you are, then you can have a grand feast. A feast fit for a King."

"Why is it so important for you to know who I am?", asked Heldring. "I was not harming anyone. In fact, I was checking to make sure a friend was doing okay."

"We have been following you since you entered the city. The man you were seeking was no friend to Drakken Aruhl."

"Why have you been following me?", asked Heldring.

"We just told you. Drakken Aruhl should be dead. Wouldn't your interests be piqued if your friend, thought dead, suddenly appeared inside your city walls?", asked the Boss.

"I guess so," answered Heldring.

"Now, tell us who you are," said the badger, Gabriel.

"Untie me and I will tell you what you want to know," said Heldring. "Even though it appears to me that you already know who I am, as impossible as that may seem."

The Boss nodded to one of his henchman. The henchman untied Heldring's hands and feet but kept a tight hand on his shoulder. Not that Heldring would have any idea as to where to run. He was outmanned and would have to see this act of his life story through, even if this encounter shortened it considerably.

"I have one question before I disclose my identity," said Heldring. "I would like to know to whom I am speaking." The Boss displayed an insignia that had been sewn into the inside panel of his tattered jacket.

"It can't be," whispered Heldring.

"It is, although Pettimen has been hunting us like animals these last couple hundred years."

"How did you know it was me?", Heldring asked.

"Olaf. He has a big mouth when he drinks. Him and that fool Gorgos, your 'friend' whose house was in flames."

"We had to grab you before Pettimen did. But we had to be sure." The henchman removed his hand from Heldring's shoulder; all of the men in the room, badger too, went down on one knee, bowed their heads, and said, "Your Majesty."

"Do each of you bear the insignia?", he asked.

"Yes," said each man as they, one-by-one, slid their sleeves to reveal the insignia of the House of Heldring tattooed on their forearms. Tears came to Heldring's eyes. He stood in front of each man, and badger, and offered his hand in thanks.

"Please return to your seats and tell me how this is possible," said Heldring.

"We stayed guard in your tomb after you were laid to rest. We hid and listened when the hag would show up to do her conjuring. We heard her talking to you, taunting you, but none of us could undo her magic. So we stayed close and waited. There were always several of us in the Tower, even after Her Majesty dismissed us. You know, we have always been one face, had one purpose, to protect the House of Heldring — our fathers, and their fathers before them. We are fewer in numbers, now. Pettimen has seen to that. But, there are still enough of us to make a difference."

"I am overcome by your loyalty and dedication in my absence these last eight hundred years. I also find myself returning to great turmoil in these lands that I so love. I would gladly give my life to have each and every one of you represent my house, represent me, Your King, Nicolas Heldring."

"Your Majesty," said the men as they took to a knee once again.

10: Broken Wards

"My goodness, how in the world did you get to Chelsea Manor?", asked a still recuperating Pearl.

"I give many thanks to my new friend, Gordon. He's the reason for my occupancy and our subsequent reunion," laughed Deiter.

"If only Ben were here. He'd be so pleased to see you. We left in such a hurry," said Pearl.

"It's not like you had much of a choice," said Deiter, "what with Dipsacus ordering everyone about, your meeting with the King, and the destruction of the Amethyst Tower. It's a miracle you're even alive!"

"Oh brother-in-law, it's so good to see you. Can you sit for a while? I'd like to go to the gardens. It helps to speed my recovery," said Pearl.

"I am yours, fine lady. Lead the way."

$$++++$$

Several hours later Gordon knocked on Rho's door and slipped into her bedroom. Madeline and Rho were sound asleep, but he noticed there were hundreds of flowers all around the room. Some were growing from the walls, the floor, even the dressers and nightstands. He crawled into bed next to Rho. He was most familiar with her body and didn't want to be all clumsy and such. His need heightened as he stroked the length of her velvety body. She awoke.

"You're back," she sighed. "We were so worried."

"Everything's okay," he said. "I don't even have

any cuts or scrapes this time." She cupped her hands around his cheeks and pulled his lips to hers. He smelled freshly showered and shaved. She was grateful for that.

Madeline was much slower to awaken. It seemed to be a side effect of her multiple integrations. Once she was awake, she was lively and energetic. It was those few minutes that could turn into hours if one weren't persistent in goading her from the bed.

Madeline awoke to heavy breathing and rather petulantly said, "Hey, why didn't you guys wake me up?"

"We tried," panted Rho. "But you were having none of it." The lovers reached their crescendo and moved apart from one another.

Madeline sat up and pouted, "It's not fair." Rho reached up and pulled the sulking woman to her breast.

"We just have to wait a few minutes, that's all," she explained.

"When did Gordon get here?", asked Madeline.

"About an hour ago," Rho replied.

"An hour ago and you couldn't wake me up?"

"No dear, we tried." Rho kissed her forehead, her cheeks, and her nose before settling on her full strawberry-colored lips. She gingerly rolled Madeline over so she would be in the middle between herself and Gordon. She knew he only needed a few minutes to recharge his battery and would be thrilled to find his first true opportunity to be with Madeline. Gordon awoke to find flowers growing from underneath his pillow and his body.

"What's that all about," he whispered.

Rho laughed, "It seems to happen when Madeline is ... shall we say ... elated."

Gordon laid his head back on the pillow and looked at Madeline's white skin. He could see blends of pinks and purples as her skin blushed with exertion. He ran his fingers through her silky blonde hair, down her neck, over her shoulder, and then down her spine. Each place turned a different color. It was like she'd adsorbed all the colors of the visible spectrum, but they couldn't always be seen.

She rolled over to meet his gaze as if she was truly seeing him for the first time. There was no nervousness or fumbling in their expression of love, only the comfort of old friends whose needs matched each other's.

Flowers poured forth from the windows and climbed to the rooftop as the three lovers, enflamed in passion, played throughout the night. The next morning, residents wondered how all of the wonderful flowers had been planted on the side of the manor. Ira and Maize knew.

"We have to separate them or move them. We're going to be overrun at this rate," they laughed. The lovers were awakened by the ground trembling.

"I didn't know they had earthquakes in Innes," said Gordon.

"I've never heard of one," said Rho. Madeline had turned several shades of green.

"I'm going to be sick." They could hear her wretching into a waste can in the next room.

"Something terrible has happened," she said. "You have to help me get dressed." She seemed so weak, so completely different than she'd been just a couple minutes before.

"Gordon, please go get Maize. And hurry!" Gordon threw on his pants and ran out the room. There was another tremor that shook the lamp off of the bed stand. Madeline stumbled, her weak legs barely able to carry her to her own room. She knew she still smelled of a nighttime of lovemaking but couldn't hide that now. Something much more important was occurring. Maize, Ira, and Iris came into the room.

"They have cut down two of the ward trees in Silent Spring and they're not going to stop there," said Madeline.

"How can that be? Those trees have stood for a thousand years," said Iris.

"The border wards that protect our world must be breaking down. Someone from outside has been given the chance to cut down the trees," replied Ira.

"But who can be doing this? And why?", asked Iris.

Gordon, as if struck by lightening, knew all too well who was responsible for this outrageous trespass. He wouldn't run away and hide from him this time. That was a promise.

"I must get to the trees," said Madeline. "They are bleeding, and I'm the only one that can help them."

"I'll take her," said Gordon.

"Fine, but Gordon, please don't do anything…well you know," said Ira.

"Crazy?"

"Yeah…crazy. You still have a couple of pieces to acquire, and, in degrees of importance, they are considerably more. I need you whole. Okay?"

"We'll just go and look. No interaction, I promise. At least not this time. I'll wait until we've completed our arrangement. After that I cannot say."

"That's fair enough," said Ira. Gordon drew a doorway to Silent Spring and the point of assault. He had to carry Madeline through the doorway as she wasn't strong enough yet to pass through on her own. They stepped out of the doorway, Madeline tucked protectively in his arms. She was still green with sickness.

Her eyes glazed in fever; she implored him, "Please

kiss me." She immediately started to feel better. He gently kissed her again, and she took that energy so she could stand on her own. He kissed the back of her neck as she faced the damage the developers had inflicted.

She was trying to heal the border wards, but the trees were inconsolable. Two of the oldest males in Silent Spring had been cut down. Gordon held onto Madeline, his energy merging with hers to help fuel the repairs. She was nearly finished when the crash of a third tree could be heard not far from where they stood. She cried out as she doubled over in pain.

"Make them stop, Gordon." He looked helplessly at Madeline and back to the trees. He'd made a promise to Ira. He couldn't jeopardize their entire future for a few trees, as important as they might be, and yet he didn't like what this was doing to Madeline.

"I promised I wouldn't interfere. Not now, anyway. But I can try to help you." He lay down on the soft moss and took Madeline in his arms. He kissed her forehead, eyes, cheeks and neck. He loosened her blouse and put his hand over her ample bosom. She responded by following his actions, allowing him to lead their lovemaking. She responded to his love, and the competing stabs of pain by producing swaths of new roots that burrowed deep into the ground and from the new roots sprang forth new shoots.

Louisa, the clan leader of the Painted Lady Clan, appeared in the surrounding vegetation. She and her clan members sprinkled fairy dust on the ground and over the new shoots to help them grow more quickly. As Gordon and Madeline climaxed together, hundreds of new plants were added to the ecosystem. She wove the fibers of a new tapestry and integrated it into the damaged wards; the fairies added fairy dust to augment the healing wounds.

No one could put the old male trees back together –

they were dead, and that was that. The forest would grieve the loss of their regal denizens. Madeline hoped the bonds would heal before the developers could do more damage. The fairies coaxed Gordon and Madeline away from the damaged forest. They had a secret, which they knew would help Madeline herself to heal. The group blinked out of Silent Spring and reappeared in the middle of a snow storm, for which neither of them was dressed.

"What were you thinking?", asked Gordon of Louisa the Ladies Clan leader.

"You'll see," she replied. "Hurry now, we're almost there," Louisa encouraged as she led the way.

They found themselves standing at the opening of a cave. Gordon could see the back of a man with long hair tending to the fire. He could see bits of something sleeping on the other side of the fire, but he couldn't really tell what he was seeing. Madeline walked into the cavern and stood next to the man as she warmed herself at the fire. He stood and turned to see the new arrival.

"No way," they both said almost simultaneously. He picked up Madeline, twirled her around, and then hugged her for a long time.

"I can't believe it. What are you doing here?" Madeline turned towards Gordon and said, "Do you remember my brother, Michael?"

"We've met a few times," said Gordon as he shook Michael's hand. He looked to see others coming from the back of the cave to see the newcomers. Madeline saw her father and ran to him. He picked her up and twirled her around the way Michael had.

Louisa sat on Gordon's shoulder, "See, she's much better already. But there's also a surprise for you." Gordon shook Bernie's hand and was introduced to Beastly and Crooksey, with whom he was completely taken aback, but didn't show it outwardly. Gordon and Nate saw each other at the same time.

"No way," was all they could say as the two old friends embraced, laughed, and wrestled each other.

When they'd finished roughhousing, Ben said, "Hi Gordon."

"Granddad," said Gordon as he hugged him with all his might.

"Easy, Gordon," he laughed. "I'm an old man."

"I can't believe this," said Gordon. "Ira told me that you were at the Manor. I was really upset that I missed you." Gordon looked around the cave and saw Madeline on the other side of the fire talking to....

"Gordon, I'd like to introduce you to our last resident. Ailith, meet Gordon; Gordon meet Ailith. Ailith is the reason why we're living in Crooksey and Beastly's cave." Gordon still didn't understand.

"She's still a baby and would freeze to death in this cold," said Michael.

"Gordon, Ailith is Michael's dragon," said Madeline. "She's his dragon; he's her wizard. They're connected, like you and me."

"Oh," he blushed.

"Well, not completely like you and me," she corrected herself.

"Oh," he said again.

Nate walked behind Gordon, "You're not that scrawny kid that went camping so long ago."

Gordon laughed and said, "It looks like you've grown out of tall and gawky yourself. Well, maybe not tall, you must be six foot five inches."

Nate laughed. "Come on in the back. Let's get caught up." Gordon turned to look at Madeline who was sitting next to Ailith on one side, and her brother and father on the other. Ben, Crooksey, and Beastly had excused themselves to take a little walk outdoors.

Nate saw the look Gordon gave to Madeline.

"She was always a pretty one," Nate ribbed his old friend.

Gordon punched Nate on the arm, "Yeah, she is." He turned and looked at her again.

"Come on, you can live without her – for a few minutes anyway." Nate laughed.

Gordon took the offered chalice of wine. He could feel it warm the chill he'd felt deep in his bones. The two friends began to recount their stories since entering Innes so many months ago. The other folks sat down at the table and joined in the conversation.

Ben asked Gordon, "How's Pearl?"

"She's up and around a little more each day. I stopped in to visit her yesterday," he replied.

"She told me to come back with Bernie and the boys when we complete our mission," said Ben. "She told me, 'Ben Sutton, you're making me a nervous wreck hovering over me. Go back to Michael's cave and leave me to heal.'"

They all laughed but were glad that she was no longer at death's door.

"Has there been any news of Emily?", asked Michael. Bernie removed the obsidian star from his pocket.

"Not since we got this from Willard," he said as he turned the star over and over in his hands. "We can only assume she's been taken to Deorc. Beyond that, we've heard nothing."

"Or Will," added Gordon.

"Ted McShane and I saw Will when we were in Dosk, but no word since," said Nate.

"He was with that assassin named Draedon."

Crooksey hissed at the mention of the name, "You might as well forget about your friend if he has thrown himself in with that lot. That one's bad news amidst bad news."

"That's what Ted said when we saw him," replied Nate.

"Your friend Ted is pretty smart," said Crooksey. Nate nodded his head in agreement, although he still wasn't going to give up on Will. They were blood brothers, after all. After an extended silence, Beastly placed the topic of the impending war on the table.

"We've been lucky so far," he said. "The weather has held them at bay in the Wastelands, but that won't last forever."

"Ted, Jacob, and Caleb have gone on ahead to Leoht," said Nate.

"Jacob?", asked the long-quiet Ben.

"Yeah, Jacob Daggerstein is on his way to Leoht," answered Nate.

Ben shook his head, "These are strange days." Nate recounted the story of finding Jacob passed out on the trail and how Gordon had tripped over him and how they'd carried him into Antero's Run to beat the storm.

"He was summoned away by some strange looking ghost-like creature. That's how they took Will as well," added Nate.

"A wraith?!", spat Crooksey.

"One of the Dream Stealers, Pearl had said at the campsite," replied Ben.

"It was really creepy," said Nate. It occurred to Ben at that moment that maybe they'd confused their target and got the wrong person. He thought about the lie told to Belac and Mortifera that their only natural child had died during childbirth. It had been a difficult labor, as Nate was none too quick to enter the world at his birth. He'd been taken away and swapped with another child who'd been stillborn, delivered by one of the maids in the castle, if he remembered correctly. The maid and her husband smuggled Nate out of Deorc, over the

Dragon Spire Mountains, and into the Amethyst Tower.

It was the only time Arisaema would see his grandson before the grand show of Ben and Pearl's expulsion from Dagung. Ben and Pearl had quietly bought up all of the land bordering the eastern boundaries of Innes. They knew the Parkers already owned all of the lands bordering the western boundaries. The southern and northern boundaries were protected by magical wards. When Gordon started to talk about the trees being cut down in Silent Springs, he realized the wards were diminishing and the attack was coming from multiple fronts. It was especially bad news to learn that Lorelei, Pearl's twin sister, had been murdered. Without the power of the twins, he didn't know how long Innes could possibly remain in the light.

After hours of conversation, Gordon excused himself. "I need to stretch my legs," he said, as he walked into the front cave where Ailith appeared to be asleep. He stepped outside of the cave. It was snowing lightly again. The cold air felt good as it snapped him out of the sluggishness he was feeling from the heat and smoke of the inner caverns. A strange scent mixed with the clean air. It reminded him of something, like funky smelling socks or a wet dog.

"Don't go too far from the cave opening," said a voice in his head. "He's been looking for you."

"What? Who said that?"

"I did," said Ailith. Michael stepped out next to Gordon. "She can speak with you directly in your brain – telepathically."

Gordon looked at Michael. "That's a bit spooky. Can you do the same with her?"

"Yeah, it took some getting used to, having someone always hearing your thoughts. It can get a little crowded, but you learn to have respect for each other's space."

"You're telling me," said Nate. "When Heldring was in my head, I thought I'd go mad. He was always telling me what to do and what not to do. Like a mother hen." The three friends laughed.

"Ailith told me not to go outside because someone was following me."

"I'd listen to her, then. She's usually spot on."

"It's strange, though, I smelled that smell a couple of days ago when I was using the travel wand."

"Did you use it today?" asked Michael.

"Yes, when we went to Silent Springs."

"Did you notice the smell then?"

"Now that you mention it, yeah I did. But it slipped my mind when the fairies showed up and with all of the excitement," he shrugged his shoulders in an attempt to dismiss the fearful fact that someone or something was intruding in his personal space.

"Be careful," said Michael. "Sometimes magical items carry a signature; it could be of the maker or the previous user. If it does, it will allow the proper owner of the wand to trace its location through the use of a beacon of sorts. The beacon could be a light, or horn, or an animal with, let's say, a wet-dog smell. In all likelihood, the magi won't be pleased that you're using his property without his permission. Just be aware," said Michael.

"Thanks, I didn't know," said Gordon.

"When do you think you'll be able to leave here?", Gordon asked Michael.

"Not until the spring," he said. "She'll be full grown in a couple more months, and then we can go."

"Nate, what're you going to do?", asked Gordon.

"I'll leave when Michael leaves," he replied. "There's little I can do right now, so I'm going to hang out for a bit. I've been working strategies with the fairy clans and need to finish that business before I leave."

"How about you Gordo? What's your plan?"

"I have one or two more missions to complete for Ira, and then I'm not sure. I suppose it depends on the war. I am a knight in Daedalus' personal army," he lightly bragged. "I know I have to leave early tomorrow morning because I was supposed to leave again tomorrow. Ira will be worried, as it is," he looked at Michael, "but I want to give Madeline some more time with you and your dad."

"She sure has changed," said Michael. "My dad was explaining some of her transformation, but you really can't understand it until you see her. I've been watching the way she looks at you, Gordon. You don't have to tell me, but do you two have something going?"

Gordon paused a few moments before answering, "Yes."

"Be gentle with her, Gordon. She's very delicate. She feels things very deeply. She's really the opposite of Emily, who'd always been more headstrong and self-centered." Gordon nodded in understanding.

"You're a good guy, Gordon; I'm glad it's you."

"Thanks, man. I didn't know how you'd feel about us," Gordon said as they shook hands.

"Let's go back inside. I need to check on Ailith. The Painted Ladies are talking her head off, and she's getting a little cranky."

"Where can we sleep?", asked Gordon. "I'm done in. We need to be up early because we have to back by first light." Nate showed Gordon a smaller room on the left off the dining room.

"We're all sleeping in the three rooms to the right."

"This place must be huge," Gordon said.

"Crooksey and Beastly used it for a long term hideout. I guess when they were in really hot water, so to speak. It's got all of the comforts of home – well except for TV and a microwave. But you learn to live without that stuff and don't really miss it after awhile."

"How did you meet those two?"

"They're friends of granddad," said Nate. "They've been friends like forever and are really protective of Michael's dad, too."

"Why are you staying here with Michael instead of leaving with the others?", asked Gordon.

"It's really more about the fairies than Michael. I told you I was to be put to death for killing Serpentia, but instead they made me a mediator of sorts. It was supposed to be between Innesians and fairies, but it's mostly been among arguing fairies. I've been trying to organize them into factions for spying, fighting, and healing and such. The problem is they just don't like working together: 'Why do I have to do this?' 'Why does she get to do that?'," he mimicked. "They're like a bunch of disagreeable little kids."

"Maybe I can suggest some strategies. I've been studying with Daedalus's knights since we got into Innes. Maybe it will help." The two friends talked about strategies and fighting and how they'd managed to get by so far. It wasn't until Madeline walked into the room yawning and stretching that Nate left the room for the night.

"Don't leave without waking me, okay?"

"Okay," replied Gordon. Madeline snuggled into the crook of Gordon's arm and fell fast asleep. Her even breathing helped Gordon fall off quickly.

Bernie lay awake in his bed. He'd seen the way that Madeline and Gordon looked at each other, and the way she sought him out with her eyes when he left the room. There was no doubt in his mind that they'd become lovers. Michael confirmed it before falling off to sleep. He knew something of the troubles in Gordon's family, knew they were both too young to be so serious, and knew the same had happened between himself and Ashley when she was seventeen and he eighteen.

They'd had a good and happy life together until all of this craziness began. Madeline had grown so quickly. She wasn't his little bear anymore, but a young woman. He could feel the sadness within her, far more than her years should have accumulated.

He worried because they were to be separated again tomorrow, and he wasn't certain of his return. She was returning to the Manor where she'd be safe and he on another perilous mission. He had to know Emily's status; they were going to talk to an individual who supposedly could point them in the right direction. He'd found two of his kids; he'd find the other if it took him down the path to hell. As he fell asleep, he realized it probably would.

++++

"I will not marry that man, I don't care what they do to me," she sobbed. Bhodi put his arm around her shoulder.

"The wedding isn't taking place until the spring, which means we have several months. We'll have to think of something in the mean time." She nodded her head; bloodstained tears marred her perfect white skin.

"Have you told Will yet?", he asked.

"No. I haven't really seen him since the other night. I think they're intentionally keeping us apart."

"You're probably right."

"I'm afraid that if I tell him, he'll go and do something stupid. He does have a bit of a temper, you know, and he can't afford to lose control here. Not now."

"There must be an answer. We'll just have to keep searching for a clue."

"Bhodi...?"

"Yes, Emily."
"Thank you."
"For what?"
"For being here for me."
"You're welcome."

$+ + + +$

Will paced his rooms for the thirty-third time. He felt caged and bored and certainly disillusioned. He didn't sign on to be a canary in a gilded cage. He'd tried to leave, but the doors were firmly bolted from the outside. Had Draedon abandoned him to these people? Will had been entranced by Emily. She'd been beautiful before her transformation, but now she was spellbinding. He couldn't take his eyes off her at dinner the other night, and their first kiss, left him reeling. He saw the proverbial fireworks and shooting stars and any other celestial body that might describe the overwhelming flush that took hold of his body.

The thoughts of Emily just down the hall increased his anxiety and desire so much so that he considered finding a length of rope and scaling the slick obsidian walls of the tower. Death was better than this eternal confinement. He heard the bolts slide open on the outside of the door. He had tried to leave the first time the butler opened them; he'd found out quickly that as lanky as the butler was, he was no one to mess around with. He'd knocked Will onto the floor with the sweep of one arm. He didn't remember if he'd even touched him, it happened so fast. This time he stood well away from the doorway and allowed the butler to enter the room completely. Several staff members followed behind him with clean bedding, a wash tub, scents, pails of hot water, and thick bath towels. Several newly tailored suits were hung in his wardrobe. Several pairs of highly polished shoes, silk cravats, and starched button-front shirts were hung next to the suits.

"When you're in your rooms, you may dress as you please, but when called, you'll dress for dinner. When you're finally allowed to leave the tower, you'll be told the appropriate attire to wear. Tomorrow, you'll begin your studies in the ways of wraith, including business and warfare. The master wants to know your talents and skills. Do not disappoint him."

"I won't," said Will. Servants piled books and notepads, pen and ink, and pencils on the desks in the neighboring room that the butler opened and allowed Will to enter for the first time.

"This is your workspace. If you need anything to complete your assignments, write it down on this pad," which he produced from his pocket. "The items will be in your rooms within twenty-four hours. Please plan appropriately because last-minute requests will be deemed mismanagement of your time and you'll lose credits on your next assignments. Do you clearly understand everything I've told you?"

"Yes, I think so," replied Will. "May I ask one question?"

"Yes," replied the butler

"When can I leave my rooms? When can I visit my friend Emily?"

"One question," the butler said. "You will leave your rooms when you've earned the privilege or if the master or mistress requires it. I suggest you study hard. Your life depends on it." With that, he left the room, and Will was alone once again. He looked through the pile of books. He pulled a small soft cover book from the pile, The Word of Wraith. He sat in an overstuffed chair in the corner of this new room, turned up the gas lantern, and opened the book.

...and so it shall be told from this day forward, all

Innesians of the Obsidian Tower will follow The Book of Wraith. Darkness has banished the rays of light from the realm of Deorc as it will do throughout the entirety of Innes. It is the way of the wraith to embrace the darkness and to conquer the light that attempts to occlude the path to darkness.

The aspirants must attend to their daily ritual of cleansing themselves of the light and embracing wholeheartedly the way of wraith. It is the union within the darkness that allows the aspirant to embrace in its entirety the way of darkness and its subsequent goal of dreamlessness. Not all aspirants have the ability to follow the way of wraith and many must be denied and succumb to the needs of those who are able climb to the heights of its truth. The needs of the few outweigh the needs of the many.

The wraith aspirant must embrace the darkness that resides in all hearts and harness it to do the work of wraith, that being the conquest of light and collection of the dreams and lives of those unworthy to attain the honor of wraith. The power of their blood will support our bodies; the power of their dreams will support our souls.

The wraith are a dreamless race, which have been sculpted into perfection and delivered from defect. We have learned how to harvest humankind's innovations, hopes, dreams, and aspirations for our own needs, pleasures, and fulfillment. It is the word of wraith that all of the faithful will know and say when our divine ruler, and Lord of Wraith himself, requires it.

And so it went for another fifteen pages. Will dog-eared his last page and placed the book back on the pile. He looked at the other titles: How to Survive the Manufacture of Wraith, The Superior Race and Their Divine Rights, and so it went for about twenty titles. He did see a business title and an Innesian Law book.

He wondered how their laws were different than human laws. He picked up the law book and started to read the first couple of paragraphs. He remembered the butler's words with a shiver, "Study hard, your life depends on it." He could hear the bolt being removed in the other room. A lovely maid entered the room with a silver dining tray. He watched as she placed it on the table beside the empty bookshelves. She carefully eyed him as she turned to walk away.

He looked at her, "Hey, you look familiar to me. Come here. What's your name?"

"I'm sorry, sir," she muttered as she hurriedly closed and bolted the door. Will sat down to his lunch.

"Who was that? She looked so familiar," he said again. He noticed a new drink on his tray, very pale red with a slight iron taste.

"Cherry flavor, nice," he said and cut into his pot roast. He was flushed by the end of the meal and decided to lie down for a few minutes. He thought about the maid who had served his lunch. The name Aggie Bisbie popped into his head.

"It couldn't be," he thought as he drifted into dreamless sleep.

Several days later, she returned with his lunch tray. This time he stood in front of the door preventing her escape.

"Take off your hat," he commanded. She did as she was told. "Let me see your face." She refused. He walked towards her and took her chin in his hand. "Let me see your face," he said again. She acquiesced. "It is you," he said breathlessly. "Aggie Bisbie!" She winced as he said her name.

"That's who I used to be," she replied. "Now I'm just maid two-nineteen."

"I knew it," he said as his mind reeled from the truth of his discovery.

"I can't stay any longer," she said. "If they find out we know each other, I'm history. Please, I'll try to come another time, but right now I have to go." Will let her go out the door.

"Please come back," he whispered.

Aggie Bisbie, or Agatha Jane Bisbie by birth, had gone to school with Will, Gordon, and Nate until the end of eighth grade. They'd been friends through an after-school theatre group until Aggie's disappearance in May of their eighth grade year. There had been the usual gossip: she was pregnant and sent to a girl's home, or she was kidnapped and murdered. No one could find Aggie, and, after years of searching, he supposed people just stopped looking. He'd known her parents. They were devastated, Aggie being an only child.

Will wondered what his parents must be feeling now. He was an only child, too. Were they still looking for him? Did they hang signs on telephone poles? Have you seen this person? It was shortly after Aggie's disappearance that Will's own family had moved from Pine Woods to Whispering Bluff. It had just occurred to Will that maybe his own family moved as a result of Aggie's disappearance.

"I guess it didn't matter after all," he figured. He decided to keep this secret to himself, even if he did get to see Emily again. He began to explore the possibilities of others being in Innes. He hadn't seen or heard anything about Nate, Gordon, or Jacob. He wondered how many others would turn up in Innes against their will or otherwise. He knew that Emily hadn't seen her family since being brought to Innes. He started to think of home and his friends. Maybe he'd made the wrong choice when he agreed to come with Draedon. What choice did he really have? Draedon had gotten him out of that dungeon. "From one jail cell to another," he smirked. His tutor was preparing for their afternoon lesson: Wraith and the Art of War.

"Let's begin," the tutor said. Will didn't really care about war. His thoughts again drifted to Emily and his friends as the tutor droned on.

11: The Gold Compact

"Where have you been? We've been worried," said Ira.

"I'm sorry. Fate took us in a different direction, but we're here now."

"So you're not going to tell me where you disappeared to?"

"I will Ira, but Madeline and I were both safe, and I think we should get on with the mission. I know how important this is," said Gordon.

"Okay, you're right." Ira hesitated a moment. "Look Gordon, I'm not your father. You don't owe me any explanations. But I want you to know that Maize and I look at you as our own son, and we were worried."

Gordon looked at Ira and then gave him a bear hug, "Thanks Ira. You don't know what that means to me. Come on, let's get on with this so I can come back and tell you of Madeline's and my adventure. It's a great story, but I could really use a rest and a shower before I leave."

++++

"Why did you stay away all night?", she cried. "We were worried sick. I couldn't sleep at all last night."

"I'm sorry, Rho, I truly am," Madeline said as she held Rho in her arms. She kissed away her sugary-tasting tears.

"We should have returned to the Manor, but it's been so long since I've seen my brother and my father too. You have no idea how surprised we were to find

158

them in the middle of the forest. If it weren't for the Painted Lady Clan, we would have never known they were there. I'm not sure why my father never told me about Michael and his dragon, Ailith, when he was here."

"Michael has a dragon?", asked Rho in awe.

"Yes, and she's beautiful. Her skin is like a metallic yellow-green that changes in the light. Sometimes she looks green, sometimes she looks yellow. She's so smart; she's just a baby, but getting huge. She can't travel until the spring because otherwise, she'd freeze to death. That's why Michael's still living in a cave."

"Oh Madeline, your brother is so lucky to have his own dragon," Rho sighed. "I would love to have my own dragon. I would call her Wynn."

"Why Wynn? What does Wynn mean?"

"Friend. What does Ailith mean?"

"Seasoned warrior, although she seems much too nice to be a warrior," said Madeline.

"Warriors don't necessarily have to do battle on a battle field you know," said Rho.

"That's true," said Madeline. "I hadn't thought about it like that. Well, maybe one day you'll get your Wynn. If there is one baby dragon, then it would only seem logical that there must be more, somewhere in Innes."

"I'm going to make it my task to find another dragon in Innes. All the better if I can raise it from a baby like your brother."

"You'd be a good dragon mom. They do eat a lot you know. She can eat a sheep or a deer every other day."

"Well, there's lots of sheep and cows and deer – plenty for the dragons to eat."

"I don't think the farmers would like them much,"

said Madeline.

"They could put out a daily penance, like they do for the church, except it would be their oldest chicken, goat, or cow that the farmer would put out for Wynn's supper." Madeline giggled and kissed her on the cheek.

"What's so funny? She'd be the grandest dragon in the land, except for Ailith, of course."

"I'm sure she would, especially with you as her mom," laughed Madeline as she put her arms around Rho.

"We'll start researching dragons tomorrow. I'm sure Maize won't mind if we use the library," said Madeline.

"That's a great idea," said Rho as she snuggled tighter to Madeline. They fell asleep in each others arms. The warm late afternoon sunlight streaming into the largely windowed room belied the snow-laden, cold outdoors.

The following morning Madeline woke before Rho. She decided to let her sleep for a while longer. As she walked to the window to see if it had stopped snowing, she noticed a small gold makeup compact on Rho's dresser. There was a small red light that was flashing, so she innocently picked it up and opened it.

"What is your report," asked a translucent-skinned woman. She was not looking into the mirror and obviously didn't realize that it was not Rho who had answered this strange device. Madeline stammered to find an answer.

"Come on, girl; speak up when I ask you a question." The woman's handmaiden was applying her eye makeup as she spoke into the device. Madeline tried to copy Rho's voice.

"There's nothing to report today," she said.

"What's wrong with your voice?", she asked.

"I have a cold," replied Madeline who tried to think

quickly. Thoughts swirled through her head. Who was this woman? And what connection was she to Rho?

"So be it. We'll speak again at the end of the week," the woman said and was gone. Madeline closed the device, slipped it back onto the table, and walked to the window. She turned and looked at the still sleeping Rho and then back out the window. Hopefully, it was her mother, but Madeline was sure she'd said that she was orphaned. She had a bad feeling in the pit of her stomach — a feeling she didn't want to believe.

++++

"Hey Crooksey, do you think we can get one of the fairy clans to blink us to the Lacewing Clan's fairy ring. We could sneak into the southern border of Skullduggery and cross over the Botes River. I think we should hear some kind of news about Bernie's daughter in Brigand's Notch."

"Sounds like a good plan to me. There's plenty of scum who'd be willing to take a kidnapping contract in that town," replied Crooksey.

"Sure enough," agreed Beastly.

"I'll go see if the Morpho King is available; maybe one of his clan can take us," he said as he left the cave entrance. Bernie walked into the main room, his pack in hand.

"I'd try to lighten your load a bit, Bernie. We'll be travelling fast and light," said Beastly.

"I thought I'd bring some travel clothing for Emily... in case we find her," he added.

"If we find her, we'll grab items in Skullduggery," said Beastly.

Crooksey returned to the cave. "We're a go in a half hour."

"Is Ben going with us?", asked Bernie.

"I'm not sure if he's decided. He's talking to Nate right now." Crooksey stuck his head in the doorway.

"We're a go in a half an hour," he said.

"Thanks," said Ben.

12: We Always Have a Choice

"You have no business here, witch! We don't want your kind in Kuhnston Derry."

Emily turned from the willow tree and looked straight at Ing. "Don't you recognize me?", she asked.

"I know who you are and what you've become; we don't hang with your type."

"The last time I was here, we parted as friends. What has happened between us to change that?", she asked.

"You are wraith! That is enough!"

"I look wraith," she countered. "That doesn't mean that I am wraith."

"Words of deceit," Ing retorted. "What are you doing here anyway?"

"I was allowed to leave Deorc for the first time since my incarceration," she replied.

"I wanted to get a message to my family and I know of no other way. I am being watched and am risking much even talking to you right now."

"What makes you think I'll carry your message?", he retorted. He did little to hide the contempt he felt. Anyone watching would interpret the encounter as unfriendly at best.

"I thought maybe," she said, her voice trailing off.

"Be quick about it," he said.

"Please tell them I am alive and well. That you have seen me with your own eyes and can verify that I am alive. Please don't tell them what I have become. They will never understand. Also, tell them that I love

163

them. No wait – tell them I will always love them, but they must let me go and not come looking for me."

He shouted at her some more, waving his arms in the air as he shouted. "I will do this one favor," he said. "Don't come back here again."

"Thank you," she replied, as one blood red tear streamed down her right cheek. "Thank you, Ing. I am sorry. I had no other choice."

"We always have a choice girlie," he replied, and was gone with a flash. She stood and looked at the willow for some moments longer before turning towards the town. She knew this encounter would be reported. It was a chance she had to take.

13: The Wolf Mage

Gordon loped through the knee-high snow; his long sturdy legs had little problems with the accumulating powder that began the night before. The dull gray sky met the horizon and told Gordon it was unlikely the snow would be ending any time soon. At least he had several points of refuge, if he needed them. He could even stay in the caravan if it came to that, although he wasn't sure if the heater still worked. But it was an option.

He stopped and drew a doorway with the translocator pen Ira had given to him. He stepped through the doorway and emerged at the Red Admiral fairy ring. The strong smell of wet dog hit him as he removed the key from his pocket. He surveyed the forest outside of the fairy ring, and, while his eyes registered nothing, his sense of smell was overwhelmed by the odor. He noticed that each time he used the translocator the smell was more pungent and closer, somehow, as if he were standing right next to it. His eyes saw nothing, however.

He plunged the key into the key hole, turned the knob, and stepped inside. He shut the door quickly, as if to block a cold wind that had caught the back of his neck and sent a chill racing down his spine. He removed his winter coat and sat down on the edge of the bed. He wondered if Michael's warnings held any truth as related to his situation. He stuck the translocator into his back pocket and then looked through the bag of items he'd carried on his back. He stashed all of the food except for the meal he was about to eat in the caravan.

He split the roll of bills into two parts and stuffed one of them deeply into his pockets. He pulled two additional items from the bottom of the bag. He'd never seen these items before and wasn't really sure what to do with them. Ira assured him he'd know what to do with them when it was time. He stuffed one object in each pocket and memorized his travel routes as he ate lunch.

He lay down on the soft bed for a short nap. He was very close to sleep when the door knob started to turn and the door rattled as if someone was trying to open it. The heckler became more persistent when he realized the door was tightly locked and wouldn't allow passage into the caravan. Gordon stayed perfectly still as he listened to the wind gusting through the trees and carrying what he thought sounded like wolves' howls coming from deep within the trees. He could hear a lone alpha wolf voice closer and louder, harsher and more demanding than the lesser voices.

Gordon listened carefully to each voice as if he could distinguish who was speaking and what was being said between individuals. He couldn't understand their howls, of course, but he was surely interested in how it was being said. He supposed he could surmise what they wanted this time, anyway. They were after him, of course, for what, he had no idea, other than the warning from Ailith. But a pack of wolves? The melee subsided after about a half an hour; they must have figured him long gone by now. He was thankful the caravan's little windows were curtained. He felt certain of his privacy and closed his eyes.

He lay perfectly still listening for movement after his nap of several hours. It was well into the evening, a good time for him to make his next jump. His next stop was the Well Road in Dagung. Ira had explained this road was the best into the Amethyst Tower. He removed the translocator from his back pocket. A strange pulse ran up his arm as he held the object in his hand. He listened carefully for any sounds and felt certain he was alone. He stepped outside of the caravan, walked three steps, and removed the translocator from his back pocket. The translocator felt alive in his hand as he drew a doorway in the air.

He stepped inside and was surprised by a loud clap of thunder and the stark white bolts of lightening against the completely black background of the nether world. He squinted to minimize the veracity of the light. He thought he saw the outline of a man-wolf coming towards him with each flash of lightening. By the third flash, the man-wolf was upon him. Gordon raised his hands instinctively to ward off the blow his body anticipated. He could feel the tear of his flesh on his arms and the long nails as they raked the flesh on his back. The storm raged as Gordon fought off his attacker. His attacker screamed, as Gordon landed a punch square to his jaw. He could feel the warmth of a liquid pour over his hands as he fought off the next offensive. The two men raged on, with Gordon in a fight for his life.

Gordon sensed the man-wolf was tiring, and, in the moment when his attention flagged, Gordon threw his knee into the man's stomach and slammed him to the ground as he doubled over in pain. Gordon stepped over his attacker, not stopping to see if he was dead, and ran to his destination. He threw the outer door closed none too soon. He could feel his attacker throwing himself against the heavy, wooden door trying to dislodge it from its hinges. Gordon sat down on the sidewalk, covered in sweat and blood, his clothes torn to shreds. The banging quieted; Gordon decided it was safe enough to move on. He needed some new clothes and a shower.

He reached deep into his pocket; fortunately the money was still intact. He grabbed a clean shirt from a clothes line and threw his tattered shirt into a trash bin on the street. He needed a room and some medicine to take care of these wounds. He wandered through the back alleys until he came upon a likely inn, The Boiling Cauldron. He paid for two nights, asked for hot water, a meal, and bandages to be sent to his room immediately.

"Where's the closest tailor?", he asked the innkeeper.

"Two blocks over," she replied.

"I'll give you an extra twenty if you'll have him, and a barber, come by my room in two hours."

She hollered for the stable boy, "Run, tell the barber and the tailor to be here in two hours."

"And no questions," he added as he handed her an extra twenty.

"My lips are sealed," she replied. "Would you like a pint with your supper," she added.

"Thanks, that'd be great."

"Your room is up one flight, end of the hall, room nine. It's a little more private, if you know what I mean." He didn't really. He never really understood "private meanings" or entendres, but found it much easier if he acted as if he did.

"Have the hot water and bandages brought up immediately. I want to clean up first." She nodded her head and set about making it so. He climbed the stairs, fatigue deep in his bones. His mind raced as he tried to figure out who his attacker was and why. Who attacked him? ... and why? Who were the other wolves? Were they trapped apprentices or hapless users like himself? Were they really wolves or something else as Nate suggested? ... Werewolves? Suddenly Michael's words came back to him. Could it be that the translocator's maker was a wizard and that he's somehow trapped inside the wand? But why attack Gordon? Why not try to ask Gordon's help to leave the translocating wand?

His mind was awhirl when the inn's help brought his bath water and bandages. He carefully removed his shirt as the blood had clotted to the material; besides, he didn't want to rip open the newly formed scabs. He sunk deep into the tub, allowing the warm water to remove the kinks from his tired muscles. He soaked for almost an hour, scrubbed every inch of his skin, and washed the junk out of his hair.

He looked at the tray the innkeeper had sent up. He noticed a needle and thread. Smart woman, he thought. He set about cleaning and closing his wounds. The ones on his back were a problem; he'd have to get the tailor to help him with those. Ninety minutes later the men removed the bath and bandage tray and replaced them with his supper and a pint. She had made a marvelous chicken stew with a dough crust, several slices of heavily slathered homemade bread and butter, and peach cobbler. He paid the tailor to sew the claw marks in his back and to make two new sets of clothes. The barber cut his hair and shaved his rough beard. He dismissed them all and lay down upon the soft bed. He was asleep in minutes. His dreams were fraught with signs of danger and death. This trip wouldn't be as easy as he'd originally thought. He wasn't even sure exactly where he was. Thank goodness for Ira's planning. He should have enough money to last for some time. He didn't dare to go back through the translocator door, even though it would take him back to the caravan he knew so well. Tomorrow was another day, he thought as he drifted deeper into sleep.

Gordon was stiff all over his body when he awoke. He groaned as he tried to sit up. The new stitches pulled his skin together to keep the wounds closed.

"Yes?", he said in response to the knock at the door. The innkeeper stood in the open doorway.

"I'm finishing the breakfast service and was wondering if you cared for something before I close the kitchen?" Gordon smiled and thanked her. She'd anticipated his hunger. He looked at her from head to toe and found himself with that familiar tingling sensation. He wondered what else she'd anticipated. He winced as he stood up from the bed and slowly came towards the innkeeper. She visibly shuddered at the sight of his well-toned, angular body. She came more fully into the room and closed the door behind her.

"What is your name?", he asked.

"Lily."

"Hi Lily, my name is Gordon." His large hands closed around her small waist. He pulled her close; her breath warmed his chilled skin.

"I'd like to order three eggs, pancakes, bacon and coffee," he said as he nuzzled her soft neck.

"I'm afraid your order is going to take a few minutes," she replied. "There seems to be a new demand for the innkeeper's attentions." He laughed as he picked her up and carefully laid her on the soft mattress. He winced again as he climbed into the bed beside her.

"Your wounds are so deep," she said as she ran her fingers around the inflamed areas. "Like you were in a battle with a bear or wolf."

"I'm not really sure what the animal was," he said. "It was very dark and all I could feel were its claws on my back and its teeth on my neck." He held her closer as she shuddered; she kissed away his pain.

An hour later as the lovers voraciously ate their breakfast together he asked her, "Lily, could you tell me where I am?"

"My inn is called The Boiling Cauldron, and you're in the Jahandhi Wastelands on the border of Dosk and Deorc."

"Really?", he said.

"Yes," she confirmed. He was definitely off course and this miscalculation would put him considerably behind on completing his mission.

Lily excused herself. "I have to attend to my other customers," she said.

"Do you give them all the same level of service?", he teased. She blushed as she shrugged him off. He overheard her talking to a man who had just entered the inn.

"I didn't expect you back so soon."

"Did you get my money from Pettiman?"

"Yes, I have it in the back." Gordon sat on the staircase, taking note of the tall, thin man dressed in black. He noticed the man's handsome appearance. Handsomely dangerous, he thought. He could tell by the man's mannerisms that he and Lily had been lovers. He hoped it wouldn't be problematic for her that they had lain together just this morning. He returned to his room, quietly dressed, and packed the few items he'd successfully held onto. It was no longer safe for him to stay here. He left some bills on the dresser and quietly left the inn.

He was about fifteen blocks away when he heard the fire bells pealing. He turned and saw smoke coming from the general area he'd just left. He sat down on a bench outside a sweetshop. Gordon hoped she didn't suffer a painful death. He felt sorry for her. She didn't deserve to die for the kindness she'd shown to him. There was nothing more for him to do. He stopped by the tailor, changed into one of his new outfits and then walked in the opposite direction of the burning inn.

His thoughts turned to the completion of his mission. He was considerably off course, his destination being a small farm in Pickering Cross. He wasn't sure how he was going to achieve his goal without using the translocator, at least not by Ira's deadline. He decided to spend a few more nights in the city. He was going to be late regardless of his choice, and, if he had to face the beast again, he wanted his strength returned and his wounds mostly healed. He altered his path and turned towards the center of town.

A horse drawn cart carrying straw offered a comfortable ride and some rest. He watched as the cart passed the now darkened shop windows, which signalled the end of the work day.

"Do you know of a decent place to stay in town?", asked Gordon.

"I'm going to stay at The Wicked Palace," he replied.

"Can a guy get a hot bath and a decent meal at this place?", asked Gordon.

"Damned if I know," replied the farmer. "I go for the company. Friends tell me of a place a couple of blocks down if you're looking for some peace and quiet."

"That would be for me," replied Gordon. "At least for tonight," he added.

The farmer laughed. "Ask for Lucy, she'll take good care of a young fellow like you. Tell her Frank sent you."

"Thanks, Frank," replied Gordon. He walked across the street in the direction the farmer had pointed him in. He really did need some rest and a good meal.

He walked through the front door just as supper was

being served.

"Great news, I'm famished," he said to the waitress as he took a seat in the dining area. He looked around at the clientele: merchants, shepherds, and a few soldiers. He decided it would be a good place for him to hole up for several days. He attacked his plate of food when the waitress placed it in front of him.

+ + + +

Draedon walked away from the burning inn. It was too bad, really. He did care about Lily. He thought about the psychic's reading. He'd decided to see if there was any truth to her ramblings. He'd actually felt good about his decision to ask Lily for her hand. He knew his affair with Cereus was over; he'd heard about her arrest and decided she was too difficult to continue on with.

Lily was easy to be with, didn't require all his attention and was trustworthy, at least with money. He hadn't expected her to be faithful to him. Their arrangement never called for such commitments. However, when he found out she had been with another man on the very morning that he intended to ask for her hand in marriage that was too much.

"At least I was merciful," he said aloud. He'd broken her neck before setting the inn on fire. In all fairness to her, she hadn't known his intentions. He shrugged his shoulders and proceeded down the street. His thoughts turned to his future as he walked away from the inn. The fates had stepped in and taken away another choice. He liked to believe that he made his own decisions and that his life decisions were his own to choose, but he was beginning to think that fate had some design on his life, as if his future and his dreams were being manipulated by others.

An image of Mortifera's newest prize flashed into his mind. What was her name? He paused to think for a moment ... Emily; that was her name. She was a pretty one, inexperienced for sure. He could tell right away. He didn't normally like inexperienced women. He didn't like the role of teacher, but there was something about her. He couldn't put his finger on it. She just seemed so seductive in her innocence. He would talk about her future to Mortifera when he returned to the castle. For now he felt deprived of his playtime and was going to satisfy his desire one way or another. I know just where to go, he thought, and walked two blocks further before making a left towards the heart of the city.

14: Ben's History Comes Full Circle

The wind-driven snow blew out any opportunity of a fire from the tiny spark wrung from the flint. Fortunately, Crooksey and Beastly had an extra layer of protection they used for warmth. The four friends huddled close, the two humans tucked between the large tom cat and the mastiff.

"I sure could use a hot bath and a bed right now," said Ben between chattering teeth.

"You gonna git your wish soon enuf," said Crooksey. "We'll be in Skullduggery on the morrow. It's a good thing you boys let your hair and beards grow long. You'll blend in much better with the thieves and skalliwags, not as recognizable — just in case. You ne'er know who may be skulking about."

"Speaking o' which, you'd better look out for that lovely little doxy — what was her name — Kitty?", Beastly laughed a hearty laugh. Bernie smiled.

"She nearly had him altar-bound, three steps from the chapel door," Beastly laughed again.

"Me — me!", Crooksey retorted. "At least I weren't playing house with some unsuspecting dowager, you old dandy."

"She was a dandy Dinmont Terrier, purely bred and of some social standing, I might add. A fella could do a lot worse," rebutted Beastly.

"Tis truth," admitted Crooksey.

"Are you two done with your taunts? I need sleep," said a cold and cranky Ben. He hunkered down in his bedroll and pressed himself closer to Crooksey's warm body.

"What's crawled into your britches?", laughed Crooksey. "You musta had some close escapes. A fine looking man, such as yourself, could bring the fillies in from miles away."

"True that," agreed Beastly.

"I'll have you both remember that I'm a happily married man," retorted Ben.

"Yeah, we know — and a fine wife she is — but some pretty little lass musta had eyes for you before you met your Pearl," said Crooksey.

"Well, there was this one girl," replied Ben. "I haven't talked about her in over five hundred years."

"Tell us about her," said Crooksey.

"I was seventeen the first time I saw her. Her family was summering at their Pickering Cross estate not more than two miles from my family's home. We were of modest means, and, as you may well guess, I should have been unsuitable for her company. At first we used to meet secretly under the large red oak that stood at the edge of the fields of her family's estate. We lay under the shade of that old oak wiling away the warm summer days laughing and holding hands."

"Didn't her parents find out about you two?", asked Beastly.

"Yes, they did eventually. But they were so in love themselves, they apparently didn't see the harm in our young love." Ben paused. In the process of Ben's story, Bernie remembered he'd stashed a couple of packs of matches and was starting a most welcome fire when Ben went silent.

"Hey Crooksey, ol' Bernie here has been holding out on us."

"No I wasn't, you old fur-ball. I didn't remember until just this minute," he added defiantly. The group laughed and welcomed the warm flames. Ben's prolonged silence worried Crooksey. Ben had been through a lot lately and wasn't a young man any more.

"It's alright Ben, get it off your chest," said Bernie.

"The troubles started in the beginning of August a full year later. Her father was poisoned at the estate, apparently by a servant. I never really knew who was responsible."

"Were you accused of the murder?", asked Beastly.

"No, fortunately I wasn't. But I had other concerns. Elizabeth had taken to her bed as she was deep into a troubled pregnancy, and Elizabeth's mother was in shock at the loss of her husband. Three days later, Elizabeth went into labor and delivered a beautiful baby girl, Abigail June." Tears streamed down his cheeks.

"My first wife, Elizabeth Abigail Sutton died less than twenty-four hours later from complications of the birth." Ben sighed. "I've never told this story to anyone … not even Pearl." He stared into the fire's flames for a long time before he spoke again. "I've left out several details of the story, thinking they weren't really necessary. But I can see now, that this information may be useful and even necessary in the upcoming weeks."

"Ben, who were Elizabeth's parents?", asked Crooksey cautiously.

Ben hesitated, "Nicolas and Cereus Heldring." A gasp went through the circle as the friends began to comprehend the importance of Ben's narrative.

"Ben, there are no stories of Heldring's grandchild. How can this be?", asked Crooksey, who was somewhat of an historian.

"I told Cereus the child died along with her mother. I had no idea how an heir to Dosk would be received, especially since her grandfather wasn't even dead a week and I was not of noble Innesian birth. She was removed from Pickering Cross and taken to the Devil's Hole Forest. I never saw her again, my own daughter.

But that was the agreement. The fairies would have it no other way," he said, and then paused for a few minutes. Bernie poked at the fire; something nagged at the back of his consciousness. Some bit of information that suddenly seemed relevant, but elusive.

"Fate has a funny way of twisting back upon itself," Ben continued. "Many years later after Pearl and I had married, I met my great-great-grandson."

"How did that happen?", asked Crooksey.

"He was in the process of building what would eventually be a landmark estate and a boundary ward to protect the Innesian borders to the west," said Ben.

"How did you find out he was your grandson?", asked Crooksey.

"Well, the fellow got to talking about the name of the estate and how one woman in each generation had been named Abigail: his daughter — Abigail Rose, his sister – Abigail Jane, and so on, until his litany arrived at his great-grandmother — Abigail June. Can you imagine how excited I was at the possibility that he was talking about my Abigail June? My heart nearly leapt from my chest. I remained quiet, because the idea of finding my children after hundreds of years was improbable.

As we conversed and he continued to share his family history, I became more certain that his great-grandmother, Abigail June, was my daughter. I asked him pointed questions about his great-grandmother, but he didn't know much about her or her parents. Apparently, Abigail June's parents had died or given her up when she was a baby and consequently she had been raised in an orphanage. But he did tell me that she had married a dealer of fine jewelry and artifacts, had two children — a son, Samuel and a daughter, Abigail Sue — his grandmother."

"Wow, that's wild," whistled Crooksey.

"I couldn't believe my good fortune," said Ben. "I was so delighted at the prospect of finding my family, but still reluctant to speak of the possibility out loud, for fear that my conversation with this young man was nothing but a dream."

Beastly coughed and scratched his head, "This is some wild story Ben. I canna believe that yi worked out the ties that bind yi."

"I can't either, my friend," said Ben as he patted Beastly's knee. "I guess I shouldn't be too surprised, however, what's the saying – 'like follows like'. I read somewhere once, that friends and families travel in pods throughout time and every time they are reborn into flesh, their families and friends are born with them, in different genders and roles, certainly. Did you ever meet someone and feel like you'd known them your whole life?" Ben gauged his companions' responses as they nodded their heads in unison. "Well, that was my reaction when I met Bernie I." He continued, "My nephew married his lovely wife, Madeline, and they had two children — a son, Bernie II and a daughter, Abigail Rose — for who their lovely manor was named.

Bernie III looked hard at Ben, the many circuits in his brain working overtime to clearly understand what was being said to him. Sometime, during Ben's discourse several of the fey clans landed in the treetops surrounding the small group of travellers.

"I, along with my new wife Pearl, purchased a large farmstead adjacent to the Monkshood Forest, to protect the eastern boundaries and over time we became friendly with the Parker family." Ben sighed and hung his head. The crackling of a log on the fire broke the silence.

"The fey folk have done an excellent job of raising and protecting the family of Heldring, so much so that the Heldrings themselves still have no idea of their descendants' existence. For myself, I'm most grateful to have had this opportunity to spend time with my grandson, even if he is a few generations removed." Ben's companions all sighed at once, as if they'd been holding their breath during the last part of his tale. Bernie stood, left the circle, and walked into the shadows of the forest. Ben stood to go after him.

"Maybe you should give him a few minutes to sort things out Ben," said Crooksey.

"You're probably right," he said. He sat back down and stared into the fire for some minutes before speaking again.

"I'm sorry to have burdened you with this story."

"Nonsense, it's no burden," said Beastly. "Every man has a past. Sometimes he carries the burden of his choices as scars, sometimes as prizes. We all have 'em."

"Why haven't you said anything sooner?", asked Bernie from the shadows of the trees. "Why haven't you told Pearl?" Ben looked to the fey folk for advice.

"You must tell them," said Sidney yellow socks.

"Yes, you must," chimed the rest of the clan members.

"Bernie, I'm sure you must have surmised from my story that you are part Innesian, from one of the oldest bloodlines to settle Innes and my grandson, with a couple of greats attached. What you don't know, yet, is my history."

"Go on," said Bernie.

"What I haven't told anyone is who or what I am. As you can probably guess, I am not Innesian. My ancestors did not come here from the stars seeking a better way of life. My forefathers lived in these parts for thousands of years before the Innesians arrived. My father was Lord Galwin, King of the sole remaining elven clan. Other tales have described the elves leaving earth because it was the time of men. What few know of are the clans that stayed. My father's clan, the Catalpa clan, stayed in the trees, protected the trees, protected the forests. I was born to the House Catalpa around 800 years ago."

"What of your parents?", asked Crooksey.

"They are long dead, shortly after the first remaking of the world. I had a sister, as well. She was killed during the second remaking of the world. Her tree was struck by lightening during the Phase of Storms that shattered so many of the ancient forests of these great lands. There are few of my kind that still roam as free elves. Many chose to follow the other elves over the oceans, or they became dormant, choosing instead to merge or blend with their trees. Did you ever notice that some trees have faces, or maybe even multiple faces? They are the remnants of my clan. Don't misunderstand me. The trees have their own personalities, don't let them fool you. They're not very talkative and only choose to orate when the winds leave them no choice.

The elves live in a symbiotic relationship with their tree, a mutual arrangement that is beneficial to both parties. My family was here long before the Innesians came from their space ships. We lived in harmony with the fairies and the gnomes.

"Like I said, I left the trees to walk amongst the Innesians and the humans that left their technologically chaotic world for a simpler life. When I first left the trees, I travelled a great deal, meeting trees from all walks of life. I talked to the Japanese Maples of Japan, the bamboo of China, the baobabs of Africa, and to the cottonwoods of Hawaii. They all had the same story to tell of how their elves left them to cross the waters and how they were lonely and longed for the companionship forged through millennia. They also whispered of a new wonder, that none of this planet had ever seen. They whispered of an alien race, the Innesians, who had come to the earth seeking freedom from persecution. They landed in these very lands, my homelands. Their arrival brought me home. The rest of the story is as I told it." With that, he sat in the midst of a large silence. No one dared to speak, for no one could believe Ben's tale. The embers from the fire swirled and popped in the lengthening silence.

Ben continued, "I have lived in many lands throughout my life, but know none such as these, even down to the language of the trees. My family left these trees to walk amongst man and the Innesians when they arrived. Through the years we have mediated many treaties, resolved land disputes, overseen marriages, births, and deaths. My family has translated between the races for as long as the races have intermingled.

"The Heldrings wrote a doctrine called the Book of Dreams. The Book of Dreams was written as a charter among Innesians, fairies, humankind, and all other living things to protect peace and to encourage hope, dreams, innovation, creativity, free thought, and reason throughout the lands of Innes. The idea was that the world of dreams and fantasy provided the stimulus and the safest place to create new thoughts, to foster new projects, to explore hopes, and to pursue higher aspirations.

Above all, the book was to bring unity and peace to the inhabitants of this utopia in process. I was brought to the estate to moderate the final signing of the book among man, the fey, and the Innesians. There were some minor details that needed to be sorted out before any party would put their final seal to paper."

"Ahem," sang the King of the Monarchs. "Not so minor in some cases, you might well remember."

"Yes, Your Majesty, I'm sorry. I did not mean to

misspeak."

"Quite right," he sang.

"I thought the book was from fables," said Crooksey.

"My mum used to tell me bedtime stories from the Book of Dreams, although she sometimes called it the Book of Fey or the Fair' Book," said Beastly. "I just thought they made up that sort o' stuff. I ne'er really put any kind 'o stock inta it. I just thought me mam was a bit off her rocker," said Beastly.

"No," said Ben. "Your mam was put together just right"

"I shoulda known. Me mam was always right," said Beastly musingly.

"I still don't understand the importance of this conversation," said Bernie. "How does all of this relate to Emily's disappearance and how we're going to get her back?"

"Patience, young Parker," sang the Monarch King. "This tale has great history; much relies on the preservation of the book and its contents. For you see, this book was not something that was written once and then finalized. Rather, it's a document that continues to be written and rewritten as needed. The length of the volume is extended as imaginary or creative thoughts are added."

"The book must be huge by now," said Bernie.

"The book is only ... the root of the tree, shall we say. The effects of the book have manifested all around you. Everything you see around you has been written in the book and revealed as it materialized."

"That's a crazy story," said Bernie. "Life doesn't exist because it was written in a book. It's the other way around. Books exist because of life and someone has taken the time to write about life."

"We certainly see your point," sang the Monarch

King, "and wouldn't normally argue against it. But the Book of Dreams manifest thoughts, just as they are written down — it makes them real. Do you see the dilemma? Someone wrote down their thought of this Lucky Rabbits' Foot tree that I sit in, by their dream or something they imagined.

That was the book's purpose, as a repository for free thought. But the book itself had something else in mind as it evolved; the trees, flowers, much of the wildlife started to change what they looked like or even how they functioned. It was most unexpected the first few times the book was rewritten. You can't possibly understand what it was like: the first remaking of the world. We've gotten a little better at weathering the effects of each subsequent remaking – that is, until this time around."

"What makes this time so different?", asked Bernie.

Hisses went through the fairy clans as the Monarch King replied, "The Dream Stealers." Beastly spat at the mention of Belac and Mortifera's collective.

"Mortifera is a vain creature and would have the Book of Dreams rewritten in her image; that is, all things Mortifera first, and then all things Wraith at the second.

One of the most amazing occurrences in Innes is the diversity of its beings and the ready acceptance of those beings: alien, fairy, human, or dragon. The world of dreams and imagination must be protected. It's the last bastion of free thought.

The Dream Stealers would stifle all free thought, innovation, ideas, hopes and dreams, and rewrite the book as a corporate war machine, with a homogenized, uniform, and unimaginative doctrine of life — cast all into permanent darkness — The Way of the Wraith," sang the Monarch King.

There was a lengthy pause before Ben picked up the

conversation. "This is where Emily comes into the discussion, Bernie."

"Go on," said Bernie.

"Information about Emily's whereabouts has come to me through one of the fairy coalitions."

"Where is she?", demanded Bernie.

"She was seen several weeks ago talking to a sprite, name of Ing, in Kuhnston Derry."

"Why are we wasting our time going to Skullduggery? We should be going to Kuhnston Derry to talk to this fellow Ing," said Bernie, rather heatedly.

"I know Ing," said Ben. "He wouldn't hold out on her whereabouts if it wasn't important."

"I don't care," replied Bernie. "This is my daughter we're talking about."

"This seems to be part of the problem," said Ben. "The fairies who saw her talking to Ing didn't know it was Emily. Ing told them as much."

"I don't understand," said Bernie. "They've all seen pictures of her. She shouldn't have changed that much — longer hair, maybe."

"That's the crux of the matter; she was completely unrecognizable."

"How can that be?", Bernie said.

"I'm sorry, Bernie, but you need to know ... your daughter has gone through the change," said Ben.

"Change?", asked Bernie.

"She's become Wraith," said Ben.

"No, that can't be. Emily's too strong. She wouldn't," he cried, his face buried deep into his hands. His world cast upside down.

Beast put a paw around his shoulder, "We'll find her Bernie, dunna yi worry none." One by one, the fairy lights silently blinked out as the rays of the rising sun began to find their ways through the canopy.

"Come on, let's get our gear together, we're just

outside of Skullduggery. We'll certainly find something out about Emily, and where she's being held," said Crooksey.

Ben walked over to Bernie. "I'm really sorry to lay all of this on you."

Bernie shook his head, "I'm not sure what to call you now."

"How about Ben, that seemed to work fine before." The two men shook hands with a new understanding between them – the ties and trust that family brings.

The travellers entered Skullduggery nigh on lunch time tired and hungry. After another half hour or so of weaving through rat-infested back alleys, they came upon their destination, The Squirming Lassie, a saloon with the lowest of the low in reputation. The main support beams of the room — ancient thick timbers — gave the appearance of a ship's mast. Evenly spaced gas-lit lanterns were low cast so as not to direct light on the faces of the customers, many who chose to remain unnamed or unseen.

A thin layer of saw dust sopped up the spilled spirits that covered the well-worn floorboards. The walls were lined with all sorts of relics, pirate — ropes, nets, crates. The room was filled with the smells of grease, pipe tobacco smoke, and body odor from men too long at sea without the niceties of civilization. Scantily-clad women brought mugs of the house ale to table patrons, some playing cards, others looking for trouble.

Beastly led the party towards the back wall, "tis better to be watching than being watched," he said. A tall slender brunette took their orders for spirits and food. She passed a note to the lead cook, who took his towel from the service window and dried his hands as he walked to their table. Crooksey stuck out a paw to shake the hand of the new occupant.

"Boys, this here's Cap'n Abel, the finest scum and

best mate around these parts," said Crooksey.

"A real societal stand-up he is," jeered Beastly. Cap'n Abel laughed and clapped them both on their backs before sitting at the table. The waitress returned with the drinks and food many minutes later.

"Did you get my message?", asked Crooksey. "I know it's kinda last minute, but we're in a bit of a hurry and don't want too many questions asked. If'n you know what I mean?"

"What's new?", replied Cap'n Abel. "You boys never was ones to stick around long anyway. Too much heat on your trail," he laughed. "I got what you asked for and let me tell you, it weren't no easy task neither. Ain't the likes of us good enuf scum? That you have to go entering the castle and all, probably gittin yourselves kilt real good. You couldna pay me enuf to enter those blood suckers' house, no way," he said as he slid a skeleton key with a piece of paper attached to it. "This is what you need. That and a new braincase I'd say."

"Thanks mate," said Crooksey as he slid a thick, sealed envelope across the table. Cap'n Abel deposited the envelope quick as a fiddle and was back in the window shouting orders to the cook's assistants as if he'd never left.

"There you have it," said Beastly. "Our rooms are upstairs."

"I don't know about you lot, but I could sure use a bath. I stink worse than the rest of the scum in this place," laughed Ben.

"I agree," laughed Bernie.

"We'll leave after breakfast tomorrow," said Crooksey. "Does everyone agree?"

"Yes," they all agreed.

After a night's rest in a bed and a sufficient breakfast, the travellers let out towards Necromancer's

Notch. They didn't dare use the front roads as the number of soldiers would make travel difficult. They carried kerosene lanterns to light their pathway and to push the never ending darkness back against itself.

"At least I understand the scum in Skullduggery," said Crooksey. "This lot in Necromancer's Notch is a breed of a different color."

"Dunno trust anyone," said Beastly. "These necros use the blood suckers' dead bodies for experimentation. Bring 'em back to life, they say."

"I never seen 'em myself, but that's what I've heard too," said Crooksey.

"I have seen them," said Ben. "Shush," he said as he shielded the lantern. "Up ahead." They could see a large fire as they crept nearer to the chaos in the woods in front of them.

Two reanimated figures twirled like rag dolls around the campfire. Their faces horribly disfigured, leather lacings sewed their mouths shut; another large male was trying to copulate with a smaller female. Two necromancers were arguing to see how they were to divide the three live human captives who were tightly bound to the wheel of the wagon.

"Trussed up like chickens, they are," said Beastly.

"Always thinking with your stomach," chuckled Crooksey.

"Would you two get serious," said Bernie.

"Why? It's not our problem," said Crooksey.

"We can't just leave them to the necros," said Bernie.

"They was stupid enough to get caught," growled Beastly.

"Crooksey's right," said Ben. "We can't get side tracked. Besides, we can't be responsible for them either."

"Let's just cut them loose and then leave. I'll do it

if you don't want to." Bernie started to carefully creep through the underbrush. Any noise they made was drowned out by the now-warring necromancers. Sparks flew overhead as the wizard's battle escalated.

Beastly crawled next to Bernie, "I couldna let yi do this alone." He stuck his straight blade between his teeth and moved noiselessly through the thicket until he cleared the brush. He gave the signal to Bernie to move forward. Beastly sawed at the tough ropes that bound the boy's arms and feet together. The necros were so involved in their spat that they never noticed Beastly and Bernie hewing through the ropes.

The reincarnated humans increased the tempo of their riotous dance as the chaos of the magical displays increased. Beastly, Bernie, and the now-freed prisoners started to back away from the hideous scene when the one girl tripped and fell in among the unfettered zombies.

They were on her, ripping flesh from bone before the necros realized their blunder. Ben's one hand held the other girl tightly while the other hand covered her mouth. Crooksey had charge of the boy, but he had stopped struggling once he realized this group was friend and not foe.

The necros didn't seem too concerned as the group blended with the forest and made off into the night. They returned to their argument. This time, it was about whose fault it was that they'd lost their prey and they would have to start over again.

The group travelled until long after they thought they were being pursued. When they did finally stop, Ben was quite adamant about going separate ways.

"We cannot take them with us. It's far too dangerous for us… and for them."

"We can't leave them here to get picked up by those necros again or maybe something even worse," said

Bernie.

"We cannot take them to the Obsidian Tower, period." Ben was emphatic.

"Maybe we could help them get somewhere relatively safe and then they're on their own," offered Crooksey.

The young man stood amongst the four friends, "I can help you get into the Obsidian Tower," he said very somberly. The four friends were quiet as the young man relayed his story. They came to find out that the surviving girl was his sister and the girl who was killed by the zombies was her best friend. She hadn't spoken until this minute, as she walked over and stood next to her brother.

"We can get you into the tower," she said flatly.

"You won't survive without our help." Ben spoke to deny them again.

The young man asked, "Have you ever been in the tower?"

Ben was silent for a moment. "Yes…but a long time ago."

"We're just came from there not two weeks ago, so we know our way around."

"Why would you return to that horrible place willingly?", asked Bernie.

"You were willing to risk your necks to save us. It seems that we owe you," said the young man coolly.

"You don't owe us anything," said Ben. "Least of all, this."

The young man pushed a small pile of dirt with the toe of his shoe and reluctantly said, "We were kinda hoping you'd help us if we helped you. We left a lot of friends behind and it's only a matter of time before they become raw material for the necros." There was a long silence.

Finally the young man said, "You know…they're

building an army."

"Yeah, we know of the army coming outta Dosk. We saw it with our own eyes," said Beastly.

"It's an army coming out of Deorc, to meet up with the one from Dosk," said the young man. The four friends looked at each other.

"What do ya mean, outta Deorc?", asked Beastly.

"Belac and Mortifera are building their own private army, a real freak show if you ask me," said the young man.

"What is your name? It's really hard trying to have a conversation without a name," said Bernie.

"John. John Dunne and this is my sister Fiona."

"Where are you from?", asked Bernie.

"You wouldn't believe me if I told you," said John.

"Try me."

"Boston."

"Boston?"

"I told you that you wouldn't believe me."

"You mean Boston, Massachusetts?" John and Fiona gasped at the same time.

"You know it?", asked John.

"Only a little, I've only been there once or twice," replied Bernie. "I'm from Pennsylvania."

"How can that be?", asked Fiona.

"There is much you don't know," said Ben. "But it appears that we can help each other, for now. If my fellow travellers are in agreement, I suggest a temporary alliance." All others shook their heads in agreement.

"John, you said earlier that Belac was building an army. How do you know this?", asked Ben.

"I was a personal servant to Belac. Always at his side in case he needed something. I tasted the blood that he drank every day to make sure it hadn't been poisoned."

"How did you get away?", asked Bernie.

John hung his head, "I started to change. So I was dismissed – to become necro-fodder."

"I don't understand," said Crooksey. "Isn't that their goal – to make everyone wraith?"

"Oh no," replied John. "Only the special ones are turned. Like the new girl they just brought out of the dungeons. She's someone special – that one – you can be sure because Mortifera turned her herself. Calls her daughter and everything." Bernie started to pace.

"Does this girl have a name?", he asked carefully.

"Not really sure of a name," said John. "But I saw her face once. She's beautiful, even as a wraith. She's tall, has long-curly black hair and silky-white skin.

They said she was going to become a very powerful witch who would help them destroy the Amber Tower. She's to be wed to that horrible man Draedon in the spring. I overheard them talking about it one night in their chambers."

"Agatha Bisbee said she cries herself to sleep every night," said Fiona. "They have to hide the blood-stained pillow cases and wash them special so the mistress doesn't know. She's so nice to all of the servants; no one wants to get her in trouble."

"Aggie has become one of her personal servants," said John.

"Aggie says she's in love with the new boy. Aggie says she knew him from school, before she was captured and taken away."

"What is the new boy's name?", asked Ben. "Take your time, think about it."

"Oh that's easy," said Fiona. "Agatha chatters on about him — his name is William, but she calls him Will." Both men gasped.

"It must be Will Tipton," said Ben.

"It's got to be Emily. She had a huge crush on him

before his parents moved out to Whispering Bluff."

Bernie's pace increased. "How far do we have to go? Was she okay? Turned to wraith? Maybe she won't remember me," he emoted while furiously wringing his hands and then clenching them into fists, as his mood changed from anxiety to dread to anger.

"Calm down, Bernie," said Beastly as he put his paw on his back for reassurance. "We'll find your lassie, dunna yi worry." John shook his head.

"You two can't go into the Tower," he said as he pointed to Crooksey and Beastly.

"Damned if'n I won't," growled Beastly. "Ain't no kid gonna tell me different." It was Beastly's turn to be calmed down.

"You would be spotted, captured, and gutted; it would be your last hundred breaths. My plans of entry include: the witch's father and myself; that's all." Fiona looked to her brother to say something contrary.

"Not even you, Fiona. That's final." Fiona nodded her head and looked at the ground. John wrapped his arm around her waist, as he said, "We must enter silently, hide within the cracks in the wall, move with the rats."

"How will we get Emily out?", asked Bernie.

"You won't be able to get her out...."

"No, she's coming back with us!", railed Bernie.

"She won't come, and, if you push her or try to kidnap her, you'll just screw things up," said John with equal vehemence. "I know these things and what they're capable of – you don't."

"The kid is right Bernie – take my word – you can't half imagine the circumstances and the events that Emily has endured. We must trust John; of this I'm quite certain." A long silence ensued.

"So what's your plan?", asked a calmer Bernie.

"I was figuring the dog and the cat...."

"Hey, watch your mouth," growled the still-riled Beastly. Ben put his hand on Beastly's back.

"Calm down, brother, let him speak freely. This is no time for niceties."

"Go on," gruffed Beastly.

"I said earlier that Belac is creating an army of the undead. I was thinking you and your cat friend could stay in necros' territory, move closer to the army being assembled in the north along the Deorcian border and then reconnoiter in a location of your choosing. You," he said, pointing to Ben. "I hope you'll take my sister to the Sapphire Tower. She has her own destiny to follow."

Fiona shook her head adamantly. "I'm coming with you, John."

"You cannot escape your destiny, Fiona," said John.

"You know that. You must take the information to the Amber Tower. Daedelus must be warned. Belac's spies reported that Leoht has four legions on the march. They should meet with Pettiman's men by the thaw. Belac intends to use his undead army to flank Daedalus from Dagung."

"How do you know all this?", asked Bernie.

"I told you I was always present at his side. I've learned the 'Wraith Art of War' from the originator himself. I learned early on: keep your eyes and ears open, your head down, and your mouth shut."

"What do you hope to gain from this plan?", asked the long-quiet Crooksey.

"Revenge," John replied. "I hate the wraith, and now I'm becoming the very thing I hate. There is no way back for me."

"No, John, no," cried Fiona.

"You know I'm speaking the truth," he said as he wrapped his arms around his trembling sister. "I won't be leaving with you," he said.

"What will you do?", replied Bernie. "How will you survive?"

"I will steal their blood, live amongst the rats until I have completely changed. They won't know of my existence until it's time."

"Well, my friends, it appears that we each have our paths to follow," said Ben. "Come child, my new granddaughter, it's time for us to go." Fiona had her arms and legs wrapped around her brother.

"You must go, Fiona. Do the Dunne name proud. Remember: I'll always love you and be with you." He hugged her for the last time and handed her to Ben. He turned and walked away. Bernie grabbed his gear and started after John.

"We'll hang around the saloon in Skullduggery for a few days before heading to Leoht," said Beastly as they turned to the north to wait for the undead army.

15: Rho Dora Unmasked

Madeline was thrilled with the Innesian history book she'd discovered on a high shelf at the back of the library. She turned the thick parchment gingerly, not wanting to put any creases or bends in the pages. She was delighted by the ornate drawings of the castle's dragons. She knew so little about dragons, but was intrigued since meeting Ailith.

The first discussion was about Thryth, the Amethyst Dragon. She knew from Michael that Thryth had passed away, and Ailith, her daughter, had been born to take her place. Michael wouldn't take her back to Dagung because the Amethyst Tower had succumbed to the armies of the Obsidian Tower. Madeline turned the page to the Amber Dragon of Leoht.

"Look, Rho, he's a splendid dragon."

"What's his name?", asked Rho.

"Hang on, let me read about him ...," said Madeline.

"Oh look, here comes Maize and Iris. I wonder what they want," said Rho.

"Hi girls," said Maize.

"Rho, we'd like to speak with you in private for a moment."

"Okay," said Rho. "But you can say what you have to say in front of Maddy. We have no secrets."

"Are you sure about that?", asked Iris, as she removed the gold compact from her pocket.

"Where'd you get that?", snapped Rho. "Were you searching my room?"

"So, you don't deny that it belongs to you?", asked

Maize.

"Why would you search my room? I haven't been a problem."

"We didn't search your room, Rho. We went looking for you; we wanted to tell you that the Treaton School agreed to send a tutor for you as well. Your compact was ringing when we entered your room," said Iris.

"I opened it and said hello," said Maize. "I was quite surprised when I realized with whom I was speaking. I'm afraid your cover has been blown, both here and with your mistress."

"What is she talking about, Rho?", demanded Madeline. "You told me you kept in touch with your mother. I just assumed...." Rho hung her head, the fight gone from her.

"Whom do you speak with, Rho? Tell me!", Madeline shrilled.

"... the Queen of the Obsidian Tower," mumbled Rho. Madeline gasped.

"Maddy, I had no choice," pleaded Rho. "My mother is Morifera's personal handmaid; she threatened to kill her if I didn't report back once a week. That's how I know she is still okay. Mortifera would allow me to speak with her once in a while. Please, forgive me," she sobbed. "I didn't want to lie to anyone. But, I didn't know what to do."

Madeline spoke after an intense few minutes. "You should have trusted that Maize and Iris and the sisterhood would know what to do."

"I know," cried Rho. "But, I was afraid."

"Rho, you should have trusted me," said Madeline

"I'm so sorry. What can I do to make this right?", pleaded Rho Dora.

"I need time to think," said Madeline. She turned to walk out of the library.

Rho reached for her hand. "Please Maddy, don't hate me."

"I don't hate you, Rho. But you have broken my heart," she said, tears falling freely over her cheeks. She turned and walked out of the room.

"Please don't throw me out," begged Rho.

"Your fate will be determined by the council. You're to be in council chambers within one hour to give testimony. We called an emergency meeting once we realized the lie that had been perpetrated upon everyone in this house and in the Guild. We're very disappointed and saddened by our discovery," said Iris.

"We suggest that you figure out what you'll tell your mistress. In the meantime, you'll return to your room. You've lost your privileges to move freely about the estate," said Maize. "These guards will see that you get to your room and the council chambers on time."

Rho hung her head, her embarrassment glowing dark purple on her cheeks and neck. The light had gone from her eyes. Moments ago she was looking for her dragon with her best friend, in the only place she truly felt at home. How could her life have gone so horribly wrong, so fast? Maize and Iris watched her go.

"You know the council will look to your wisdom, Maize," said Iris. "What are your thoughts?"

"I think she's truly sorry — mistakes of the young and inexperienced. Ira thinks we should give her another chance, and, even though he doesn't generally speak on the Guild's affairs, we're living in very precarious times and I'm inclined to agree with his decisions. Besides, we can turn the tides and make her useful to our needs."

"You are nefarious," clucked Iris.

"Practical, my dear, practical," Maize said as she pulled Iris close. "We're at war, and she's a direct line to Mortifera herself. So much misinformation we could feed her. We have yet to understand how useful she might really be."

"Do you think it's fair to Madeline?", Iris asked, as she pulled Maize closer towards her.

"I have a feeling they'll work their differences out, given some time. At the very least Gordon will see to it when he returns," Maize chuckled. "Besides, those three needed some cooling off. Have you seen the walls, both inside and out?" Iris laughed.

"Oh pooh, look who's talking about needing cooling off," she said as she delicately bit Maize's top lip. Maize laughed and blushed deep yellow.

"Well, at least we don't go broadcasting our affairs about the estate for all to see. Maize, lest I remind you, Chelsea Manor is Ira's family estate. He could run around naked all day if he chooses to." Maize laughed at the image that popped into her head.

"He's too much of a gentleman," she said.

"That he is," agreed Iris.

"I'm so glad he's our gentleman," said Maize.

"Me too," laughed Iris. "At least we know one of Madeline's talents for sure." They both laughed at that and walked towards the council chambers.

"I hope everything is alright with Gordon," said Maize. "He's two days overdue."

"Have you any news on the chatty stick?", asked Iris.

"No news regarding Gordon directly, only rumors and a string of seemingly unrelated deaths. All women: an innkeeper, a psychic and her maid, and this morning two prostitutes, were found lying next to each other, strangled to death."

"It can be a dangerous world for a woman," said Iris.

"I guess it depends on the company that you keep,"

said Maize as they hurried along the hall way. Additional thoughts were left unspoken. Many hours later, Rho Dora was found guilty as charged. Against all advice to keep her as an operative for the Guild, Rho was stripped of her membership in the sisterhood and asked to leave the premises immediately. She was to be escorted to the dungeons in the Amber Tower of Leoht in the morning.

Several days later, Madeline moped about the estate. Her teacher had not yet arrived, and Gordon was still amongst the missing. When she thought she couldn't stand it anymore, Ira turned up with a proposition for an outing. He proposed a that she stay just a couple of nights with the only ones who could soothe her, her brother, Michael, and his friend Nate. She was delighted. They went into the garden and were gone in a flash.

"Michael, Michael," she called. But the cave was empty. She walked up the trail a piece and saw the now almost full-grown Ailith basking in the warm, late winter-early spring sun. Lying next to her were a dozen fairies who were braiding flowers into each other's hair. Madeline walked into the clearing. "Hello," she said. She startled the fairies who had been too involved with their chatter to hear her approach.

"Hi, Madeline," said Ailith. "Please join us, Michael will return soon. I'll let him know you're here."

"No, don't, I'd like to surprise him."

"Your choice, but I will have him come back shortly. I have to hunt soon and I don't want you here alone."

"She wouldn't be alone," said the fairies. "We'll keep her company. You can go hunt."

"Okay, if you're sure. But you can't leave until Michael or Nate return. Agreed?"

"Agreed," they responded.

"Madeline, can we braid your hair again?", the fey-

Ailith in the Morpho Fairy Ring

folk asked in unison.

"I'd love that," laughed Madeline. Ira waved and turned to go.

"I'll be back in three days. Your teacher should be at the estate by then."

"Thank you, Ira," she said.

"You're welcome," he said. With that he winked and then blinked out of sight. Madeline spent the next three hours being primped and preened by the fairies, as if they knew they were diminishing her grief.

"Don't worry Madeline, it'll all work out — you'll see."

"Thank you," she replied and closed her eyes as the fairies delicately brushed her hair.

"Hey, how long have you been here?", asked Michael as he entered the fairy ring. The snow had retreated back under the dark canopy — its cold crystals were no match for the warm, early spring sun that warmed the still-frozen earth.

"I was out of my mind with boredom," replied Madeline. "Gordon is several days overdue and Rho...."

"What?", asked Michael. "Rho, ...what?" Madeline started to tear. One rolled down her pink cheek. "Rho got kicked out of the Guild and off the estate grounds."

"What for?", asked Michael.

"She was a spy for Mortifera in the Obsidian Tower."

As he breathed deeply, Michael whispered. "She was a spy?", he asked.

"She says not. She was doing it to protect her mom. How could she lie to me? I'm so embarrassed," she cried.

"Maybe she wasn't lying to you. Maybe she had to report just like she said."

"But, why didn't she tell me?", asked Madeline. "We shared everything."

"Would you have told if you were in her shoes?" Madeline hesitated.

"I don't know," she said after many minutes passed. "Maybe not."

"You would do anything to protect our mother, wouldn't you? I know I would," replied Michael. Ailith landed in the fairy circle just as several members of the Red Admiral clan appeared.

"Ahem," said the Captain of the Guard as he cleared his throat. "Please forgive the interruption, but we have come with urgent news." It must have been important for the Red Admirals to send a Captain to do a courier's job.

"Ira Pufflehump, himself, asked us to come." Just as the Captain was about to speak, Nate rode up on Arion.

"Hey, what's going on? Did I miss anything? Hey Madeline, what are you doing here?"

"Ira brought me here early this morning," she replied.

"Ira, himself, personally brought you here?", asked Michael.

"Yes," she said. At which point the Captain of the Guard, not to be forgotten, interjected himself physically into their line of sight.

"Please, I come on urgent business."

"Sorry to interrupt," said Nate. "State your business."

"Master Pufflehump has asked us to let you know that Miss Rho Dora has escaped her guardsmen and run off into the Devil's Hole Forest to the south. She is being hunted as a fugitive of the law and if caught will be tried and executed for treason against the state. You must find the 'Rider of Wynn' before she is caught.

Secondly, the Lady Madeline is not to return to Chelsea Manor."

"What?", she said.

"The Guild has become unstable. The business with Miss Dora has many members paranoid and calling for room searches and house arrests. They fear infiltration from the lands of darkness. Many members of the Guild are saying that you must have known and are as guilty as Miss Dora herself. They say that, as her lover, there is no possible way that you could not have known."

"That's ridiculous!", shouted Madeline.

"Master Ira, Madame Maize, and Miss Iris want you to stay here with your brother until it's safe to return."

"I love Rho, that's true, but I have no love of the Obsidian Tower. None at all."

"The master knows this and that's why you were brought here and why I'm here now," replied the Captain. "Stay away from Chelsea Manor, Miss Madeline; it's not safe for you there." With that, the Red Admirals popped out of view.

"What's that all about?", asked Nate.

"How are we going to find Rho?", cried Madeline at the same time.

"What did he mean — the 'Rider of Wynn'," asked Michael.

"Wynn is Rho's fantasy dragon," said Madeline.

"You and this Rho Dora were lovers?", asked Nate. Madeline blushed, several deep shades of pink.

"What about Gordon? I thought you were with Gordon?", said Nate.

"We're both with Gordon," said Madeline very quietly.

"That dog," whistled Nate. "How'd he keep that information to himself?"

"That's hardly the point, Nathaniel Sutton," Madeline chided.

"What do you mean, Rho's fantasy dragon?", asked Michael.

"Who cares about any of it? Didn't you hear what the Captain said? We have to find Rho, and fast. How are we going to do that?", demanded Madeline.

"We'll find her, Madeline. Don't worry, we have the fairies to help us. But first you have to tell me who Wynn is," said Michael.

"I already told you, Wynn is Rho's fantasy dragon. When I told her about Ailith, she freaked, and said she wanted to be a dragon rider more than anything in the world. I'm not sure what the Red Admiral Captain meant though," said Madeline. "We couldn't find any reference to a dragon named Wynn in the Manor's library."

"That is because dragons are not found in libraries," said the long-quiet Ailith.

"Do you know of Wynn?", asked Madeline.

"Yes," said Ailith. "She belongs to the Moldavite Tower. She's the green dragon of Twe-Leoht."

"But the Moldavite Tower has fallen," said Michael.

"That must mean the dragon has fallen as well," said Madeline.

"She is not dead," said Ailith. "I can feel her; but just barely. She's in a state of hibernation, waiting…."

"Waiting for what?", asked Michael.

"Waiting for her rider," said Ailith.

"We must find Rho," said Madeline. "But how?"

"The fey folk can help," said Nate. "The Sidneys are in the south right now, you know, they've gotten a little rambunctious with the coming of spring. I can get word to them. What does she look like?"

Madeline started to describe Rho Dora to the group. After she was done, she looked to Michael.

"What am I to do? I've been removed from my

home for something I didn't do."

"Well, you'll stay here of course," said Michael.

"But I have no clothing, nor my books, and my lessons were supposed to begin again," she said. "Oh, this is terrible."

"Hey Madeline," called Nate from the cave opening. She walked to the edge of the overhang.

"Hey Madeline," Nate called again.

"Yeah," she said.

"Come here. I think you should see this," he shouted. Madeline ran down the hillside to the cave opening. She gasped. Lined against the right wall were several trunks, piled next to crates, piled next to several heavy cotton bags. They could hear someone moving about inside the cave.

"My, my, this just won't do — too primitive — yes, too primitive." They could see a myriad of colors flashing within the cavern accompanied by curious bangs and clicks.

"What is going on?", asked Nate who was bewildered by the show.

"It can't be,' said Madeline.

"What can't be?", asked Nate.

"My teacher came here," said Madeline.

"Your teacher?", asked Nate.

"From the Treaton School," said Madeline. With that, a brown furry critter walked upright into the front cave.

"Oh my, please excuse me. I hope you don't mind my redecorating, but the décor was terrible. I couldn't possibly stay under these conditions. No, not possible," he murmured.

"Who are you?", asked Nate.

"Oh right," he muttered. "Introductions. I'm Willard Wombat, Madeline's teacher from the Walter Treaton School of Mystery, Magic, and Mayhem."

He stepped forward, "You must be Madeline," he said.

"Yes," she said.

"Hey wait, weren't you Emily's teacher before she … before she disappeared?" asked Nate.

"Yes," he said. "Or I was to be, anyway. Poor Miss Emily." He hung his head in sadness. Nate had moved into the next room of the caves, his curiousity was too strong.

"Wow!", he exclaimed. "This is unbelievable. Come here you guys, you have to see this." With that, Michael entered, Ailith immediately behind. Bringing up the rear were a couple handfuls of fairies, a few brownies, and a stray pixie or two, all of who had taken up residence since Ailith's introduction. Willard saw Ailith and gasped.

"Oh my, no one told me about a dragon. This is very unusual, to be certain."

Michael stepped forward, "Dr. Wombat," he said as he gestured towards a handshake. "Do you remember me?", he asked. "I'm Michael, Michael Parker."

"Why yes, I remember you. That was a long time ago Master Parker. You're considerably taller than last we met."

"Please, Dr. Wombat, come with me. There's someone I'd like you to meet." He stepped forward tentatively.

"This is my dragon, Ailith," he said.

"Your dragon?", he asked. "This is most unusual."

"Yes, sir; I'm her rider. Well, at least, I'm learning to be," he laughed. "It's not as easy as it looks."

"Mademoiselle," said Willard as he bowed to Ailith.

"Dr. Wombat," she said. "It's good to meet you."

"Now that the necessities are finished, can you …Come here!", hollered Nate from the next room.

"I hope you don't mind, Michael. It's your cave,

isn't it?"

"No. It belongs to some friends, but we're here for the duration as it appears that none of us are moving to Chelsea Manor anytime soon."

"Michael, you won't believe this: a fireplace, a proper stove with a tea kettle, and thick furry carpet," squealed Madeline as a pair of hands sprouted from the carpet and started to massage her feet. There was a heavy cook pot on the stove top emitting a wonderful smell. A soft concerto played from within a newly made bedroom.

"I'm sorry Michael, but there was nowhere for me to sleep." Michael nodded his head as he went from room to room, noting the upgraded bedding. The cave was splashed with gorgeous shades of blues and greens. As they spoke, the front room, Ailith's room, turned a lovely shade of violet. A thick large cushion appeared next to the fire. Multiple chairs and benches, large enough to hold a fairy clan, were attached to the cave walls.

"I see we are beneath a fairy ring," said Willard. "Which clan?"

"The Morpho Clan," replied Michael. Willard turned to his left and created the loveliest flat-topped podium for the King.

"Let's eat," he said. Dishes and silverware marched themselves through the air as glasses and salt and pepper shakers followed suit. Several slices of still-warm, fresh-baked bread with pats of butter were at each table setting. A ladle, free of hands, poured the heavenly smelling stew to each table occupant.

Even the brownies, who normally preferred grasshoppers and crickets to cooked human food, found a thimbleful of the delightful stew waiting for them. Michael kicked his chair back and pulled his tobacco and pipe from his pocket. Jonah had acquired a new one at Chelsea Manor, leaving Michael as his old pipe's master.

"It has been many full moons since I've had such good food, thank you kind sir," said Michael.

"You're welcome," replied Willard. "It seems that we have many items to discuss," said Willard. "Master Nate, if you would be so kind." Willard handed Nate a quill and paper. "We must prioritize and strategize," he said.

"Divide and conquer," suggested Nate.

"Quite right," replied Willard. "One question I must ask: I was hoping to see my old friend Jonah Hobken. It was my understanding that he was in residence here."

"Normally, you'd be right," said Michael. "But Jonah went with the Monarch Clan about three weeks ago — to document their music. He was thrilled when the Monarch King agreed."

"He's not due back for another couple of weeks," added Nate.

"We could get him," suggested Lt. Clay of the Red Admiral Clan.

"It may come to that," said Willard. "Let's see." The group stayed up long into the night, discussing matters at hand. A travelling party, consisting of Nate on Arion, several of the Sidneys, and two Red Admirals left at dawn. It had been decided that finding Rho Dora took precedence over all else. Michael took flight on Ailith and headed to the southern lands of Dosk and the Sapphire Tower. He was nervous, as this was only his third time atop Ailith, and never over such a long distance.

"We'll be okay, Michael. You're a natural."

"I wish I had your confidence," he replied. He patted her neck and pulled his purple robe closer to prevent it from flapping in the cool wind. Inside the

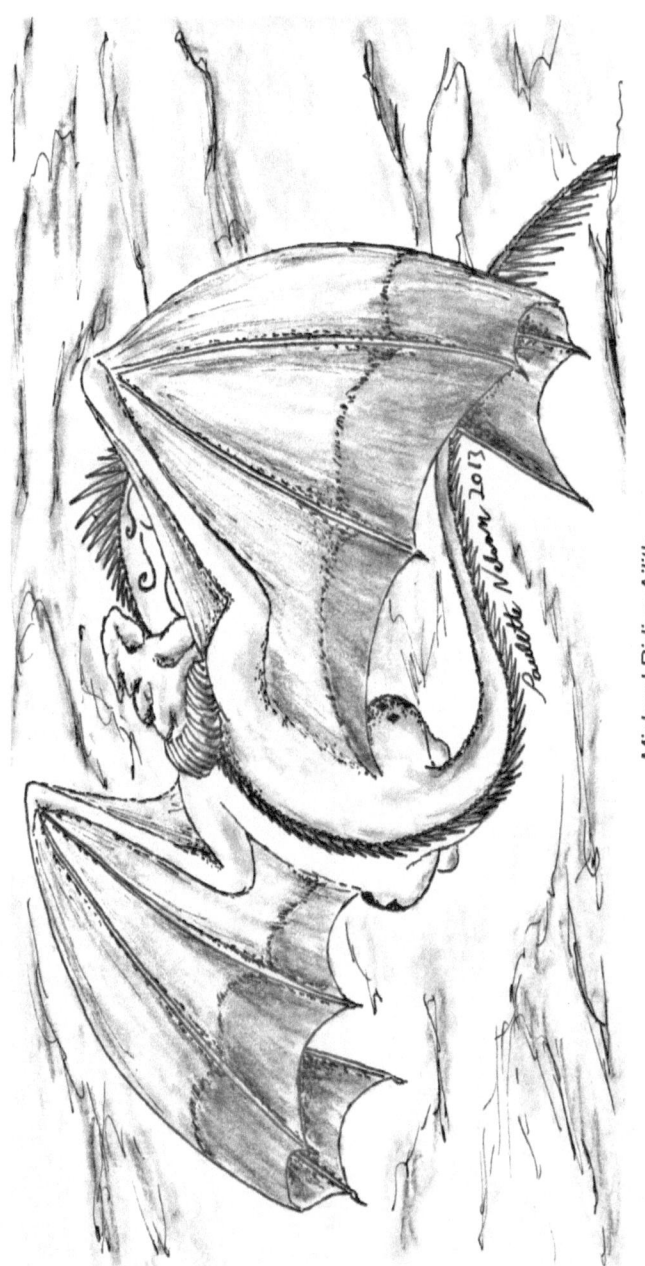

Michael Riding Ailith

caves, Madeline prepared for her first lessons in magic with Dr. Wombat. As excited as she was about finally learning magic, her mind still wandered. Would they find Rho before the Leohtian soldiers? Assuming they did, what would she say to her when they were face to face? And where was Gordon? He was already a week overdue. She assumed that Mr. Pufflehump would send Gordon here to the caves, with the unrest at the Manor. He would be implicated, just as she herself was. Ira would be unable to fend off the hundred or so flower hybrids in residence at the Manor.

Madeline had been correct. Ira had been unable to fend off the hybrids staying under his roof. What Ira hadn't told Madeline before they left that morning was that two of the new hybrids, Dottie Dill and Rosa Ramirez, had been found dead in their rooms. Suspicions fell to Madeline. Rumors of Madeline's revenge or the dark sorceress' involvement were rampant throughout the Guild, as such, many fled. Those that remained wanted justice. Their sights were set on Ira. In their opinions, he'd helped the wretched polyhybrid freak escape and now they wanted his blood.

He was losing the authority to carry out the rules of his own house. There was no other option left to him. He had to save the Pufflemals. He closed and locked the doors to his Pufflection. He pushed a series of buttons and pulled a couple of levers. This separated the estate into two pieces, a feature he'd added to the estate after the last re-making. The piece he was in was a virtual Noah's Ark — a cross between a large sailing ship and a Victorian-era submarine. Very steam punk, he reflected. He was sad to see his beautiful home torn apart, but it was necessary for him, his family and their few remaining friends to find a safe harbor. Maize and Iris would join him later, either tonight or tomorrow.

The Guild could fight about the balance of the estate, stand or fall; it was the end of Chelsea Manor as it was known. Those who had not allied themselves with their kin and their Gods would not survive this remaking. Ira was quite sure of that fact. They would go to Pickering Cross first. Gordon, a week overdue, must have been captured. He would have to see to the Book of Dreams himself. His ship hovered over the estate briefly and then made its way to the Red Admirals. "See to the safe passage of my wife and her confidante," he said to the Captain of the Guard. He was glad he had safely moved Madeline and her teacher earlier in the week. He'd hoped that the paranoia would have calmed down and a more sensible approach taken.

"Oh well," he sighed aloud. He'd taken Madeline to the safest place he could find for her right now.

+ + + +

Pearl slowly made her way amongst the Pufflemals, feeding and petting each little member of the troupe. Maize and Iris met her half way through the labyrinth of pens and corrals.

"How are you feeling today, Pearl?", asked Maize.

"Every day is a little better, thanks to you two," she weakly smiled. She'd also found that Dieter's unexpected company was helping her heal more quickly. He always did have a quick wit, she mused to herself. "But the nights are still difficult," she added.

"Are you still having nightmares?", asked Iris.

"I guess you could call them nightmares," she said. "Although my dreams feel different somehow, as if someone is trying to enter my mind and manipulate or remove my thoughts and dreams."

"It's probably the effects of the galraugs," said Iris.

"Most folks don't recover from their venom, especially not the dosage that you were exposed to. I think you can thank Madeline; she seems not only to have the ability to rehabilitate tissue, but to reanimate it as well. Not in the undead sense, as do the necromancers, but literally to create new life where old life had once existed."

"Especially when her hormones are active," said Maize. Pearl looked questioningly at the two women.

"Sorry, we don't mean to be rude, but the estate has been undergoing a bit of a transformation since Madeline's alliance with her friends, Gordon and Rho Dora," said Iris.

"With Gordon?", asked Pearl.

"Yes," said Iris.

"What's this about her ability to create new life?", she asked.

"It seems that when she is in the throws of — shall we say — passion, she has a habit of growing flowers, trees, and vines. So far, we haven't seen signs of new animals, but that remains to be seen," said Maize.

"That's interesting," Pearl said as she absentmindedly scratched the little pufflion cub that had been born just two weeks ago.

"You know that she's the first triple hybrid that has survived in the last one thousand years," said Maize.

"I figured as much," said Pearl. "Not since my sister...," she trailed off. Pearl gave the little lion cub one more scratch on the chin and said to the ladies,

"I'm feeling a bit tired, please excuse me. I think I need to lie down."

"Certainly," said Iris. "We can come by later and do some healing if you'd like."

"That would be nice," said Pearl. "Maybe a hot cup of tea as well?"

"That's easily accomplished," said Maize.

"Oh, and by the way," said Pearl as she stopped on her way out of the door. "Has there been any news about Gordon?"

"No, I'm afraid not," said Iris.

"Keep the faith," said Maize. "That boy seems to have a gambler's luck. He'll be alright."

"I'm sure you're right," said Pearl as she turned back towards the doorway. Her thoughts and worries were not only for her husband – of whom it had been too long since they'd seen each other – but also for her grandson, who she'd not seen since their arrival in Innes. Ben had told her that he'd had some troubles when he first arrived, but was currently doing okay. That news was a month old; the last time she'd seen any member of her family.

Speaking of family, her thoughts drifted to her sister, and, contrary to what everyone else was saying, she knew her sister to be alive. She could feel the twin tie, a tie that never went away no matter how far apart or how long since their last meeting. She'd kept that bit of information to herself. Her sister must have good reason for wanting others to think she was dead and gone. Three days ago, Ira had come to her rooms to warn her to stay within this section of the estate. He was reluctant to speak his mind even though she knew that a lot was going on.

Two days before that, she'd run into Rho and asked her why she was crying. She'd said something about getting caught speaking to Mortifera and that she was being banished from the estate. There was much for Pearl to catch up on, but, for now, she needed some rest. She stopped by the kitchen for cookies and tea and then made her way back to her rooms. A healing session would be really nice, she thought. Maybe she could figure out who's trying to tamper with her dreams.

16: Unknown Magic

Gordon hadn't been in touch with Ira for over a week. His injuries were far worse than he had originally considered and had kept him confined to his room for over four days. He sat at a window seat overlooking the street; three eggs and a thick slice of ham were placed before him, when the stranger he'd seen the week before at Lily's place came in to be seated for a meal. The tavern was busy and the only available seat was the one across from him. The server sat the man opposite Gordon, curtsied, and took his order. Gordon nodded towards the man in acknowledgment and started on his morning repast. He could tell that the man was watching him, trying to ascertain his strengths and weaknesses.

Gordon stuck out his hand in a gesture of friendship. "Name's Gordon," he said unceremoniously. He'd completely caught the man off guard by the gesture. Draedon had found most men rather boring and stupid, and with very little courage unless it was bolstered by money or alcohol. There was something different about this man, though. He would proceed with caution.

"I'm Draedon," he replied as he slipped his long, smooth hand in Gordon's large, calloused hand to complete the gesture. "What brings you to these parts?"

"Actually, I'm off course," Gordon replied. "I was headed for Dosk and was mugged in the night. The thieves scraped me up pretty badly and left me for dead.

Fortunately for me, a farmer found me and dropped me off here. I've been tending to my wounds for the last few days. Gordon had rolled his sleeves up prior to breakfast as it was his last clean shirt. The claw marks that the mage wolf had left on his back and forearms were still markedly noticeable. The gouge across his cheek and forehead had healed quicker it seemed. He figured the tailor had taken some extra time with the stitches so as to lessen the scars a bit.

"There will be scars," said Draedon. "It's a shame."

"How about you?", asked Gordon. "Are you from these parts?"

"No, I'm passing through, just like you."

"Where you from, if you don't mind me asking?", said Draedon. Gordon had considered this type of question and had decided he would say he was from Aquilegia Falls, in Leoht. He'd been there the one time and could describe the area well enough to satisfy most curiosities.

"I have a small farm in Leoht," replied Gordon. "How about you?"

"I'm from Deorc," said Draedon as the waitress put his breakfast on the table. Both men finished their meals in silence.

Upon completion, Gordon handed the waitress some cash, stood up and said to his table companion, "Well sir, it was a pleasure sharing such a fine meal with a gentleman. I must be going on my way as I still have a long journey ahead of me." Gordon shook his hand for the second time, his face not betraying what he knew to be true — that these were the hands of a bona fide killer. He slipped out of the door and made his way to the nearest clothier. He wanted a change of clothing as the ones he had on reeked of death.

Draedon, who found himself suddenly amiss, walked to the brothel across the street, picked out two ladies and climbed the staircase to a room. After an hour of being unable to perform, he slit the throats of both ladies, casually dressed himself, and silently left down the back stairs. He couldn't shake the picture of the man he'd shared breakfast with. What was his name ... Gordon? Right, Gordon. There was something about Gordon that shook Draedon to his foundation. He couldn't put his finger on it though. He walked up the street in the opposite direction of Gordon's choosing, his mind filled with all sorts of questions. He ducked into a tavern, and, while it was a little early, he needed some time to clear his thoughts.

"Whiskey, neat," he told the barkeep. There was something in the demeanor of that man, somehow uniquely familiar, as if he wasn't from Innes at all. He was from outside. He remembered the first time he'd met Will Tipton. He had that same demeanor, even though he'd been imprisoned for months. It was the certainty of their presence, adaptability, and courage.

That man, who'd sat across from him this very morning, was another piece of the puzzle, one of the very keys that Mortifera herself sought. He was certain, as certain as anything in his life. This man, Gordon, had mesmerized him, had prevented him from seeing the truth as they sat together and broke bread. What sort of magic did these outerworld humans possess? He'd lost the ability to study his first capture. Mortifera had trumped his ace, plus she'd already collected one and changed her for herself – like her own personal play toy. But he could play games too, especially high-stakes games. He knew some of the old legends.

There was one that was something about the six keys and the Book of Dreams, but he'd figured they'd meant actual keys, not some metaphor for keys. He needed some information. Maybe that old gnome that never left Emily's side could tell him a few things. He decided to return to Doerc, at least for now, to see what he could discover about the legends, and then set off for Dosk. Maybe he'd even visit the Queen; maybe the dungeons had tamed her somewhat. He was doubtful. He thrust his hands in his pockets and started towards the stables and his horse. He whistled a little ditty he'd heard somewhere. What was it called? He couldn't remember. He dismissed it and continued down the street with his goal clearly in mind.

+ + + +

Ben and Fiona sat at the edge of the woods for five days. They saw legions of men, Innesians, orcs, and other foul creatures disembarking from their winter headquarters. They'd spent several days travelling closely to the Obsidian Tower so they could avoid the bulk of the armies spread between the Bowerstein Brine and the Jahandi Wastelands. Ben had known of a town in the Wastelands where they would find a bed and a hot meal without too many questions. No one had seemed very interested in an old man and a young girl anyway.

As he lay in his bed, his thoughts turned to Pearl. He wondered how quickly she was healing; he shivered at the extent of her injuries; few recovered from the touch of a galraug. Their venom caused not only bodily injury but if left long enough, also corrupted their ultimate goal — the soul. He hadn't seen her for weeks and missed her terribly.

He'd grown accustomed to the conveniences in their other world. Simple things like a telephone could allow him stay in contact with his wife and rest more easily at night. He also found that he missed his truck and his recliner. I'm getting soft, he thought. He knew that success was important, and even though this was no longer his world, the continuation of his world relied on the continuation of Innes. He was, after all, almost eight hundred years old. His roots, his lifeblood, were based in Innes and so was his continued existence.

It was time for breakfast and their departure from the Wastelands into Dosk. It had been many years since his return to the home of his youth. He'd felt especially hungry this morning and was grateful when two table spaces opened for him and Fiona. He had a full view of the occupants of the dining hall and mindlessly scanned the diners as he waited for his breakfast.

The door opened and a cold breeze raced around the room, making many of the patrons shudder. He watched the exceedingly handsome young man be escorted to the other side of the room and seated across the table from a man hidden behind a newspaper. Ben's breakfast was placed in front of him, and the hostess asked if he wanted anything else. He thanked her and sent her away as he poured the syrup over his and Fiona's pancakes. The smell of the hickory-smoked bacon nearly drove him crazy as he stuffed an entire piece in his mouth. Fiona said very little, instead seeking solace in her buttery breakfast treats.

When Ben was finished with his breakfast, he returned his eye to the young man in black. He couldn't believe who he saw sitting across the table from this stranger. He was paying his bill and readying to leave.

Ben turned and said, "Come on Fiona, we have to go, now." She looked dismayed as she hadn't finished her breakfast, but she stuffed the remaining pieces of bacon into her coat pocket and jammed as much pancake into her mouth as possible. She grabbed her gear and followed Ben out the back door. Ben watched as the man walked onto the street and allowed him to gain some distance between them before following. He knew there would be watchful eyes near all of the inns and decided to play it safe. They followed the man for most of the day, coming nearer to the edge of the city and the wastelands. Fiona began to tire from the day of traipsing across the city. Ben decided he must make his move now, before she could go no further. He picked up the pace to close the distance between the two parties until he was standing beside the man.

"Oh, thank God, it is you," Ben said.

Gordon smiled and said, "I wondered when you were going to catch up." The two men laughed, embraced, and clapped each other on the back. Gordon winced.

"Sorry," said Ben, "but you have no idea how happy I am to see you."

"I think I can guess," Gordon replied. "And who is this?"

"I'd like you to meet my newly adopted granddaughter, Fiona Dunne."

"Pleased to meet you," said Gordon.

"Hi," said Fiona.

"Where you headed?", asked Ben.

"Dosk."

"So are we. Any thoughts about how you're going to get in?"

"Not yet," said Gordon. "We're going to have to use some unknown magic, that's for sure." He could hear the dice rattling in his mind again.

"Come on. Let's grab some dinner and see if we can arrive at a plan."

+ + + +

Bernie never knew such a place could exist. He'd seen plenty of horror movies on television, but nothing could prepare him for what he saw on the outskirts of the tower made of obsidian. The stacks of bodies that filled the moat had no smell because they were frozen solid under the biting cold that swirled down from high atop the JaMuto Mountains.

He pulled his collar higher in an attempt to lessen the ache that gnawed at the nape of his neck. John explained that these corpses would be reanimated by the necros, like the ones they ran into in the woods several days ago. John and his own sister, Fiona, had lain in and amongst those bodies, pretending to be dead, until they could make their own escape. Fortunately, we didn't have to do that, Bernie thought. I'm not sure I could have, he reluctantly admitted to himself as he felt the backlash of stomach acid burn his throat.

The sun never shone here; the oily blackness barely retreated under the gas-lit lamps that lined the streets. John Dunne moved in and out of the few shadows as deftly as a cat. How he'd learned to move like that Bernie didn't know, but he did find himself slightly jealous at this moment. In part, because he felt so obviously out of his comfort zone, everyone knew he didn't belong. But he also felt very old, and resented the lack of youthful agility, especially at such a crucial time. John stopped in a nondescript alley and peered around the sooty brick wall. Most of the tower guard were not in residence, having been shipped to the frontlines in Dosk. That was an unexpected benefit for the interlopers.

The residents of Deorc seemed to live very close to the margin, at least this section of town. John didn't want to move in the better neighborhoods. The likelihood of discovery was too great. Folks in these regions minded their own business; mostly they didn't want to become wraith fodder. While it was true that the wraith dined mostly on humans, they were not above the occasional Innesian, elf, or fairy, for that matter. It was mostly a matter of opportunity and appearance. It was bad business to consume your neighbors; besides, nobody really seemed to care much about humans, at least not in Deorc. So they became their regular food source.

Bernie's mind switched to an image of his daughter dining on some nice well-fed merchants who didn't provide the contracted services as outlined by some agreement. He turned to the wall and vomited the empty contents of his stomach. They hadn't stopped to eat since breakfast two days ago. Bernie could see how food nauseated John, but he still needed to eat.

"Wait here," said John. "I'll be right back. A few minutes later John returned with biscuits and a chunk of cheese.

"Thank you, John," he said and offered John a biscuit.

"No, thanks," he said. "I seem to have lost my taste. But I do need to eat," he said. "Wait here. I should be back within the hour."

"Okay," said Bernie, who settled himself behind several empty beer barrels. He'd rather smell the stale hops and yeast than the cold clamminess of death. The biscuits and cheese tasted like a gourmand had spent hours preparing them. He dug around in the boxes that sat next to the empty kegs and found a full bottle of beer. He leaned back against the wall with a sated stomach and closed his eyes. He awoke an hour later, John sitting on the stoop next to him waiting for him to awaken.

"You ready?", he asked. Bernie scratched behind his ear.

"Yeah, I guess so."

"I was in the Tower," said John.

Bernie sat upright, "Did you see Emily?"

"No," he said with true remorse in his voice. "But I can take you to her. This will be the best time as Mortifera and Belac are not at the Tower. They frequently like to hunt in the northern lands. But we must hurry. There's no telling how long they'll be away, and you must see your daughter and then leave, NEVER to come back. Agree, or else I'll leave you right here." Bernie could tell that John was firm in his resolve. "You cannot be here in the final phase. This is not your place. Go back to your friends in the south. Take care of your other children and my sister. In return, I will take care of Emily – with my life, if need be." He looked long and hard at Bernie. "Do we have a deal?"

Bernie hesitated a moment more. "Yes. But I must see her at least once, and then I'll honor our agreement." Bernie hoped he could go through with it when the time came. He figured John had some plan in case he faltered and went back on his word. He was glad that John Dunne was on their side, on Emily's side. Belac definitely erred in underestimating this young man. Bernie thought that Belac would pay dearly for that mistake.

"You promise to take care of Fiona as if she was your own?", John asked.

"Yes," said Bernie. "And if you find yourself clear of this mess and can leave this horrible place, you will be as my own son." A small red tear rolled down John Dunne's pallid cheek.

"I think I would like that," he said. "It's time to go. Now!", he said as he stood and walked to the alley's end.

17: Finding Rho Dora

Nate had it on good authority that Rho Dora had veered into the swamps where the Sidneys played war games. He carefully managed Arion through the difficult swamp, trying to track Rho's movements through the endlessly shifting environment. The dense Spanish moss trailed from the ancient cypress trees and passed through Nate's hair and over his shoulders, making him feel itchy all over.

He could hear a low monotonous sound coming from somewhere over his left shoulder and tried to turn Arion in the direction of the sound. Whatever it was, must be keeping a distance between it and Nate, for he could hear the cries, but never got any closer to the maker. He'd become so engrossed in finding the creature that he'd forgotten his main task – to find the girl. He was quite surprised when he came upon a beautiful purple human flower hybrid standing at the water's edge drinking through her toes.

Aside from Madeline, he hadn't seen any other flower hybrids. He supposed their varieties were only limited by the varieties of flowering plants that existed. She was really beautiful but in a haunted sort of way. Her skin looked like translucent white paper with a purple hue. He wondered if that changed with the lighting. He dismounted from Arion as quietly as he could, considering the shifting sod clumps. He led Arion to the water's edge so he could drink, and slowly edged his way towards the girl. He fully expected her to run when she caught sight of him. She didn't let his expectations down. She gasped and turned to flee deeper into the swamp. Fortunately, the Sidneys had also expected her retreat, and flanked her from the sides and rear to prevent her escape. She collapsed onto the narrow trail and began sobbing uncontrollably.

"I didn't mean for any of this to happen," she cried. "I had no choice. She would have tortured and killed my mother. Please don't hurt me," she wailed.

Nate stood in front of her, "Please, I'm not going to hurt you. Ira asked me to look for you."

"It's a trick," she squealed. "You just want to take me to the horrible dungeons in Leoht." Nate laughed at that.

"What's so funny?", she snapped. "You think that me sitting in a jail cell is funny?"

"No, I guess not. But at least you've stopped that horrible caterwauling." She laughed in spite of herself.

"Are you telling me the truth?", she asked.

"Yes," he replied. "What could I possibly gain by lying to you?"

"A reward?", she countered.

"Is there a reward for your capture?", he asked innocently.

"I'm sure there must be," she said. "The women of the Guild had me out as the worst human being in Innes."

"Are you?", asked Nate.

"No!", she replied annoyed once again. "You do like to provoke, don't you?", she said. Nate laughed again.

"My grandmother used to say, I liked to needle her. Did you meet my grandmother, Pearl Sutton, when you were living at Chelsea Manor?", asked Nate.

"She was injured very badly," said Rho gravely. "For many months only Gordon and Madeline were allowed to see her. But shortly before I was asked to leave, I saw her ambling through the gardens. She was definitely healing. Madeline told me the galraug had almost completely sucked out her soul and that your grandmother fought not only for her body but also to recapture her essence: her dreams, goals, fears, and desires; everything that made her who your grandmother was, is, and will become."

"I had no idea," said Nate. "My grandfather said very little. I guess he didn't want to worry me."

"At least she's feeling better," said Rho. An awkward silence hung between them, neither one knowing what to say to the other. Sidney gold-foot landed on Nate's shoulder.

"Where are you going to take her?", he asked.

"I'm not really sure," he replied. "I know Madeline is crazy worried about her. I could take her back to the warren," as Nate had come to commonly call it.

"But what about the other?", Sidney pink nose asked cryptically.

"You know I'm sitting right here in front of you. You can talk to me directly," she said.

"Oooh, she's a little spit-fire," said Sidney brown socks.

"That, she is," laughed all of the Sidneys.

"I think we should take Rho to meet her. She's waiting in the meditation grove," said Sidney gold foot.

"Ailith says we need to find her before Pettiman's soldiers do," said Sidney brown socks.

"Well, then, let's go and fulfill our destiny, shall we?" Nate lifted Rho atop Arion. He didn't have a pack horse, so they'd have to ride double. It suited him just fine. They travelled well into the day, stopping only briefly to stretch their legs and for a quick bite to eat. Finally, they came into a small clearing amidst a dense grove of old-growth oaks. The ground was firmer and easier to stand on.

"I think we'll make camp here," said Nate. He

started to build a suitable fire to cook a light supper. Rho wandered to an interesting-looking rock outcropping and climbed to the top. She had little scenic advantage on the top of the rock but instead found a comfortable flat surface to lie down on. She looked into the fading blue sky and imagined herself flying atop her imaginary dragon, Wynn.

She'd never really had much control over events in her life. She was born into slavery, her backyard the Obsidian Tower courtyard. By the time she was seven, she helped the washer women hang the sheets on the long drying lines. While there was never any light in the land of Deorc, they did have lovely cool summer breezes from the north.

She was very pretty, her waist-length black hair liberally curled in all the right places. She was not just pretty. She was beautiful. And as such, Mortifera had taken a great interest in her long before she was sent to penetrate the Women's Guild. Mortifera used to ply her with treats to get her to answer questions about what the servants were saying and doing. She thought it was a normal part of life to report the goings-on of the castle staff.

When she was told to report the operations of the Guild, she thought that was normal. However, she met Madeline early in her tenure at Chelsea Manor. This changed her opinion of what she considered to be back-wash folks. The fact that she had fallen in love with Madeline was unexpected and had definitely grayed the areas of conflict.

"Is it true that you're a spy for Mortifera?", he blurted out as Nate climbed to the top of the rock and sat down beside her.

"You don't waste any time on the niceties do you," she retorted.

"I was curious, that's all," he said. "What's it like

in Deorc? I mean, I know it's a big question, but is it all scary like the stories say?"

"Yes," she answered gravely. "That and more." He sat back on his elbows and sucked on a piece of grass that he'd picked on his way up the hilltop.

He thought for a long moment before he said, "I never knew my parents. They died when I was little."

"I'm sorry," she said. "Have you ever been faced with a situation where no answer seemed to be the right answer? And no matter how hard you tried to figure it differently, the option presented seemed the only way."

She paused briefly. "That was what happened to me. I didn't want to spy for Mortifera. I hate her. But what was I to do?", she asked.

"Do you believe your mother's in trouble now?", asked Nate.

"I suspect she's already been put to death," she said as she started to cry. Nate put his arm around her shoulder for comfort and support. "Thank you," she sniffled. They sat like that until Nate excused himself to stir the cook pot.

"You know that you can't run forever. Sometime you're going to have to face the charges. I know, because I had to face them myself when I killed Serpentia."

"You killed Serpentia?"

"Yeah, and I had to face the penalty of death, too. It seems I'd broken some forbidden law by setting the Sidneys free."

"Obviously, the mess was resolved," she said.

"What makes you say that?", asked Nate.

"Because, you're sitting here."

He laughed. "Yeah, there was a happy ending for me. And maybe there'll be one for you too."

He handed her a plate. "Hope it's okay." They sat in silence eating their meal. The woods seemed silent, as well, with the exception of a constant moaning noise coming from somewhere close to their path.

"What is that noise?", said Nate. Rho set off into the trees to find the source. The full moon hung low in the sky, casting an otherwordly light into the thicket of trees. She could tell she was getting closer to the creature that was groaning. She jumped when Nate came up behind her so quietly. She never heard him coming.

"What is that?", he asked. He could barely see a shape through the trees.

"I don't know. Let's get closer," she said. They stole through the trees, quietly stalking their prey. They were less than ten feet away when Rho realized what she was looking at.

She gasped, "Wynn?" The dragon turned its head towards her and called.

"Was that a sound of relief?", asked Nate. She walked towards the creature.

"She's beautiful," said Rho. The pale-yellow feathered pearlescent wings matched the thick furry underbelly. Her long body and long neck had a furry dark-green background with contrasting light-green tiger stripes. The antlers and long legs made her appear deer-like.

"She looks nothing like Ailith," said Nate. "But I'm certainly no expert on dragons. I thought they were from fairy tales until I came to Innes." Rho scratched her neck and petted her body. Wynn nuzzled Rho's neck and rubbed herself against Rho's body just like a cat. What a strange-looking animal, thought Nate.

"See if she'll follow us back to our campsite," said Nate. Rho led the dragon to their campsite. It didn't seem to mind Arion, as the beast curled its legs under its body and lay down next to the fire.

"She seems to have that in common with Ailith," said Nate. He waited until they had finished their meal and settled in for the night. "I think we should go to the caves tomorrow."

Rho, who had curled up next Wynn, said: "I'm sure no one will want to see me — Rho the traitor."

"I wouldn't be so sure of that. Madeline was pretty broken up, and what with still no word from Gordon, she's been frantic. The only thing keeping her together is her magic studies, and, well, Michael too, I'm sure."

"Do you hate me, Nate?", she asked.

"Hate you? How can I hate you? I don't even know you. Besides, Madeline thinks pretty highly of you, and she's usually a good judge of character."

"But what if she's wrong? What if I am that horrible traitor of the Guild accusations?"

"Somehow, I don't think so. I can't see how your dream would have come true. Remember, Belac and Mortifera are wraith ... blood suckers ... vampires ... leeches ... whatever you want to call them. Ultimately, they suck you dry and then steal your soul, but not before they've tortured you by stealing your dreams. You did what you had to do to survive. I don't see how someone can fault you for that." She looked at him through the firelight,

"You are a good friend. I can see that. I can also see why you and Gordon are best friends."

Wynn

Paulette Nelson
2013

18: Onager

"We have to get through Dosk," said Ben. "There must be twenty thousand soldiers spread across the Deorcian plain and the Jahandi Wastelands." They could see the Dark Armies slowly gaining ground from the Leohtian soldiers and allies. Hordes of dark allies collided with the mounted riders, the sounds of metal clashing along with blood-curdling screams from rider and horse alike could be heard for miles. They had been unsuccessfully trying to skirt the battle for most of the day. They watched as more dark recruits – trolls, orcs, and goblins, streamed in from the northern provinces.

"How are we going to cross?", asked Gordon. "I can't see a way."

"We're going to have to try to cross it tonight when everyone is asleep," said Ben. "We have no other choice. John Dunne was very clear in his desire to have Fiona in the salt marshes of Peddleton Prow."

"What's up with that?", asked Gordon.

"I'm not entirely sure," said Ben. "But I have a theory."

"We should get some rest if we're going to try this crossing tonight," said Gordon.

"I'd like to go further to the north to see if we can lessen our possibility of interaction," said Ben. "One more day of travel should help. They won't be expecting the carriers of light to be hiding in the depths of Deorc. It's our best chance. Let's rest here," said Ben. "We'll get an early start tomorrow." The travellers passed a chilly night on the damp forest floor.

They ate a cold breakfast of nuts and apples then started towards the northern borders of Doerc. They stayed in the darkness choosing to skirt the ever-grey lighting of Dosk.

"Gordon, you've not said why you're travelling to Dosk," challenged Ben when they stopped for lunch.

"I'm not really supposed to discuss it," said Gordon. "I'm on a mission for Ira. But I'm several weeks overdue and I'm not even sure if...."

"If your mission is still valid?"

"Well, yeah. I was thinking that."

"Why don't you go back to the Manor and find out."

"I was meaning to ask you a few questions," said Gordon.

"Shoot," said Ben.

"I was wondering if you have any experience with one of these?" He pulled the flashlight-type wand from his pocket.

"A flashlight?", asked Ben.

"No, it's some kind of a wand that Ira loaned to me. It allows me to travel from one place to another instantly."

"I've heard about them, although I've personally never seen one. It's kind of light isn't it, a bit deceiving," said Ben. "So what's the problem? Why don't we use this to get us into Peddleton Prow?", he asked as he turned it over while inspecting it.

"Well... that is what I wanted to ask you about. Michael said to me that these wands are made by a mage and that sometimes the mage's image or character stays with the instrument."

"That may be true, but so what? It's not like the mage is in the wand, right?", asked Ben.

"I'm not so sure," said Gordon as he showed Ben the still-healing scars on his arms and back.

"I was wondering about them," said Ben. "It's not usual for a man to scrap with a wild animal. I'm assuming these are claw marks."

"That's just it," said Gordon. "When I was coming here I used the wand and was attacked by a big wolf. I mean a BIG wolf. I've never seen anything like it."

"Is that the first time you used the wand?", asked Ben.

"No, it was like the fourth or fifth. But each time the encounters get worse, until I had to fight with him this last time."

"Have you noticed any differences in yourself?", asked Ben.

"What do you mean?", asked Gordon. "Do you mean like am I becoming a werewolf or something? That's only on TV."

"I would think by now you'd have realized that you're in the land of fantasy and anything, and I mean anything, is possible. You'd do best not to forget it."

"I don't think I'm becoming a werewolf. But, I guess we'll find out soon enough because tonight's the full moon."

"If you are, remember we're your family. Go and whoop some Orc butt, okay."

"Okay," agreed Gordon. Both men laughed. Fiona continued to walk ahead in silence. "The kid doesn't say much, does she?", asked Gordon.

"It's gotta be tough for her," said Ben. "The likelihood of her ever seeing her brother again is pretty small, and even if she did, he's so far into the change to wraith, I'm not sure he wouldn't eat her for dinner."

"Has there been any news of Emily?", asked Gordon.

"Fiona's brother, John, is taking Bernie to the tower. He supposedly knows where she's being kept. It's gonna be hard for him, though, as he's gonna have to leave her behind."

"Why?"

"John says that they have plans to interrupt, shall we say, the reign of the Wraith. I don't know what that means necessarily. But, I have it on good authority that she doesn't want to see her family due to the change. I saw a sprite by the name of Ing, who talked with her several weeks ago in Kuhnston Derry. She told Ing that she did what she had to do and there was no undoing it. It's a heavy burden to bear to think that there's no possibility for redemption, especially for one as young as she is. You and she are about the same age, aren't you?"

"Yeah," said Gordon. "I think she's a year younger than Nate, Will, and me. Speaking of which, I wonder what's happened to Will? Nate said that he saw him several months ago, in Dosk with that fellow in black, what was his name ... I can't think of it."

"Draedon," said Ben.

"Yeah, that's it. Nate said he looked like a real Romeo, if you know what I mean. Can't say as I blame him, there are some real pretty girls in Innes," Gordon laughed. "I met a real nice girl a couple of days ago. She was real nice, took care of me just fine, until that fellow, Draedon, showed up. Next thing I know, her inn is up in smoke. With her in it, I'm assuming. I had breakfast with him the day before you and I ran into each other."

"Yeah, I saw that," said Ben.

"You did? Why didn't you say anything?"

"I am now," said Ben. "Besides it didn't come up until just now."

"Shhhh!", said Fiona.

"What?", asked Gordon.

"Be quiet," she said. They could see she was squatting down behind a copse of trees ahead of them.

She signalled for them to get down and then pointed further down the path.

"What is that stench?", whispered Gordon.

"It looks like we found part of their undead army. I thought they were coming out of Necromancer's Notch, not the JaMuto Mountains," said Ben. They've must have been travelling for weeks. The JaMuto Mountains are at least four hundred miles from here."

"What the hell, Ben. Are they zombies?"

"Yeah."

"Being in Innes is like living inside a video game. Only this one doesn't have a reset button or endless lives."

"That pretty well describes living in a fantasy. The Book of Dreams rewrites itself all the time, differently for each person of course. We all experience a certain level of the same experiences, the trees and grass and such, but even that can be tailored to the one who is experiencing. Consider the purple polka-dotted trees found in Dagung. They evolved as a result of someone's imagination."

"Why is the book threatened? Ira told me that its very existence is threatened."

"The Dream Stealers are the biggest threat to the book's continuance. If no one has dreams or hopes or imagination, the book suffers and so does the land of fantasy."

"How do I know I'm not part of this fantasy," asked Gordon. "It seems that by all rights I shouldn't really exist unless someone else dreamed of me."

"Well, in a way, your parents did. They dreamed of a child, got a son, and named him Gordon. Your role in Innes is something else entirely. But don't ever question your existence. It is the molding of the dream that allows for circumstance to unfold."

"Will you two please be quiet," said Fiona, who

seemed to have more sense than either of her two guardians. "There is a small pack of zombies not more than two hundred feet away and you two are talking about the philosophy of fantasy. Can we please go around them?" She turned as if to go deeper into the woods, a path opened through the densely treed forest.

Fortunately for them, they were able to elude the undead soldiers. They were ill prepared for hand-to-hand battle, having no knives or guns or magic to stop the zombie band from turning them into zombies themselves. When they had travelled more than a mile from the rotting corpses, Fiona turned and said," You two are supposed to be my protectors, maybe we can be a little bit more careful in the future."

"Very grown up," said Ben.

"Yeah," agreed Gordon. "Very grown up." It took five more days of cautious travel for them to cross into Peddleton Prow. Fiona instantly set a course for the coast. It was as if she knew exactly where she was supposed to go.

"Have you ever been here before Fiona?"

"No, Ben, I haven't. But I can hear Onager calling my name."

"Who's Onager?", asked Gorgon.

"A dragon," said Ben.

"I've only ever heard about her. I've never seen her," said Fiona.

"I thought she was dead by all accounts. There hasn't been a dragon sighting in many hundreds of years, before Ailith that is," said Ben.

"Ailith found her," said Fiona, "wandering senselessly through the swamps of Peddleton Prow. She has apparently lost her way, a type of insanity or something. We have to find her before it's too late.

My brother says she is my destiny. I'm not so sure, but I guess we'll find out soon enough."

"We'd better stay close together," said Ben. "A dense coastal fog seems to be settling over us and I don't want to spend the rest of eternity searching for one of you." Gordon pulled a length of rope from his pack, "This will be long enough to tie us together."

"Fiona first, as she seems to know where we're going, but choose your footsteps carefully. These back-water estuaries are known for quicksand, and I don't want to end up at the bottom of one."

"Did anyone think to bring bug spray?", asked Gordon who was already scratching the welts left by the greenhead flies.

"It doesn't do any good anyway," said Ben. "They seem to like the taste." Both men laughed. Fiona stopped suddenly.

"What's up kiddo," asked Ben. She was pointing to something that was about twenty feet to her left.

The group walked a little closer when Fiona turned and said, "Please stay here." She untied herself and walked towards the dazzling blue dragon. She was perched on an old tree that had fallen into the water. Fiona purred Onager's name as she walked closer to the spectacular beast who was considerably larger than Fiona's five foot frame. She extended her wings from underneath the hard exoskeleton. They heard Fiona gasp as the Sapphire Dragon of Dosk introduced herself. Fiona walked out onto the petrified tree to reach for the dragon. The beast had a stunning sapphire blue and pure white exoskeleton and large saucer-like black eyes. The top of Fiona's head came roughly to the dragon's shoulder.

"She kind of looks like a hornless triceratops without the big neck skirt," said Ben. Fiona led her off the tree and onto solid ground. She patted her tough hide as she walked around the creature a full three hundred and sixty degrees.

"Can you fly?", asked Fiona. The dragon nodded its head yes.

"Gordon, can I have your rope, please?", asked Fiona.

"Sure, why not."

"Do you think this is wise, Fiona?", asked Ben.

"Look. You two were on different missions before we met. I think you should go back to your missions and I'll tend to mine. Besides, I couldn't be any safer. Onager and I are bound for life, before, now, and later as well. She's much longer lived than I'll ever be, so she just waits and pines until I'm reborn and old enough to find her again."

"You two have done this before, then," said Ben.

"Yes," she answered. "I remember now."

"Oh," said Gordon who was not really sure what else to say.

"I think she can carry all three of us out of the marshes and then we can decide what's to be done, okay?"

"I like that option much better," said Ben. "Fiona Dunne, rider of the Sapphire Dragon. It has a nice ring." The three climbed on top of the previously exiled dragon, she spread her wings, and lifted them well above the salt marshes of Peddleton Prow.

"She's going to need to eat soon," said Fiona.

"What does she like to eat?", asked Gordon who was sitting right behind her.

"She tells me that she's fond of deer, when she can catch one. It's more difficult than it might sound," she says. "She'd really rather eat fish and is a surprisingly good swimmer."

"Turn her towards the ocean," said Gordon. "Then she can catch a proper meal, and maybe even a little bit for us. I'd love to have a piece of fresh fish," he said, as he drooled a little. "I didn't realize how hungry I

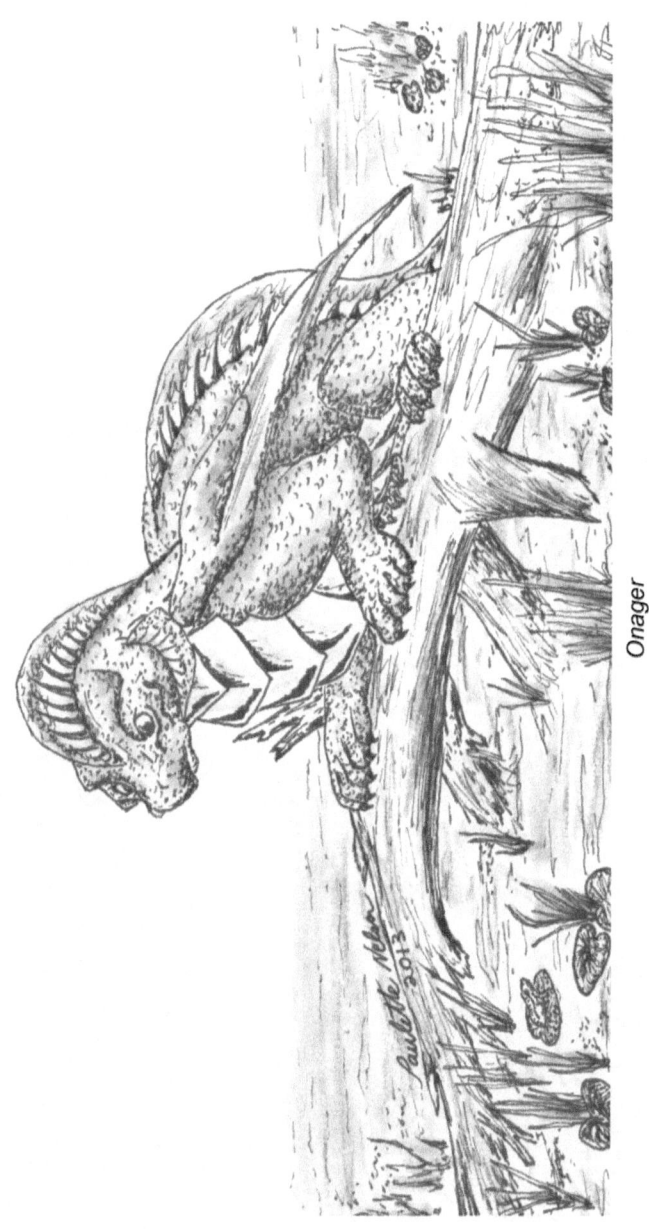

Onager

was, sorry". The travellers had a roaring fire ablaze when Onager returned a few minutes later with a fish of considerable size. Gordon cut off enough for the three of them and then fed the rest to Onager, who was only too grateful to have her fish returned. She waddled down the beach about a hundred yards and then ravaged the rest of her fish. She returned to the water a couple of times before her hunger was satiated, then curled up into a ball and basked in the afternoon sun for several hours.

"What can you tell me about Pickering Cross?", asked Gordon.

"What's in Pickering Cross," Ben asked. Gordon watched as Fiona walked towards Onager; her interest in the two men waned as soon as lunch was finished.

"I need to get there as soon as possible," said Gordon. Ben looked up from poking at their beach fire.

"Once upon a time I could have told you a lot about the territory. I haven't been back in almost seven hundred years."

"How old are you, anyway?", asked Gordon. "You and Pearl are ageless and yet you talk about time and age in a way I can't begin to understand. And I thought Ira was old."

"Gordon, in this world, fantasy IS reality. There is no separation."

"Why isn't it like this at home?", he asked innocently.

"Because people lose the ability to imagine as they get older. Not everyone, mind you — we still have hold-outs. But most folks get caught in their day-to-day lives and trade their free will for the comforts of industrialization — the automaton. Remember Gordon, when you give away your ability to think for yourself and accept the responsibility for your choices you become the fodder that fuels the automaton and its interest in, first your flesh, then your soul. That is the Way of Wraith. An industrialized, homogenous lifestyle surrounded by blood, lust, and violence."

"WOW!", exclaimed Gordon. "I had no idea. To me fantasy was just a bunch of stories my mom used to read to me when I was a little kid."

"There is a famous British band that released a piece of music called … let me think a minute … yes, that's it … Welcome to the Machine by Pink Floyd. They masterfully disclosed the basis of The Way of the Wraith."

"Will you two please stop talking about the Wraith. You're upsetting Onager," scolded Fiona.

"She will have to learn and soon," said Ben. "We are in desperate times. War is upon us. We must fight the darkness, each in our own way."

"She knows, but she wants to enjoy the last couple of days without the thought of Wraith, if possible." Ben acquiesced.

"How close are we to Pickering Cross?", asked Gordon.

"What's in Pickering Cross?", asked Ben.

"I'm not really supposed to say anything, but …," Gordon paused. "I think Ira would be okay with me sharing my task with you. I'm supposed to find the Book of Dreams and bring it to Ira. He's been collecting all of these items that somehow relate to the book."

"What kind of things?", asked Ben.

"I've collected a special pair of glasses, an old-style feathered quill and ink well, an old leather case, several books from Dagung, a book mark, and two women so far."

"Two women?", asked Ben.

"Yeah, in the fancy part of the ghetto," said Gordon. "I'm not really sure what that was all about, but the one was really nice. I took them to a farm in Leoht."

"Maybe Ira was returning a favor," said Ben.

"Yeah, I thought that at first, but then it seemed there was something more to it. I can't really put my finger on it, and Ira wasn't forthcoming in explanations. Not that he really owes me any, but these missions of his have been getting more dangerous, as you can see."

"Back to the book," said Ben. "How does Ira expect you to move the book?"

"I'm not sure. I thought it was just a book, like any other," said Gordon.

"Not at all," said Ben.

"You know of this book then?", asked Gordon.

"Yes, I do," said Ben. "Ira must think that the very book itself is in danger. This is far worse than I thought."

"What is the book?", asked Gordon.

"It's a long story, Gordon. But I will tell you this much: Once upon a time, the Book of Dreams was just that, a book. After a thousand years of existence, it has evolved into something much more than a well-written book. It has become the heart of all existence in Innes and by default our world as well. The book has remade itself twice since its inception, from growing pains you might say. This time it is different."

"Why?", asked Gordon who was plainly distracted by Fiona who was throwing a stick for her dragon.

"Gordon, this is serious business."

"Yeah, I know, sorry. I've never seen a dragon play catch before. It's a little unnerving," he said. "So the book has magical properties?", he asked, trying to return his attention to the discussion.

"I guess you could say that. It has the power to manifest thought and imagination. You might say it's the power behind the light bulb, so to speak. How did Edison come up with the idea of a light bulb, or Ford, with the Model T? They dreamt, imagined, fantasized, and then worked from sunup to sundown to put their dreams on paper and then into shape and form. That is the world as we know it. Someone dreamt of this coastline, and here it was, same with the purple polka-dotted trees and curly pink sea grasses."

"So why is the book itself in jeopardy?", asked Gordon. "It seems that it should be able to take care of itself."

"It's true that there were a few fail safes written into the bylaws, and they have allowed the book to flourish into the magnificent tree of life these last thousand years. The problem now is a problem of wraith. Belac decided many years ago that he was going to recast the book into his own image, and thus the entirety of Innes by stealing people's thoughts and dreams. I suspect that is why the dragons are coming forth after all these years of inactivity. Based on her own words, Fiona was bound to Onager before her birth. I suspect it's much the same with Michael."

"What do you mean, 'bound'?", asked Gordon.

"Think of it sort of like soul mates. They're destined or bound together. I'm sure there is a certain level of free will, as much as any of us have for that matter. In this case, their destinies are intertwined, for eternity. Only some very, and I mean very, powerful magic can break the bond once it's in place. I hope that Belac hasn't found out that the dragons have risen, it may be our ace in the hole. I'm going to get Fiona to fly to Michael's cave. Hopefully, the forest will hide Onager's reemergence, for at least a little while longer. In the meantime, let's see if she will drop us off in Pickering Cross."

"Are you coming with me?", asked Gordon.

"Yes," said Ben.

"You don't have to. I figured you'd fly back with

Fiona."

"I have a personal interest in the book," said Ben. "Someday, I'll tell you about it."

"Onager has been speaking with Ailith," said Fiona. "We're going to the cave."

"Drop us at Pickering Cross," said Ben. Fiona nodded her consent. "She actually seems happy," said Ben. "For the first time since she was split from her brother."

"Let's go," said Fiona. "We have a lot of ground to cover."

"Yeah, you should be hidden in the Devil's Hole forest by first light," said Ben.

"Let's be on our way, then," said Gordon.

19: Impossible Interludes

"Father! What are you doing here?"

"Turn around Emily. Let me see your face."

"I'm sorry, Father. I can't do that. I'm too ashamed."

"Emily, listen to me. I'm your father and I love you no matter what you think of yourself. Now turn around and look at me." There was a knock at the door.

"Pick up that tray," she hissed. "You must act like a servant. Keep your head down and your eyes averted." The knock came again. "Yes," said Emily. The door opened, and to her dismay in walked Draedon. He had liked the idea of their imminent marriage and had been following her everywhere twenty-four, seven. She found him most distasteful, worse than a mouthful of lemons. But something inside her told her that he was a very dangerous man, and she didn't want to be on the wrong side of his mood swings.

"Is everything all right in here, darling?", he asked as he glared daggers at Emily's father. "Is this servant giving you troubles?", he asked.

"No," she said, as she waved her hand in a dismissing gesture. The man nodded his head and carried the silver tray and chalice through the open doorway. "I'll see that you get better servants," he said.

"No, he was fine. You worry about me too much," she said. "I have the best of everything anything a girl could want or need. Really, Mother is very generous and sees to my needs."

"Soon you'll be my wife and I'll be seeing to your needs."

"Yes, my love, that is true," she said as she lightly kissed his cheek. Fortunately, she'd just fed because mother wouldn't be happy if she ate her husband-to-be.

"Do you mind if I lie down. I'm feeling tired and I would like to take a nap."

"Certainly," said Draedon. "I'll sit with you if you'd like?"

"Thank you for your concern," she said once again.

"It's not necessary. I just need a short time for myself." She had to get rid of him. She wanted to see her father again before she sent him away, forever. The thoughts of never seeing her family struck like a bolt of lightening. She'd thought somewhere deep inside that maybe she'd get to see her family; against all odds, she thought maybe the universe would forgive her and lead her to redemption. Since she had been in Deorc, she had learned to kill. Mercilessly and without compunction she had taken the lives of over a hundred humans, some for food, some for her magical studies, and some solely for Mortifera's pleasure of torture.

Her magic skills had grown considerably; much of her knowledge incorporated the left-handed path — the dark arts. She hadn't seen much of Will, especially since Draedon's return. In many ways their impending marriage was a death sentence for Emily. The date was looming closer, and Emily hated the thoughts of marriage, of Draedon, of Deorc. She'd seen and participated in devastation and chaos, all as a matter of fact. She was repulsed by her own actions but never asked for forgiveness. She knew that none would be granted.

Now, at the worst possible time, her real father appears. How could he have even found out where she was, let alone be HERE, in the flesh. She had cried for weeks, longing to go home, and wanting to see her parents. So much time had passed, that she'd talked herself out of ever seeing them again. She was a monster now. There would be no happy homecoming for her, no balloons, no whistles, and no party streamers. She would live with her treachery. When the opportunity presented itself, however, she would enact her vengeance.

In the meantime, she would wait and learn and bide her time. She would marry this horrible creature, Draedon, because it was required of her. While her true love resided down the hall from her, learning the ways of wraith, she would marry the assassin. This time there were no tears; this was a woman's resolve bound by a woman's fomenting scorn.

++++

Will didn't like that he'd seen so little of Emily. He was certain they were being kept apart intentionally. He looked at the calendar on his desk. The wedding was only a month away. Mortifera had wanted the wedding by the equinox, but Draedon's continued reluctance had thrown her schedule off. Will was glad of it, but the last few weeks Draedon told a different story – that he'd marry Emily to appease his mother.

"I care little for the creature," he confided one day while sitting in Will's study. "But it seems so important to my mother. I just don't understand the big deal."

"Why don't you leave Deorc for a month or two? I thought you had a love interest in the Jahandi Wastelands."

"I did," he said. "But, I had to kill her. I found out that she had lain with another man the very morning I was going to ask her to marry me. I couldn't forget that. So I killed her and burned her inn to the ground."

"A little melodramatic wouldn't you say?", replied

Will, whose eyes were affixed to his nightly studies."

"What would you have done?", he asked.

"I wouldn't have killed her. If I killed every girl who disappointed me, there would be very few girls remaining at my old high school."

"Have you ever killed anyone before?", asked Draedon.

"Not before coming to the Obsidian Tower, no," he replied.

"How does it feel when you do kill someone?", asked Draedon.

"Do you mean, do I like killing?", asked Will. "If that's your question, then no, I don't like killing. But, I get so hungry that I don't really have the choice anymore."

"So you think that you kill just to sate your hunger?"

"Yes," said Will.

"Well, I kill for much the same reason, although I don't eat my query. But I do get paid handsomely and I don't really care one way or another whether my targets live or die. It's inconsequential to me. But, I don't take any great joy in killing. We're both predators," said Draedon. "We just have different goals."

"I thought Belac was going to turn you," said Will.

"He was, but I talked him out of it."

"You did? Why on earth would you do that?", asked Will.

"I'm much more useful in my human form. Once a wraith, I can only roam in the darkness. I'm not ready to give up the light yet."

"That's treason," said Will.

"Not for the best assassin in Innes," Draedon gloated, as he swung his leg over the arm of the chair.

"It has been my purpose far too long to abandon it so readily."

"So you really do like your work … like killing," said Will.

"I guess when you put it that way, I do," he replied, as he scratched two day's hair growth on his chin. He rarely was unshaven and suddenly decided that he liked the look. The lack of mirrors in the castle was a bit of a nuisance, especially for someone as narcissistic as Draedon. He constantly fussed with his hair and clothing to make sure he was neat and tidy. He hated it when people were dirty and unkempt. They were only slightly above the vermin that ate his crumbs and lived in the sewers.

"The 'Way of Wraith' is very clear on the issue of predator and prey. There are those that eat, and those that are eaten," said Will. "But I'm not sure why only humans and the rare fairy or elf are eaten. Why not an Innesian? There's no clear answer on this question."

"Don't you know that Innesians are alien?"

"What do you mean, alien? From another country, you mean?", asked Will.

"No, I mean they're true aliens – from outer space." Will let out a whistle of surprise.

"Didn't you find it suspicious that they are multicolored: pink, yellow, green, and blue? When was the last time you saw a green human?"

"I haven't really seen very much, if you'll remember. I came straight into the Doskian dungeons, across the Jahandi Wastelands, and into Deorc. I've not really seen anyone, except for you and that horrible Official Pettiman."

"I haven't really thought of that," said Draedon.

"I'll see if Father will allow me to take you out on the town one night soon. You've been training in your books way too much. I think you need a night out with libations and company."

"Can I drink alcohol?", asked Will.

"Why sure, not that it'll have much of an effect, you being wraith and all."

"Why don't they just call themselves vamps and get if over with?", asked Will.

"Because, they ... you, are not really a vampire. I think you'd need to come from a human lineage to qualify for the role of a vampire. I think alien DNA is way too different."

"But, I'm human," said Will.

"Are you? Do you know that for certain?", asked Draedon. "You may appear to be human, but, like your friend Emily, I suspect that you're something more than human. That is why Mortifera is so keen on having you as her pets. There can be no other explanation. She doesn't collect useless items."

"I've been meaning to ask you for some time now. Why did you save me from the dungeons of Dosk?"

"I'm not sure, really. I will tell you, however, if I had known that you were from Outerworld, I would never have brought you here. I would have taken you home and kept you as my own pet. Now Mortifera has two of you locked away in her tower. And I will marry Emily and take her as my wife. With that marriage will come the power to do with her as I please."

"What's that supposed to mean?", asked Will heatedly.

"I know you love her Will, that's as obvious as the nose on your face. Believe me when I tell you, you will never have Emily. Ever! Mortifera will see to that. Once again she has stolen my dreams by taking away my Lily and replacing her with a witch. I will make that witch my own; I will use her until she is used up and then I'll destroy Mortifera's pet, as she destroyed mine." Draedon's eyes blazed like hot coals. His longing for the young virgin witch was suddenly overwhelming. He stood and abruptly left Will's chambers.

Will laid his desk chair back and put his feet up on the desk. He stared out of the window to the bustling streets below. It had been weeks since he'd been outside. He missed the cool night air and the bawdy laughter of the drunken sailors on shore leave. He also loved Emily; that much was true. He hadn't really realized to what extent until Draedon's diatribe. "This marriage cannot proceed," he whispered to the room. "I must figure out a way to stop it, for I am certain that her life depends upon it.

++++

Emily's father sat on the edge of her bed. He carefully pushed the lock of curls out of her eyes and slid his fingers over her cheek. She was crying again, the red tears staining the thick cotton sheets. Bernie handed her a handkerchief to wipe her nose and eyes.

"Father, please listen to me. You cannot stay here. You're jeopardizing everything by being here, and if you get caught, I will not be able to do my part. Please, leave now, while I know you still can. They will torture you and make me watch. Mortifera will probably leave it to me to kill you, as a final act to show my love and undying devotion to her. Please, don't make me do that."

"Shhh, you're not going to have to kill me. I want you to come with me, but I know you won't. John Dunne told me he would look out for you. I know you don't need it," he said in response to her hand gesture.

"Let him do it for me, to satisfy my need to protect my little girl." She hugged him and then turned her back.

"I love you, Emily."

"I love you too, Daddy. Go now. Please!"

++++

Draedon walked up the hill towards his house. He needed a woman, now. Fortunately, there was a blonde and a red-head standing on the corner he was approaching. He would have them both.

"Hi, girls," he said.

"Are you looking for a party?", asked the red-head.

"I sure am," he agreed. "For both of you." They tittered and left with the predator. They were found several days later in the back of a dark alley. He'd used them within a block of where they'd met and left them for trash on the street. He walked back to his place, drank a cup of tea, and went to bed. His desire temporarily satisfied, he slept soundly through the night. He awoke to the sound of a thunder storm that had rolled up in the early morning hours. He lay in bed and watched as the lightening raced across the permanently darkened sky. He thought about taking a trip to the ocean before his wedding. Unlike the wraith, he still needed to see the sunlight. It had been sometime since he was at the beach.

He lightly dressed for the warm day and called for his horse. He hoped the back roads between Deorc and Peddleton Prow would help him avoid this ridiculous war that Pettiman and Belac had started. He scoffed at the thought of world domination, too much work entirely. I'll take the money, any day, he thought. That's where the real power was. A completely zany idea crossed his mind. What if I went to outerworld? How would I go about doing it? Is that why Mortifera needed the six? Would it give them access outside of Innes?

Then, the most devious thought occurred to him. Belac is not about ruling these alien freaks in Innes; he wants the outside world as well. That's his true goal.

Draedon couldn't believe he hadn't seen the truth before now. If Belac voids the realm of fantasy, the outerworld will be unable to withstand his armies or his ability to void their world of light as well. Their hopes and dreams would be gone, replaced with the world of wraith. Draedon had seen some of Will's books. The tome that kept nagging at him the most was 'The Book of Wraith'. Belac had rewritten the ageless human bible. The first words Draedon clearly remembered. 'In the beginning was the word and the word was Wraith'.

He steered the horse wide of the fields teeming with creatures both undead and dying. The clash of metal to sinew was sickening. He couldn't remember how many people he'd killed in his short life time. Hundreds, he was sure of that. He had never seen so much death displayed for his enjoyment. Somehow, he didn't find it as entertaining as he'd hoped. In fact, it was rather repulsive to see such waste, both light and dark. There was no finesse, no precision, nor beauty as in a well-planned execution. The carnage was brutish, boorish, and ugly. His stomach rolled at the repulsive smell of death in the air – a smell he was very familiar with.

He wasn't afraid of death, but he didn't court this churlish display. He unsaddled himself and stumbled to the nearest tree where he hurled his lunch. He wiped the greasy sweat from his forehead, took a drink of water and spit it out, trying to clean the taste of bile from his mouth. He crawled back on his horse, unsettled by his response to the bloodbath below. He turned his horse away in hopes of a clear path to his destination. "Am I getting soft?", he muttered.

He stayed within the boundaries of Deorc as the fighting didn't cross the border for some reason. After many hours of zigzagging his way, he crossed into Peddleton Prow. He climbed off his horse at the far end of the beach-front property he owned. He could see smoke in the distance but decided to settle himself in the crude shack he'd built last summer. He sat in a chair on the beach and allowed the repetition of the waves to lull him into a meditative state. He wasn't happy about the turn of events in his life. This was supposed to be his and Cereus' hideaway. He missed her and thought about the possibility of visiting. She was the only woman who'd truly satisfied him. Maybe it was because he was slightly afraid of her being Innesian and about a thousand years old. He didn't know how, but deep down inside he knew that Cereus was changing and would no longer be receptive to his overtures.

Feeling peckish, he opened his bag of supplies and took out a few items, tossed them into a pot and set it on the edge of the small fire he'd built. He saw smoke billowing a few hundred yards up the beach and decided to take a little walk. He wanted to see who was hanging about. He hummed his favorite ditty as the surf splashed over his bare feet and calves. He loved the beach more than any place he'd been. He hoped that their wars stayed far removed from this place of beauty.

He was close to the interlopers, almost close enough. "No ... it can't be," he whispered. Standing not more than thirty feet from him was the man he'd eaten breakfast with a few mornings past. He rubbed his eyes thinking they were playing tricks on him. No, there was the outworlder with two others and a ... dragon? What strange company these people kept. He started to advance towards the party; they hadn't noticed his presence yet. Twenty feet, fifteen feet and then they were gone, on the back of the blue reptile, and he was once again by himself. What was this dance of fate about?

He walked to their spent fire looking for any

indicators of their direction. Not that he'd really needed any, up to this point. It seemed they were destined to meet again. When, he couldn't be certain. But he knew with all his blackened heart that they would meet again. He turned to walk back down the beach. He thought all the dragons were dead or at least out of commission. Clearly he was mistaken. What other crazy turns would these outsiders bring forth? He couldn't wait to find out. At that moment, Draedon decided to stay here in his shanty, away from court, and out of the melee. His network would keep him posted on upcoming events.

$$+ + + +$$

Nate awoke with a cramp in his neck. He rubbed at the cramp as he sat up, took stock of their camping area, and decided to throw a log on their diminishing fire. His grumbling stomach reminded him that he was long past breakfast. Time was lost deep in the Mirthless Swamp and if you stayed long enough, so would be your will to live. Rho was still snuggled next to the strangest dragon Nate had ever seen. Not that he was an expert or anything, but pictures of dragons could easily be found on the internet.

"She can't be that bad," he said to the fire. "She didn't try to kill me in my sleep." Arion whinnied in response. "How ya doing, boy?", he asked as he rubbed his velvety soft muzzle. Several fairies popped onto Arion's back and neck: Monarch, Painted Ladies, Morpho, and, of course, several of the Metalmarks, who really never left Nate's side since finding out about King Heldring.

"Nate," said Louisa Longfingers of the Painted Clan. "We have come to tell you that the battle front has entered the lands of the Ladies. Legions of trolls, orcs, and goblins have merged with the humans and Innesians of Dosk. Soon they will overrun our lands. If they take possession of our ring, they can access our magic, which will kill us."

"Tell the fey to move their ring."

"Did you hear that?", asked Nate. Sidney red stocking shrugged.

"Nephew, tell the Ladies to move their ring. But they must do it now before it becomes tainted."

Nate relayed the message to Louisa. "You must move your ring before they mess it up."

"But how can we move what has been forever fixed?"

"Wait," said Nate as he held up his finger.

"Tell them to chant:

Nimbus Rhombus
Clouds are askew
The unclean are attacking
We must be free, to do what we do
Move the fey ring to a place that is safe
And out of reach from orc, demon, or wraith.

"How do you know this?", asked Louisa.

"I don't know exactly," said Nate. "It just popped into my head. You should hurry, NOW! Send word when all the Ladies are safe." With that, Louisa and her companions blinked out of sight.

"It sounds like the Leohtian soldiers are losing ground," said Nate to Arion, who whinnied and stomped his hoof. "I wish there was something we could do. But I'm no soldier." He started on Arion's daily brushing, hoping that Rho would wake soon. He was famished. He started to speculate on the voice in his head. It definitely wasn't Heldring's deep baritone.

"I told you I'd contact you when I needed you," said the voice. Definitely a woman, thought Nate.

"Who else would call you nephew?"

"Aunt Lorelei? Is that you?"

"Yes, it's me."

"How can you do that?", he asked.

"Do what?"

"Talk directly into my mind."

"Oh, that. It's not a big deal, a parlor trick really. What is important is that I need for you to bring Rho and her Wynn to me — today."

"How today? We're at least four days ride and I know Wynn can fly but not with Arion."

"Which fairies are with you?"

"Metalmark and Morpho. The Monarchs left with the Ladies."

"Send the Morphos back to the cave with the following message: 'Dr. Wombat, please assist the Ladies in their ring transition. You must recite the mantra specific to the Treatise on the Protective Wards of 1654. There can be no gaps or breaks when the ring is being moved.' Tell him, he will understand." Nate relayed the message and out blinked the Morpho fairies.

"Now tell the remaining Metalmarks to bring you to my cabin. They know where and how to access it without alerting the soldiers. I'll see you shortly." Nate walked over to Rho and tapped her on the shoulder until she awoke.

She put her arms up and stretched. "I'm starving," she said. He poured the remaining stew for her.

"Sorry, I couldn't wait," he said. He called Sidney red stocking to the fire and told him that in ten minutes they would leave. Nate explained what Lorelei had said. Within fifteen minutes, they were seated in Lorelei's living room Nate, Rho, and the entire Metalmark Clan. Nothing had been said yet, but Nate could hear Lorelei's thoughts. They were going to rescue Ben and Gordon?

"Aunt Lorelei, what do you mean a rescue mission for granddad and Gordon?"

"They are walking into a trap, set by Belac himself to ensnare the One Who Will Be."

"Will be … what?", asked Nate.

"King over all of Innes."

"Gordon is going to be the King of Innes?"

"I didn't say that," said Lorelei. "But they are walking into a trap."

"I thought those legends were malarkey," said Nate.

"Apparently, Belac doesn't think so." Rho sat very quietly by the fireplace. Gordon was in trouble. She could barely stand it. Lorelei watched Rho as she spoke her next thoughts.

"Belac must not capture either Gordon or Ben. It would be better to sacrifice their lives than to let them be captured and taken to Deorc."

"Arion and I are ready to go right now," said Nate as he stood to lead Arion out of the front door.

"You cannot go, Nate," said Lorelei.

"What? Not go? Impossible!", exclaimed Nate. "I'm sorry, Aunt, but this is my grandfather and my best friend we're talking about."

"I know, Nate. There will be major consequences if you and Gordon are captured. They have two of you already: Emily and William. Right now, the war is weighted to Leoht's favor. If one of you is caught, the game is even. If two of you are caught, and especially you, the possibility of Leoht's survival diminishes significantly. We cannot take the risk. But your friend Rho on the other hand …" Rho's eyes were glazed and very dark.

"You will meet Fiona Dunne and her dragon Onager at the cave. Take all but four of the Metalmarks with you and resolve the issue in whatever way you have to. Do you understand me clearly? They must not be caught."

"I understand," Rho whispered.

"Nate, I want you to return to the cave and let the fairies know that we are going to war. Then I want you to go to Leoht to assist Daedalus. Michael must go to Dosk and Madeline and the Wombat are to stay put. Do you understand?"

"Yes," said Nate. He didn't like that Rho was going without him. She barely knew the dragon. What if it left her or turned on her?"

"Stop worrying, Nate. Rho and her dragon will be strong together. Now go. May light show you the way."

++++

"How close are we to Pickering Cross?", asked Gordon.

"It's not far now," said Fiona. "Onager tells me the border is over the next rise. In a few minutes we should be over the summer cottage." Ben tensed.

"What's wrong?", asked Gordon.

"It's been a long time since I was here last — a long, long time." Onager began her descent, and the turrets of the summer cottage came into view.

Ben pointed to the rolling fields beyond the estate. "That is where we will find the Book of Dreams."

Gordon nodded. He was absorbed by the beauty of the well-manicured gardens. The blue-green grass had an iridescent glow from the morning dew. He still hadn't become accustomed to the odd lighting found throughout Innes. He missed the regularity of the sunrise and the sunset. He realized he missed a lot of things about home — the familiarity of his town, his school. He especially missed his mom. His skin prickled at the thought of that man touching his mother. I won't run from him again, he thought, barely concealing his pent-up rage.

"Onager wants to know what's wrong with you, Gordon?", relayed Fiona.

He was surprised again by the acuity of these dragons. "Tell her I was thinking of home," he replied.

"Does home make you feel sad and angry?", asked Fiona. "Onager wants to know."

"No, Onager, home makes me happy. But my stepfather makes me very unhappy."

"I'm sorry," Onager said. "We are very near our goal."

"Cool. I heard her that time," said Gordon.

"Yes, she's finally remembering who she is," said Fiona. "Hang on!", hollered Fiona as they dipped and sharply banked on the outskirts of the estate.

20: Safe Passage

Jacob had not expected their journey through the Mirthless Swamp to take as long as it did. The travellers hit obstacles at every turn, from getting lost in the swamp, to the boatman Hans, to Aquilegia Falls. He wanted nothing more than to pack it in and return to the comfort of his small home at 714 Cornflower Lane. Every joint in his body ached from sleeping on only slightly dry patches of ground inside the swamp, and then hard rocks outside the swamp. He needed a hot shower, a bed, and a good long rest. He knew that was a dream, however, for they were still many miles from their destination. Fortunately, they'd emerged from the swamp into farmlands as far as the eye could see — fertile lands growing corn and wheat.

A cool breeze and sunshine brought rays of hope to the three men who'd just departed from the dreadful swamp. It was like they'd struck gold, and all three were infinitely wealthy as a result. They emerged onto a dirt road that cut through a peach orchard. Jacob wished the fruit was ready to eat, the thoughts of the sweet nectar dripping down his arm was more than he could take. They'd taken to eating what they could catch from the swamp — frogs, fish, even a snake. While it did the job of filling the gut, all of it tasted like pond algae. None of the men complained.

Ted approached the neatly-kept stone cottage. He was met by what he figured to be a middle-aged farmer's wife.

"Excuse us, Madam, but we are long on the road and in desperate need of a roof for a couple of nights. We would be glad to help you around your farm in exchange for meals and some clean straw."

"I'd be right glad of the company," she said. "I'm sure I can find a couple of odd jobs that need tending."

"Please excuse my rudeness. I should introduce myself. My name is Ted McShane. My friends are Caleb Hobken, and Jacob Daggerstein."

"It's a pleasure to meet you," she said. "I'm Anne. My husband is away in the north, attending to some work."

"Oh," said Ted. "Is he at the front?"

"No, thank the Pillars of Flame for that," she said. They all nodded in agreement.

"Well, Anne. Do you have an outside tub and some hot water, so that we can clean up a bit?", asked Ted.

"We don't want to come to the supper table smelling of swamp," he chuckled.

"You men can get situated in the barn. You'll find a suitable tub and some privacy," she added. "I'll call when the water is warm enough for the first of you."

"Thank you," said Ted. "We'll get started on the chores first thing tomorrow. I'm good with my hands and can fix most things."

Jacob led the horses to the barn. "You sure could use a good brushing," he said as he removed the saddle and tied Windwalker securely. He moved the rubber curry he'd found in the barn in a circular clockwise motion to loosen the caked dirt and mud from these last weeks of travel. It took several hours for Jacob to get Windwalker's shiny coat back in shape. In the mean time, Caleb had bathed and was in the kitchen helping the mistress put together what Jacob hoped to be a small feast. His stomach rumbled to match his thought.

By the time Ted and Jacob brushed, watered, fed

the horses, and bathed themselves, it was time for supper.

Jacob saw a tall woman glide quietly through the parlor as he took a seat at the table. Somehow, she seemed familiar to him. He looked into the living area to see if he could catch another glimpse.

"Please excuse her, but my companion cares little for conversation and takes her meals privately. Do you have any news of the war or news of any type for that matter?"

"We came from the front, but that was many weeks ago. We have been wandering around in that infernal swamp for longer than I care to remember.

"Where are you going?", asked Anne.

"We're on our way to the Amber Tower to speak with King Daedulus," said Jacob. "Do you have any idea how far the Tower is from here?"

"You're still several days of travel away," Anne said. She looked at her tea cup as she stirred the sugar into the warm brew. She really didn't know, as they hadn't been anywhere except on the farm since they had arrived all those weeks ago. Her mind wandered back to their arrival. She wondered what happened to that nice young man who had escorted them safely to her new home. She doubted that she'd ever have the chance to properly thank him.

She thanked the Pillars of Flame and hoped for his safe travels during these perilous times. Her thoughts turned to her husband. It had been weeks since they last spoke. He'd told her it might be some time before he'd be able to join her again. She was patient and would wait, but she missed him terribly. She returned her attention to the conversation as Ted was describing his search for Jacob, who had apparently wandered off during the middle of the night.

"I don't know, honestly. I have no memory of why

I left camp," said Jacob. "The only thing I remember is that I awoke to find myself in front of a festival-like audience of animals dressed as fantastical characters."

"We kept going in circles," said Ted. That infernal swamp seemed to get denser and darker when you're looking for something."

"Yeah, like an exit," added Caleb.

"I called out to you for days," said Jacob heatedly. That is before I stumbled upon the remnants of a house hidden behind sweeping clumps of Spanish moss. Seated in front of the house was a large badger who obviously considered himself the lord of the manor. He was dressed in lordly clothes, a red velvet jacket and matching britches embellished with gaudy gold brocade. He wore a black velvet beret adorned with a large egret's feather. A small wood-handled dagger in his waistband completed the costume.

Seated around him were several field mice dressed as bandoleros, plus a weasel, a fox, and a raccoon – all dressed as if they were attending a medieval masquerade party. A pair of skunks and an opossum ambled into the party as I was beginning to address the badger. He obviously didn't believe my story but was too intent on the party to worry himself about my dilemma. For him the world stopped at the edge of the swamp. I had little choice but to stay. I was cold and tired from aimlessly wandering through the swampy mire. There at least I had found food and some conversation."

"By the time we found you, you were quite alone," said Caleb. "It appears your friends were of the fleeting type."

"It was their help that finally got us out of the swamp," said Jacob defensively.

"True," said Caleb. "We could have spent an eternity wandering around in circles," he said, as he scraped the remnants of the meal into the pig bucket.

"So, did the badger have a name or any good conversation points?", asked Anne.

"No name, but he did say that that the darkness was creeping further south. He said the lavender trees in the northern Devil's Hole Forest were dropping their needles and the fruits of the cinnamon bush in Nell's Nettle had lost their spice. He continued by saying that he and his friends would prolong their party until the end because what could one badger and a few mice do against the Wraith Lord and his armies?"

"I suggested they gather their courage and fight for their homes and their families," said Jacob. "But the badger couldn't or wouldn't see things my way. There was no way to change his mind."

"That's a shame," said Anne. "I rather liked the badger, he was very charming. I met him once, a long time ago, before I was married. His name is ... give me a minute to think ... George ... no, Jeff ... no ... Gabriel ... that's it! Except when I met him he was wearing purple velvet with a white egret feather. Ha ha," she chuckled. "Isn't that funny? I haven't thought about those days in a very long time. He threw such gay parties. I was young and beautiful in those days."

Jacob placed his hand on top of Anne's hand to show his empathy. "You are still beautiful," he said.

Ted stood up from the table. "Thank you, Anne; that was an exceptional meal. I think I'll retire for the evening. Gentlemen," he said, and then turned to leave the table.

"Wait, I'll come with you," said Caleb.

"I'll be along in a few minutes," said Jacob. He turned his attention back to Anne. "Tell me more about yourself," said Jacob. "It's nice to have some female company to talk to for a bit. My only other friends, Pearl and her husband, Ben, are a long way from here.

It's been along time since I've had a conversation."

"Where should I start?", asked Anne. "I'm originally from Balliwick Prop. My dad had a shop, my mom stayed home to raise us kids. I have two brothers, long deceased, and a sister who I haven't seen in many years. Until recently, I lived in Dosk, but my husband sent me away for my safety. It's the safest place, I suppose. If the darkness makes it this far south, then all of Innes is doomed."

"How about you?", she asked.

"Well," he hesitated. "This is a little difficult to explain, but I'm not from Innes at all. In fact, I'm not really sure how I came to be in these lands. My home is in a little town called Pine Woods. My wife died fifteen years ago, and I never remarried. I retired from the military and certainly never expected to find myself in the middle of another war."

They talked late into the night before Anne asked, "More tea?"

"No, I think I'd better get to bed," said Jacob. "Thank you for a wonderful evening. It's certainly the best meal I've had in a long time. We'll get started on those chores first thing tomorrow morning."

21: Elinor's Way

Last year's leaves rustled across the moonlit tile flooring. The air was heavily scented with the smell of gardenias from the neighboring gardens. Daedalus leaned against the concrete pillars, as his daughter walked away from him. They'd just argued. She wanted to join the forces that were fighting to the north. He forbade it. A woman had no business fighting in men's wars, even if she were one of the best trained soldiers in the lands of Leoht. She was his only daughter — his only heir. He was not prepared to lose her to this war, regardless of what was at risk. He watched her walk away, so like her mother, long golden hair, the color of sunshine. It was unusual to see it hanging loosely at her shoulders. She'd rather have it tightly bound in a long braid down her back.

She spent most of her time in the training camps, preferring sword play to more typical feminine pursuits. Her long sleeveless dress showed off her tall, muscular build.

"Father, I am nineteen now and old enough to manage my own affairs."

"Don't be stubborn, Elinor; please come back in and finish dinner."

"I'm done, thank you. I'm going to my rooms." He remembered his little girl, how happy, how unaware of the troubles in the world she'd been. He knew he couldn't protect her forever, but he would try. He was the King of Leoht and all its neighboring free lands. He walked to the dining room, not wanting to be rude to his guests. Messengers had brought startling news from the front. The armies of Leoht were losing to the ever increasing numbers of dark monsters. He didn't know how the powers of light would ever overcome those of the dark. He prayed to the Pillars of Fire for a miracle. The gods knew he could use one.

He took his seat at the head of the table and raised his goblet to join in a toast that was already underway. He'd tried to contact Ira, but his scouts returned with the news that Chelsea Manor had divided and the Flower Guild had taken root on the remaining property and were hostile to any outside of the Guild. He wondered about the outworlders, Gordon and Madeline, and what had become of them. He'd thought them to be good luck charms, but so far they seemed to leave disharmony in their wake.

Daedalus would hold his opinions, however, as he didn't have the full story of the collapse of Chelsea Manor. He frowned at the thought. He loved vacationing at the Manor. Besides he and Ira had become good friends. He could always rely on Ira to tell him the truth and not what he thought a King would want to hear. He was a rare individual indeed, and now he and his Pufflemals were gone; his daughter wanted to ride off to war, and the world was turning on its head.

+ + + +

Elinor took off her crown and laid it on top of her dress. She'd dismissed her ladies-in-waiting, wanting time in private. She put on her more comfortable pants and cotton top, laced up her boots and went for a walk in the gardens. The full moon was high in the sky, close to the late evening sun. The sun always shone in different degrees, in the lands of Leoht. There had never been a time in the last thousand years since the settlement of Innes that Leoht had seen darkness. She'd heard stories from all the lands that had fallen under the control of Deorc that they were now embedded in permanent darkness. She couldn't imagine a land where the sun never shone. There would be no flowers or trees or anything green. What creatures did survive would be pallid in color, like cave dwellers. Her golden hair and permanently tanned skin were in direct contrast to the dark hair and pallid skin of the wraith.

She wandered to the edge of the garden and saw pale beams of light dancing about twenty feet into the forest. Her curiosity got the better of her, and she followed the dancing lights. She was drawn deeper and deeper into the forest, as the lights seemed to always be right in front of her ready, for her to touch. She'd been so focused on the lights that she'd failed to realize no one knew where she was or how long she'd been gone.

The sounds of the canopy-darkened forest seemed to grow louder the deeper that she went, as if the night creatures were scolding her for being so foolish. She was committed to her mission now. She'd follow those lights to the end of the lands if need be. There was a growling noise to her left. She couldn't tell what animal made such noises. The lights changed course and moved to her left, towards the growling. The boughs of the trees slapped against her chest and face as she sped her pace to keep up with the lights. The growling became deafening, more like a roar.

Elinor crouched behind a monstrous basswood tree, afraid to look around the other side where the lights appeared to have stopped. After many minutes, she gained her confidence and peered around the tree. She'd never seen any creature, large or small, as beautiful as the beast that was before her. But something was wrong. She couldn't tell what, from this angle, but the animal seemed to be limping badly, favoring his right front foot. She wanted to help the animal, but didn't know if she dared. He turned his head as the sticks snapped under her feet.

"Can I help you?", she whispered, her body tense with fear. He turned his body towards her, and, after several moments, limped to her and lay down on his side. He was breathing heavily, obviously in terrible pain. She sat down and lifted his heavy paws one after the other to determine what was ailing the poor creature. The pads on his left paw were torn and bleeding, but didn't seem to be the source of his troubles. She ripped a piece of her cotton shirt and cleaned the wounds as best she could with limited resources.

Then she picked up his right paw. He roared in pain, so much so that it scared her into dropping his paw. He laid his head back on the ground waiting for her magical touch. It was very obvious when she turned his paw over that a long thorn, maybe three to four inches had penetrated deep into his pads. How was she going to remove it? She had no pliers or needles or even a knife for that matter. "I'm too far away from the castle to run for help or get supplies, and besides, I don't know where the castle is anyway," she said to the trees.

"What am I going to do? I can't leave you like this. I won't leave you like this. I need to take you back to my rooms, but how can I do that?" He looked deep into her eyes. "Do you trust me?", she asked. His long tail whipped back and forth in agreement. "We need to go to the castle so that we can remove this thorn properly and protect you against infection. Can you help me?" He slowly stood on his three good legs and motioned for her to climb on his back.

"No, you can barely walk and you're going to carry

me?", she asked incredulously. He motioned for her to get on his back, again. She shook her head no, but climbed on top of the massive creature at his insistence. Her next emotion was one of awe. Within the blink of an eye, they had cleared the trees and were flying towards the castle that was many miles from where they had been. They circled the castle as she pointed to her rooms.

"There," she said. He landed in the courtyard. A tight squeeze it was but somehow he managed to limp into the main room of her tower. She climbed down from his back and rushed into her bathroom where she filled a basin with the still warm water that had been intended for her bath earlier that evening. She found a white cotton shirt and cut strips for bandages. She was going to have to push something through to both remove the thorn and cauterize the wound. She needed some help and something to sedate the poor creature against the pain.

"I'll be right back ..., Calthexis?" She heard him say loudly in her head. "Is that your name? I need to get my father's help; he'll know what to do." Calthexis laid his head on the pillows that Elinor had pushed under him. Many minutes later, Daedalus, King of Leoht, ruler of all things light and free entered the rooms of his daughter, rooms he'd entered many times with no fear or concern. He stopped in his tracks.

Calthexis, the King of all Dragons, the legends of his boyhood, legends that his old nan used to tell him when he couldn't sleep or was sick in bed, lay on the floor in front of him, injured and relying on him for help.

His daughter broke the spell, "Daddy, please help him. I can't help him by myself."

"Of course," he said, as he sat beside her on the floor and inspected the wound. "We need my surgeon," he said. "This is too deep for us to remove, and I'm afraid it'll become infected. Stay with the poor creature. I'll return as fast as I can." She pulled her hand lightly through his mane, caressing the beast to calm him. Several long minutes later her father and his surgeon walked through the door.

"I never would have believed it if the words hadn't come from Your Majesty himself," said the doctor.

"Remember, you have sworn your secrecy to me." The surgeon nodded his head as he looked at the extent of the dragon's wounds.

"These wounds are very serious. You did right by asking me to help." He hesitated and then chuckled, "I don't have a lot of experience with dragons, however." Several hours later the surgeon had all of his wounds treated. "I've given him a sedative. He should sleep until the morning. Give him two of these pills and rub this salve on his wounds for the next ten days. That should keep any infection away. If you have any further problems, please call me. Princess," he said, as he bowed and dismissed himself from her rooms. Daedalus walked with him. She could hear their whispers but not their words. A few minutes later her father returned to her room.

"You know I have to ask," he said. She nodded her head.

"I went for a walk in the gardens," she began. "Then a strange light beckoned me into the forest."

"You know you could have been hurt or even killed. How could you leave the safety of the castle without sending word? It was a very foolish decision. Do you have any idea what the princess of Leoht would be worth to a thief or cutthroat?"

"I'm sorry father. I didn't mean to, but the light was so beautiful, all silvery, and it just beckoned me to follow it until I didn't know where I was."

278 | Kimberly J. Rosengrant

"Fortunately for all of us, your bad judgment may have brought us an unforeseen gift in the fulfillment of prophecies and legends. Do you have any idea who you have brought into your rooms?", he asked.

"He told me his name was Calthexis."

"I thought so. Calthexis is the King of all Dragons, Elinor."

"Dragons? I thought all the dragons in Innes were dead."

"Apparently not," he said. "I've heard stories of this magnificent creature when I was but a boy many centuries ago. I think they've been relegated to stories and legends since it's been more than five hundred years since the last dragon sighting."

"Why do you think he's made himself known after all this time?"

"Maybe it was nothing more than need," said Daedulus. "It was a pretty big thorn. You saw for yourself how long it took for a trained surgeon to tend to his wounds. But I'd like to think that his presence has a purpose greater than his need alone. He was pretty banged up; I wonder what he was up to." Elinor continued to stroke the fur on his long back and neck.
"I'm going to my quarters. Send your handmaid immediately when he wakes. I will speak with him myself."

"Okay. And Father, I'm sorry. I guess I didn't think of the consequences of my actions."

"We've all learned something tonight, Elinor. Try to get some rest." She pulled the thick comforter off the bed and grabbed a couple of pillows and lay down next to her charge. The medicine the doctor had given him helped him to sleep through the night and well into the next day. Elinor refused to leave her rooms until he was awake. What do dragons eat she worried, and when her handmaiden came to help her dress, Elinor

Calthexis

stopped her at the door and refused her admittance. It was bad enough the doctor had to be called, but her handmaiden, while of good character, couldn't keep a secret to herself and one this big would be impossible for her. Through the locked doors she told the maid to have her father come to her rooms at his earliest possible convenience. Sometime shortly afterwards, Calthexis started to rouse. He sat straight up, not sure of his surroundings, took one look at Elinor and let out a large sigh.

"I was afraid ...," he paused. "That was a powerful medicine that your doctor gave me." He looked at his bandaged paws and back to Elinor.

"You can talk ... like me?", she asked.

"Of course I can. How else am I to speak with you and your father?"

"Why do you want to speak with me and my father?", she asked.

"I thought you would know by now. You are my rider. Can't you tell?"

"I didn't know what I was feeling," she said. "I just feel very ...," she paused. "Very protective of you," she continued. "It's like we're supposed to be together, for always."

"Very discerning you are. Good. I was afraid I'd made a mistake. It's been a long time since we last met."

"We've met before?"

"Of course we've met before, throughout eternity." Just then, there was a knock at the door.

"Elinor, it's me," said her father. She opened the door for his admittance, with the doctor in tow. She quickly closed the doors to prying eyes and returned to her seat next to Calthexis.

"Your Majesty," said Daedalus as he bowed before the King of the Dragons.

Calthexis bowed his head in return, "Please forgive me if I don't get up," he said.

"Of course not, you're injured. This is my private surgeon," said Daedalus.

"Your Majesty," said the doctor.

"Doctor," said Calthexis. "Thank you for your kindness in attending to my injuries."

"You were in quite a state," said the doctor. "Your paws were torn to ribbons. Whatever could have done this to you?"

"The story is sad. In fact, my presence here is disturbing."

"How so?", asked Daedalus.

"I must be needed, in order for me to have been removed from my enshrinement."

"Enshrined?", asked the doctor as he un-bandaged his paws to check on his rate of healing.

"I've been enshrined since the first re-making of the world," Calthexis said. "And I am the last to be released."

"There are others?", asked Daedalus.

"Yes," said Calthexis. "You will be meeting them soon enough. One will arrive on the morrow."

"Tomorrow? Here? Another dragon?", asked Elinor.

"Yes, another dragon, and her rider," he replied.

"Like you?", she asked.

"No. We're all different. Made from different materials, you might say; each with our own talents. What's important right now is that you find someplace to house your allies and their riders. Preferably in an area that is undisturbed by loose lips. The element of surprise is on our side. It would be best not to tip our hands too quickly."

"Let me understand this fully," said Daedalus. "The dragons are being released, to help me defeat the forces of darkness?"

"That is correct. Belac cannot be allowed to shutter the light. It would cause too great an imbalance for Innes and for the outerworld as well. Unfortunately, the light is losing; the angels of darkness are surging ever forward. They will stop at nothing to taste your royal blood." The surgeon shuddered, as he finished changing the bandages on the dragon's paws.

He looked from Daedalus to Elinor, "These wounds are healing nicely. Continue to put the salve on for the ten days. It will help to fight against infection."

"Thank you again, doctor. You've been very kind to me," said Calthexis. "I'd like to rest again, if that's okay. I'm still feeling weak."

"Eleanor, send your girl for food, meat, and a glass of cold tea for each of us," said Daedalus. "I will stay here for a while longer. Doctor, I'll let you know if your services are needed."

"Sire."

"And I remind you. Speak of this to no one." The doctor departed, leaving the three royals to discuss matters further. When they had finished talking, the King said, "Send word for the stable manager. I will see him in my chambers within the hour."

"Yes, Sire," said Elinor's attendant, who'd been waiting outside the door. The King left Calthexis and Elinor. He knew now that his daughter would ride Calthexis and become a heroine in this war, whether he desired it or not.

"I will not get hurt," she said as she tried to smooth his ruffled feathers. "Calthexis will protect me."

"With my life," he added. She'd curled up next to him when he asked to be allowed to rest once again. In many ways, Daedalus was as proud as any father of his daughter. Seriously now, how many were chosen to be dragon riders? Male or female? His daughter would ride the King of the Dragons, himself. How magnificent was that? Daedalus deeply inhaled the sweet scented spring air as he walked to his apartments. No man could be more proud. A hooded stranger stepped from the shadows to greet Daedalus.

"I was expecting you weeks ago. What news do you bring for your King? Did you have any problems finding the object I sent you to look for?"

"No, Sire," replied the man who stepped forward from the shadows, and then repeatedly stabbed the noble King of Leoht about his body. The black-clad man ran from the scene as Daedalus lay in a pool of his own blood, unable to move. He had lost the sweet taste of the air; it had been replaced by an annoying metallic taste. Within a few moments, the lights flickered and then went out.

About the author: Kimberly J. Rosengrant has a great interest in art, philosophy, and science. She blends science with fantasy and imagination to transport us to an extraordinarily crafted world. In her second novel, "The Binding", the players' roles have deepened in this fantastical conundrum where thought becomes reality. Kim lives in the enchanted Pocono Mountains of Pennsylvania.

About the Artist: These are the first of Paulette Nelson's paintings to be published. Her ability to reach into an unread story line and put the image onto paper is uncanny.   She has a Bachelor of Science in Biotechnology, is an avid reader of fantasy and lives happily with her dog Sydney in the lovely Pocono Mountains of Pennsylvania.

www.ingramcontent.com/pod-product-compliance
Lightning Source LLC
Chambersburg PA
CBHW030027180626
46810CB00001B/243